Kisses and Croissants

ANNE-SOPHIE
JOUHANNEAU

DELACORTE PRESS

Text copyright © 2021 by Alloy Entertainment
Jacket art copyright © 2021 by Carolina Melis

GetUnderlined.com

Educators and librarians, for a variety of teaching tools, visit us at RHTeachersLibrarians.com

Library of Congress Cataloging-in-Publication Data
Names: Jouhanneau, Anne-Sophie, author.
Title: Kisses & croissants / Anne-Sophie Jouhanneau.
Other titles: Kisses and croissants
Description: First edition. | New York : Delacorte Press, [2021] | Audience: Ages 12 and up. | Summary: Sixteen-year-old Mia travels to Paris to attend an elite ballerina program, and along the way meets a cute French boy, finds an unexpected rival, and discovers the truth behind a family legend.
Identifiers: LCCN 2020011557 (print) | LCCN 2020011558 (ebook) | ISBN 978-0-593-17357-2 (hardcover) | ISBN 978-0-593-17358-9 (library binding) | ISBN 978-0-593-17359-6 (ebook)
Subjects: CYAC: Ballet dancers—Fiction. I Friendship—Fiction.
Classification: LCC PZ7.1.J787 Ki 2021 (print) | LCC PZ7.1.J787 (ebook) | DDC [Fic]—dc23

The text of this book is set in 12-point Apollo MT.
Interior design by Ken Crossland

Printed in the United States of America
10 9 8 7 6 5 4 3 2 1
First Edition

To Scott

CHAPTER ONE

I RUN THROUGH the airport in shapeless tracksuit pants, my hair flying behind me. A screaming toddler stands in my way, and I leap over him in a somewhat graceful *grand jeté* before *pirouetting* past a man who's struggling to carry his giant suitcase.

"Faites attention!" a woman yells at me after I almost step on her foot. *Be careful!*

The thing is, I can be careful or I can be late, and being late is not an option right now. This American girl needs to get to the other side of Paris *tout de suite*.

"Sorry," I say as I race through the Charles de Gaulle terminal, my backpack banging into my shoulder.

The reason I'm late is that there was a crazy storm in New York last night, and my flight was delayed by four hours, then six. I stopped counting after that so I wouldn't pass out from the idea of missing my first day of school.

Well, not *school,* exactly. School is a piece of cake compared to what's waiting for me here.

I bump into a group of children straddling the entire width of the terminal hallway and almost fall flat on my face, but I manage to turn it into a *pas de basque.* Thank you, muscle memory from approximately a million years of ballet classes.

I'll admit, this is not how I imagined my first hours in Paris. I had a picture-perfect vision of what was supposed to happen: I would get off the plane on a warm, sunny morning, my wavy brown hair bouncing and shiny, even after the seven-hour flight. I'd swing my tied-up pointe shoes over my shoulder and declare something cute in French with a perfect accent—the result of months of practice—before strutting elegantly toward the best summer of my life: an intensive ballet program at the prestigious Institut de l'Opéra de Paris. *Le dream, non?*

Instead, I "gently" shove past a few people to snatch my suitcase off the luggage carousel, then search the signs above my head for the word *taxi.* That's when something truly wild happens.

"Mia?"

Um, what? How does someone in Paris know who I am?

"Mia? Is that you?"

It takes me a second to recognize that voice. I turn around, and there she is, my nemesis. Or she would be, if I believed in nemeses.

"Whoa, Audrey! What are you doing here?" I realize

it's a stupid question only after the words come out of my mouth.

"The same thing as you, I guess," she answers, looking surprised. When I booked my ticket, I was surprised by how many flights there are to Paris every day. I guess we were on different ones, both delayed by the storm. In any case, I can practically hear her wondering, *How did Mia get accepted into one of the most exclusive summer ballet programs in the world?*

'Cause I worked my buns off, I want to say.

I'm not going to lie: Audrey is one of the best ballet dancers our age in the tristate area, but, hey, so am I. I know because we've competed against each other in every major event in the dance circuit since we were basically babies. I live in Westchester, which is outside of New York City, and Audrey lives in Connecticut, so we don't go to the same ballet school (thankfully!), but several times a year, I watch Audrey snatch roles, receive accolades, and almost always come out *just* ahead of me.

"*You* got into the Institut de l'Opéra de Paris?" Audrey asks with a perfect accent, one eyebrow raised in suspicion. I can tell she regrets her question, because she adds right away, "I mean, what level did you get in?"

I clear my throat, buying some time. There are five levels in the program, and students from around the world get placed according to the skills they demonstrated in their application video.

"Four," I say, holding her gaze.

Four is great. I was *so* excited to get level four. Honestly, I was happy to just get in, especially after being rejected from the American Ballet Theatre's summer program in New York. I've worked my entire life to get into a program like this. Ballet has run in my family for generations—or so the legend goes—and I know my grandmother would have been pretty sad if I didn't get into any school, though nowhere near my own major disappointment.

"That's great," Audrey says. Her hand tightens around the handle of her suitcase, the only sign that betrays her true reaction. Yep, I'm good enough for level four.

"And you're in . . . ?" I begin, even though I can guess the answer.

"Five," she answers coolly.

I nod. Force a smile. Of course she is. It's fine, really. Audrey's technique is flawless; even I can admit that.

"Are you coming?" she asks in a clipped tone, starting to walk ahead of me. "We should share a taxi. It doesn't make sense to take two cars to the same place," Audrey adds like she's talking to a child.

"Right." I hate to admit she has a point. "But we're probably in different dorms?"

I pull up the dorm address on my phone, which Audrey reads over my shoulder. She lets out a deep sigh. "That's where I am, too. Please don't tell me they put all the American students together."

"Seems like it," I say as we make our way to the taxi stand, not bothering to hide my annoyance. There are over a hundred girls and boys aged fourteen to eighteen attending the ballet summer program, and the dorms are scattered all over the city. The minute I received my admission packet with the address of where I'd be staying, I thought I'd won the Paris lottery. Now I'm not so sure about that.

"Boulevard Saint-Germain," I tell the driver once we're seated in the back of a metallic gray car with leather seats. Even the taxis in Paris are chic.

The man frowns at me in the rearview mirror, and I don't know what else to do but frown back. I have no idea what's happening. My thoughts feel like they're trapped in a cloud. Even if I had slept on the plane, Audrey's presence would be enough to throw me off my game.

She shakes her head, then hands the taxi driver her phone, which is open to the map with our dorm's address. My newbie mistake hits me right in the face. I've researched Paris so much that I should have remembered that Boulevard Saint-Germain is one of the longest streets in the city. It snakes across most of Rive Gauche, the side of Paris south of the Seine. Basically, it's like telling a New York City cab driver that you're going to Fifth Avenue.

Audrey gives me a pointed look that seems to say, *Lucky I'm here.*

Her phone rings just as we get on the freeway: a FaceTime call from her mom. I've never met her, but I know who she is—a retired principal dancer who spent her entire career in Moscow with the Bolshoi Ballet. As I listen to Audrey go on and on about how her flight delay almost ruined her life, I realize that I haven't even told my parents I'm here yet. I send a quick text saying that everything's fine. Dad responds immediately.

Good luck at orientation! Show them who's boss! Love you.

I smile and respond.

I'll try! Love you too.

And then nothing from Mom. I keep staring at my phone, hoping, wondering, wishing. She's still mad at me. Grandma swore she'd get over it by the time I left for Paris, but clearly she hasn't.

Ever since I was little, dancing has been my whole life. To my mom, however, it was just a hobby, something fun I did on the side, an extracurricular activity to keep me busy on weekends. I kept telling her I wanted to become a professional ballet dancer, and that I would do whatever it took to make it happen, but she always shrugged it off, like it was something I'd outgrow. Luckily, between Dad and Grandma Joan (Mom's mom), there was always someone to drive me to classes, help me sew costumes for my shows, and cheer me on during important performances.

But things got really tense with Mom when I started talking about applying to this program.

"You didn't get into New York. Why would you try again in Paris?"

I'd just received my rejection letter from ABT and was doing my best not to show how devastated I was. I always knew how competitive it would be, but I figured that, after a lifetime of dedicating myself to my art, I had a real shot. But Mom didn't agree with me. "So many girls want this; there just aren't enough spots for everyone," she'd said with a sad face. It hurt a lot to realize that she was right.

"Paris is every aspiring ballet dancer's biggest dream," I'd said.

To be honest, that's not exactly how I felt at the time. Even though it's true—the Paris program is just as well regarded as the New York one—I only ever dreamed of attending ABT, and of joining their company one day. But that wasn't going to happen this summer, and I couldn't allow myself to accept defeat. Everyone knows everyone in the ballet world, and borders don't really exist. If I made it in Paris, then I'd find my way into ABT eventually. They couldn't get rid of me so easily, even if I had to cross an ocean to prove it to them. At least that's what I told myself.

Mom shook her head. "It's your last summer of high school. Don't you want to see your friends, go to the pool, to the movies, and just, you know, do other things?"

"They have pools and movies in Paris, too."

She ignored my snarky tone. "Mia, there's more to life than ballet. You need to have a plan B. Everyone should have one, especially when they're only seventeen and chasing an impossible dream."

She'd never put it so plainly before. An impossible dream? Thanks for believing in me, Mom.

Despite everything she'd said, I kept rehearsing for my video, checking the requirements—an introduction to explain my experience and credentials, a showcase of each of the key steps, then a personal routine of at least two minutes. Grandma Joan even surprised me with a new leotard in a beautiful shade of dove gray.

"It'll be your Paris leotard," she said as I dashed to my room to try it on. It fit perfectly and complemented my blue eyes.

"I haven't even been accepted yet," I told her as I adjusted the straps over my shoulders. My hands shook as I imagined myself practicing *pliés* in a light-filled Parisian studio.

"But you will be," Grandma said, her voice firm. "How could they ever say no? It's in your blood."

"Mom!" Mom said to Grandma Joan as she walked into my bedroom. She cast a skeptical glance at the Degas poster hanging over my bed. "Can you please stop saying that? It's not even true."

Grandma sighed, then turned to me. "Of course it's true. You come from a long line of ballerinas, Mia." She gave me a wink. "You believe me, don't you?"

Grandma Joan has told me the same story since the day I put on my first tutu. The first part of it is definitely true: My great-grandmother was French. She met an American man in Paris when she was twenty-three, fell in love, and moved to the U.S. soon after their wedding. But before that—and this is when things get a little murky—she practiced ballet. Like her mother before her, and her mother before her, all the way back to the late 1800s, when my great-great-great-grandmother was a *danseuse étoile,* a principal dancer, the highest, most prestigious ranking in the Paris Opera. Supposedly, this was around the time Edgar Degas created his world-famous paintings of ballerinas.

Grandma insists that Degas painted my great-great-great-grandmother, and that she was the subject of one of his masterpieces. The nonspecifics of this family legend drive Mom crazy. She doesn't believe this story, and whenever Grandma Joan brings it up, she'll happily point out that no one actually knows which painting our ancestor might be in, or even remembers what her name was. *If* she was a ballet dancer at all. Mom never lets me forget that it's most likely made up, and that there's no way to know for sure. She doesn't want me to believe in fairy tales.

But I do.

The myth itself is proof enough that ballet is my destiny—how could anything as strange as this get passed down from generation to generation if it weren't true? This story has always been part of me, of how I dance. When I'm performing, I sometimes imagine my ancestor twirling across the stage, spotlighted by gas lamps, while Degas sweeps his oil paints and pastels onto canvas and paper. I like to think she was part of his inspiration, that he watched her spin in a sea of color and light.

I wore my new leotard for my audition video, which Camilla, my best friend from ballet school, helped me film. She'd decided to only apply to local summer programs, and swore it had nothing to do with the fact that she didn't want to be away from her new boyfriend—an aspiring musician named Pedro. I think Mom wishes I had a boyfriend as well, but my dating experience so far has only proved that no one can make my heart flutter the way ballet does. To go with my leotard, I put my hair up in a tight bun, my face fully made up. And two months later, I got into the Institut de l'Opéra de Paris, just like Grandma had promised.

I close my eyes for a moment, and when I reopen them, one of the most famous churches in the world stares back at me.

"Notre-Dame!" I squeal to Audrey, who doesn't react. I press my face against the window, soaking in its beauty, the two towers disappearing off behind our taxi, the arched structure revealing itself in the back, and the grand majesty of it all. My first look at Paris! But I don't have time to revel in the moment, because our taxi makes a right turn, and, a couple of minutes later, we pull off to the side of a wide street packed with cyclists, buses, and pedestrians.

"Finally," Audrey says, looking out the window.

The driver slams his horn as a bike zooms past, and I'm definitely awake now. The cyclist turns back and yells what I can only assume is an insult. Though, because it's in French, it sounds almost pleasant to me. Our driver just shakes his head in response as he parks in front of a white stone building, about six stories high, with small double windows all with matching gray curtains—our home for the summer. Thanks to my Google Street View research, I know exactly where we are—a stone's throw from the embankments of the Seine, and the lively student neighborhood called Saint-Michel.

Inside the building, the hall is very quiet. According to my admission packet, my room is on the third floor, and I pull my suitcase up the curved stairwell one step at a time as Audrey rushes ahead with her duffel.

"I knew it!" she calls down the stairs. When I catch up, she's standing in front of a door, shaking her head.

A handwritten sign reads: *Audrey Chapman & Mia Jenrow*

I take a deep breath. Roommates. Ugh.

In the room, two single beds with metal frames are tucked against opposite walls, which are painted in dirty beige. There are also two tiny closets and a small wooden desk barely big enough for a laptop. The window looks onto the building on the other side of the inner courtyard, letting in very little light, even though it's now the middle of the day. Okay, so it's not as glamorous as I'd imagined.

Without a word, Audrey pushes past me and claims the bed by the window. She quickly pulls out fresh clothes and makes a dash to the communal showers. I grab a striped tee and a flowy navy skirt and follow suit. Ten minutes later, we're both back in the room and ready to go when I notice the cardboard tube peeking out of my suitcase. I stop in my tracks.

"What now?" Audrey asks, standing by the door. Our flight delay means that we have to leave immediately if we want to get to orientation in time.

I don't want to have to explain to her that inside that tube is my favorite painting in the whole wide world. I'd promised myself I would hang it up as soon as I got to Paris. It'll only take a minute.

"You should go ahead. I . . ." I pick up the tube and open it. "I need to do something."

Audrey gives me a funny look, her big brown eyes framed by thick but perfectly curved eyebrows. I'm sure she's going to run out the door and not speak to me for the rest of the summer. Instead, she retrieves the few pins from the corkboard above the desk and kicks off her shoes. "Quick," she says.

I'm too shocked to respond as I join her on my bed. A moment later, I smile as I take in the image I've woken up to for as long as I can remember: *Ballet Rehearsal on Stage,* the Edgar Degas painting featuring tulle-clad ballerinas rehearsing on the stage of the Paris Opera. It's so striking; I can practically sense the tension before the curtain lifts.

"It's a superstition—" I begin.

Audrey cuts me off. "I get it. I put my ballet clothes on the left side of my body first. The left strap over my shoulder before the right, the left leg in my tights, my left shoe . . . I can't dance if I don't do that."

I grin. Audrey and I may have never exchanged more than a few icy words before, but this is promising.

"It's a nice painting," Audrey admits.

With the Degas dancers watching over me, my Paris adventure can finally begin.

CHAPTER TWO

THE SUDDEN KNOCK startles us both. Our bedroom door opens, and in bursts a petite girl with brown skin and long black hair.

"Mia, Audrey, *finally*!" The girl's voice is bright, with a strong British accent. "I'm Lucy. Everyone else has left for orientation already, but Anouk and I wanted to wait for you."

Lucy steps aside, and in walks a very tall, pale, blond girl. Anouk waves and gives us a sweet smile.

I'm overcome with gratitude. These girls are total strangers, and they waited for us—who even does that? "So nice to meet you!"

"Anouk was in the program last year, and she knows Paris really well," Lucy says, motioning for us to rush out the door. "Come on, let's go."

"We'll take the ten and then the five," Anouk says in an

accent I can't place. Then, at my confused expression, she adds, "The métro lines."

"Oh, right!" I say. We might be late, but at least we won't be lost.

"Oh, and here," Lucy adds, fishing something out of her tote bag. She pulls out two croissants wrapped in paper napkins along with two mandarins. "We saved you this from breakfast this morning, in case you didn't have time to grab anything."

I hadn't realized how much my stomach was grumbling. "Thank you!" I say, accepting my half from her and immediately biting into the pastry. Whoa. The buttery flavor is delicious, and I wish I had more time to enjoy my first taste of France. "You two are my favorite people in the world right now," I say in between two mouthfuls.

Audrey mumbles a vague "thanks" as Lucy hands her the food. It's kind of rude, of course, but Audrey's not here to make friends.

I wish I could be that disciplined, too, but I *like* friends. Friends are . . . nice. I throw my bag over my shoulder and slip on my shoes. "Ready," I say.

• • •

By the time our train stops at Bastille station, I've learned that Anouk is Dutch, from Amsterdam, while Lucy is from Manchester, in northern England. Anouk seems very focused and wants to get us to school ASAP—maybe because she's been through all this before—while Lucy chats all the way, making amusing comments about Paris and giggling like we've known each other forever. I know I just met them, but I love these girls already.

As we exit the métro onto Bastille Square, I can't help but pause and stare in awe. Paris is at my fingertips and it's real, at last. I may have spent months looking at pictures of the city on Instagram, but it's so different to actually see it in person. The Opéra Bastille is right in front of us, its ultramodern glass structure standing proud over its namesake roundabout, called Place de la Bastille. From my research, I know this impressive building is one of *two* operas in the city. The original, Opéra Garnier, is a luscious palace on the other side of Paris and has been host to centuries of ballet performances. That's where Degas practically lived.

Traffic rushes by, cars honk, tourists stop to take photos. Trees line the sidewalk, their leaves the dark green of summer. I resist the urge to spin around with glee at finally being here as Anouk takes us down a quiet little street to our left. A few minutes later, our school comes into view. It's a classical building made of beige stone with a roof covered in slate tiles, like you see all over Paris. Through the open windows I can hear a piano and the count of a teacher keeping time. *"Un, deux, trois, quatre."*

There's an inscription above the dark blue double door that reads *L'Institut de l'Opéra de Paris*.

"We're the luckiest girls in the world," Lucy says with a happy sigh as we climb the marble steps.

"Especially for those of us in level five," Audrey adds.

I roll my eyes, but Lucy's smile drops a bit. She opens her mouth to respond, but Anouk cuts in. "Level four is amazing, too. . . . Pretty much no one gets level five their first year here." Her voice lowers to a murmur and she adds, "or their second, for that matter," like she's speaking from experience.

Audrey doesn't say anything back, but the corners of her mouth turn up in a satisfied smirk.

Inside, the hall is bustling with students lining up to file into the main auditorium. We're just in time for orientation—*phew*. The four of us find seats as close to the front as possible. Glancing around, I'm struck by the wide range of teenagers attending the program: some tall and lean, others short and athletic; mostly girls, but also a few boys here and there. In the space of a few minutes, I think I hear at least three languages outside of French and English. It's clear the school has brought the best talent from all over the world. A hush falls over the room as Myriam Ayed, the most famous *danseuse étoile* of the Paris Ballet, comes onto the stage. She's known for her out-of-this-world talent, but she also made headlines when she was promoted, because she is the first dancer of African descent to become a principal dancer at the Paris Opera. As a mixed-race woman— she's half-Moroccan, half-French—she was hailed as *the* change French ballet needed: a sign that classical dancing could modernize while staying true to tradition. She looks exactly the same as in all the pictures I've seen—muscular, with sharp features but warm eyes—and I feel oddly emotional just being in the same room as her.

"It's my pleasure to welcome you," Ms. Ayed says into the microphone, slowly looking around the room with a smile. She speaks in English—the official language of this summer program—but her thick French accent clings to every word.

"You've all worked so hard to be here today, and for that, you must congratulate yourselves."

She claps her hands a few times, and the room fills with applause. "I was in your shoes not so long ago, and I know that just being selected means that you have what it takes to succeed. But your work has only just begun."

As the applause dies down, Ms. Ayed continues, "I'm happy to announce that you will be dancing *Swan Lake* as your final performance. The respective *maîtres de ballet* for each level will be assigning roles at the beginning of next week, and I will be cheering you all from the sidelines."

My heart flutters. *Swan Lake* is my favorite ballet (So dramatic! So heart-wrenching! So technically challenging!), but I've only ever performed as a page girl. I would do absolutely anything to dance as Odette, but featured and principal roles will for sure go to dancers in level five. Audrey will probably be one of them.

I look over and see Audrey biting her lower lip, hanging

on to Myriam Ayed's every word. She's putting on a brave face, but I'm certain she's praying for the role in her head.

After we meet Monsieur Dabrowski, the school's artistic director, and a few other instructors, we head to the cafeteria, where we'll be having lunch every day, starting now.

My race through the airport this morning made me ravenous, and I help myself to extra cheese—a gooey Camembert—to tide me over until dinner. Afterward, we're divided into small groups for a tour. We're led through each of the five floors, which are full of glass-walled studios with high ceilings, beautiful antique wooden floors, and Steinway pianos, along with the locker rooms. The corridors feel never-ending, and the rooms are so much bigger and more impressive than the ones I'm used to, but I tell myself that I'll know my way around here in no time.

At the end of the afternoon, Lucy, Anouk, Audrey, and I meet up outside on the front steps of the school. I edge closer to our group, curious about a tiny little *major* thing. "Myriam Ayed didn't say much about the final performance. And no one else spoke about the apprentice program directors. They will come watch *Swan Lake,* right?"

While this summer intensive isn't supposed to be competitive—there are no medals at the end, and the students aren't ranked—it's no secret that many apprentice program directors for the world's major ballet companies attend the final performance in the hopes of discovering up-and-coming talent. If you're lucky enough to be chosen by one, you get to practice with a *corps de ballet* for a year before hopefully joining the company for good. I'm sure it's the ultimate goal of pretty much everyone in the program.

The rumor is that our instructors pass along the names of their favorite students beforehand to the program directors, which means we have to give it our best all summer long to make an impression. If your *maître de ballet* notices you, then it's likely a program director will as well. And if they do . . . an offer might not be far behind.

"Anouk, is that true?" Lucy asks. "Did anyone get offered an apprenticeship last year?"

The three of us turn to Anouk. If anyone knows something, it's going to be her. "Don't look at me," she says jokingly. "I was only in level three."

"But you must have heard things," I insist.

"Okay, fine," Anouk says, "but don't blame me if it turns out not to be true."

"Just spill," Audrey says sharply. Lucy and I frown at her, and she sighs. "I mean, come on, we *need* to know."

Anouk leans closer. "From what I heard, at the end of the final performance, the program directors make a list of the students they're interested in. It's usually the leads, but not always. They might decide someone in the *corps de ballet* has potential, too."

I bite my lip. So there's a chance for those of us in level four. A small one, but it's there.

"Then," Anouk continues, "they invite them to a private audition. Those happen the next day, I think. Last year there was the Australian Ballet, the Bolshoi Ballet, the Royal Danish Ballet, the Royal Ballet in London, and ABT, of course."

Audrey glances at me at the same time I steal a look at her. ABT. The American Ballet Theatre in New York City.

I close my eyes and see countless weekends of practice, my school breaks filled with competitions in faraway places, my nights spent bandaging my bloody toes—it's all led me to this. Here is the proof that you always get another chance. ABT may have rejected me once, but I'm only just getting started.

CHAPTER THREE

THE GIRLS DECIDE to take the métro back to the dorm, but I don't feel like joining them. This is my first day in Paris, and I want to enjoy it before school starts for real tomorrow.

"I think I'm going to walk," I say, surprising myself.

I've never been alone in a big city, and I don't know my way around here. I should unpack and rest. Do the reasonable thing. But I don't want to.

Lucy frowns.

"I'll see you for dinner," I promise.

Audrey and Anouk start to walk away, but Lucy insists. "Will you be okay?"

I smile. "I'm in Paris. Of course I'm going to be okay."

Instead of south, I head west toward the heart of the city. My eyes are wide as I try to take it all in at once: the tangy scent of asphalt warmed by the summer sun, the casual yet polished appearances of most passersby (no shorts or flip-flops in sight), the lovely shade of pastel blue in the sky. I've heard Paris called a gray city, but today the sun is bright, like it's putting on a show just for me.

As I walk through a hip neighborhood called the Marais, according to the map on my phone, I notice a sea of red awnings above the rows of sidewalk cafés; the narrow, winding cobblestoned streets; the pristine cream-colored buildings; and the antique signs above the shops.

I feel like I've stepped back in time. It's the Paris of the movies, the one I've been dreaming of ever since I knew I would be coming here. There's street art painted on the side of a building of a mother and daughter holding hands, a reminder that I still haven't spoken to mine. I pop in my headphones and call my family's landline. My brother, Thomas, picks up after a few rings.

"It's me," I say, stepping onto a tiny side street to get out of the way of other pedestrians. The top of my right sandal catches a cobblestone for the third time in a few minutes, and I almost trip, again. I have no idea how *Parisiennes* can wear heels. These quaint little sidewalks are like obstacle courses designed for trained street warriors.

"Oh, hi," he responds distractedly, a video game blaring in the background.

"Is Mom there?" I ask.

"She's at work," Thomas says. "It's the middle of the day."

"Right, duh." I'd forgotten Paris was six hours ahead.

"Is Aveer with you?" Aveer is my brother's best friend, and since they're pretty much inseparable, I know the answer already. I just don't want to hang up yet. Thomas grunts in response.

"Hmm, well, tell Mom I called, okay? And Dad? Tell them I'm fine."

As I speak, two meticulously groomed dogs strut toward me. The smaller one, a blond pug, stops to sniff my feet. I bend down and give it a pat on the head. It smells like shampoo, the expensive kind. And I thought *I* was fancy with my rose-scented body soap.

The woman on the other end of the leash looks at me, incredulous. *"Allez viens, Lucien,"* she says, pulling her dog away and rubbing where my hand just was. Have I committed some kind of French faux pas? Everyone lets you pet their dog in Westchester. I watch the woman walk away, gesturing to the man beside her. I wonder if she's talking about the rude American girl who touched her dog without permission. Whoops.

"Later," my brother says. "Have fun, sis."

"Wait! Did Mom say anything about me?" I ask.

"Like what?"

"Nothing. Forget it."

"Okay . . . Oh, Grandma Joan stopped by yesterday. She was talking about someone named Aunt Vivienne," Thomas goes on. "Who's Aunt Vivienne?" He pronounces it Vivian, but I know exactly who he means.

"Don't worry about it," I say. "And maybe don't tell Mom about that. Okay?"

After we hang up, I walk and walk and walk, pinching myself on the inside at how thrilling it feels to discover a foreign city on my own, but trying to look like I do this all the time by marching on without looking at my phone too much. I also think back to my conversation with Grandma Joan on the day of the gray leotard, when I filmed my audition. I was sulking in my room that evening, worried my performance wasn't good enough to get me accepted.

Grandma Joan had been over for dinner, and she was coming to say goodbye before heading home. She sat on my bed next to me. "When you get to Paris," she'd started.

I sighed. "*If* I go to Paris . . ."

"*When* you get to Paris, you should visit my aunt Vivienne. She's my mother's sister. She's quite old now, ninety-two or even ninety-three, but I think you'll enjoy her stories."

She'd slipped a piece of paper into my hand, on which she'd written Aunt Vivienne's name and number. Then, Grandma Joan had grabbed my chin between her fingers and looked deep into my eyes. "Promise me you'll get in touch with her."

I had nodded sadly. At the time, Paris felt so very far away.

"And you better brush up on your French," Grandma had said as she left my room, pointing at a few books on the corner of my desk. She used to talk to me in French when I was little, but not so much anymore. "Aunt Vivienne doesn't speak a lick of English."

I had taken a picture of the paper with my phone after she left, then forgot all about it. Until now.

I scroll through my photos until I see the cursive scrawl of my grandmother's handwriting. I know I promised, but I don't *really* want to call up a random relative who I can't even have a conversation with, do I?

Even though it's getting late, I can't go back just yet. The light is glorious—soft and a little fuzzy, like I'm seeing the city through a vintage lens. I've gone to New York City many times—it's only a short train ride away—but it seems so harsh in comparison. Paris is just . . . different. There are so many things to look at: the tidy newspaper kiosks on the sidewalks, the little blue placards with street names on the sides of buildings, the vintage wrought-iron signs for the métro stations.

I find myself on a bustling street, packed with bistros and restaurants. It's so narrow that people and motor scooters fight to share the space. Tiny round marble tables flanked with checkered rattan chairs spill onto the street. The chairs face outward, and people sit next to one another, watching the world go by.

Just then, a man wearing thick-rimmed glasses and a cap pulls out a few coins, drops them on his table, and leaves. I rush to take his place, sliding into the black-and-white woven chair. Sitting next to me is a woman with several shopping bags at her feet, talking quietly on her cell phone. A baguette peaks out of one of her bags, and my mouth waters at the intoxicating smell of fresh bread. Would she notice if I tore off a piece? I'm kidding. Sort of.

The waiter, dressed in a white shirt and black apron, looks just a couple of years older than me. He's kind of cute, in a rumpled sort of way. I hope he ignores me for now, because I don't know what I want. Or rather, I don't know what I'm supposed to want. What do glamorous French girls order to drink? The woman next to me covers her phone with her hand. She turns to the waiter and says, *"Un Perrier rondelle, s'il vous plaît."*

The waiter nods and walks off. I repeat the words under my breath. *"Un Perrier rondelle, s'il vous plaît."* I do it over and over again, trying to mimic her accent, to remember where she put the intonations.

After a few minutes, the waiter comes back with a small green bottle of sparkling water. He pours it in a tall glass with a slice of lemon on the rim. He also places a bowl of chips and the check on her table. The woman thanks him with a nod before going back to her conversation. It's not that difficult, I tell myself. I can do this.

The waiter then turns to me to take my order. *"Et vous, mademoiselle?"* And you, miss?

It sounds formal, but kind of charming, too. He smiles as he waits for me to answer. I smile back.

"Vous avez choisi?" He asks if I know what I want, not taking his eyes off me. Come on, Mia, focus. I sit up straight,

holding my head high—never *not* a ballerina—and say, *"Un Perrier rondelle, s'il vous plaît."*

"Tout de suite," he answers. *Coming right up.*

He didn't flinch. He didn't pause. He understood me on my first try. I beam.

Two minutes later, he returns with my drink, and I swear he takes as much time as possible to put everything down. His eyes flick up toward mine, and the hint of a smile is forming on his lips. Is he flirting with me?

"C'est mon premier jour à Paris," I say in a way that I hope sounds kind of cute. *It's my first day in Paris.*

"La chance!" he responds. *Lucky you!*

I nod and bite my lower lip. Someone a few tables away tries to wave him over, but he doesn't move. Okay, Mia, enough. You've never had time for boyfriends before, remember? That's what I told Cameron, anyway, after we dated for a few weeks last winter. His family lives down the street from mine, but between school and ballet, it just didn't work.

I'll admit it was nice at first, having a boyfriend. After each date, Cameron would send me a song link that reminded him of me. Then he started suggesting we spend more time together and got grumpy whenever I left to go to ballet. I liked him, but . . . I got kind of annoyed about that. One night we stayed out until midnight, chatting and kissing after a movie. The next day I missed my alarm and got to my Saturday ballet class late. My teacher didn't let me in, even after I pleaded with her. I broke up with Cameron that afternoon.

"*À bientôt, j'espère,*" the waiter says as he starts to back away. *See you soon, I hope.*

His eyes linger on me for another second, and my heart flutters.

"*Merci,*" I say. My cheeks must be bright pink.

Sipping at my sparkling water, I lean back in the squeaky chair and let the moment wash over me. I look at the reddening sky. The sun sets so late over here, like the evenings know that they're magical and should last for as long as possible. I breathe in the warm, sweet air of summer. And the best part? It's only day one. Hello, Paris. I've arrived.

CHAPTER FOUR

"TO SUCCEED HERE, you must understand that there will be no downtime, no room for error," Monsieur Dabrowski informs us as we take position at the barre for our first class of the afternoon. "You have been given an incredible opportunity. Do not waste it. I want to see complete dedication to your craft, starting right now."

I definitely want to be fully dedicated to my craft starting right now, but I'm not sure my body is up to the task. I barely slept last night, after my dreamy evening of wandering around Paris making eyes at cute waiters (okay, just the one). Now my limbs feel stiff. Mom had warned me about the effects of jet lag, but I had sort of assumed I'd be too excited to feel it. I was wrong. At least, I'm lucky that classes are taught in English and that I don't have to rack my brain to understand what our revered teacher is saying.

Lucy shoots me a furtive glance. I know we're thinking the same thing. Monsieur Dabrowski was all anyone wanted to talk about last night at dinner. We had all heard the rumors prior to arriving in Paris. Monsieur Dabrowski can make or break your career. He makes dancers cry sometimes. He only wears black to avoid distractions. He never compliments students during class.

So far he is exactly what I expected, especially after watching the few movies he's been in. He always plays the role of a ballet dancer or choreographer, and he looks just as mysterious and cold in real life as he does onscreen.

"I am going to be observing each and every one of you. I want to see how you move, where your weaknesses are. Did you give everything you had in your five-minute audition video, or do you have what it takes to survive six weeks of intensive ballet? Will you be one of the swans in the final performance? Will you have a chance to shine in front of the entire school?"

The jet lag hits me again as he talks, my mouth going dry and my eyelids growing heavy. Each *relevé* burns my calves, even though I stretched for almost an hour last night after dinner. Audrey had insisted I couldn't do it in our room, because she needed total peace and quiet, so I had grabbed my foam roller and spread myself out on the floor of the communal living area along with a few other girls. We grimaced in unison as our respective hamstrings suffered from the pressure.

I wonder how Audrey is doing, and if Monsieur Dabrowski was even tougher with her morning class. He's the *maître de ballet* for level five, but assesses the top two levels on the first day, which means that this is our first and last class with him. Thankfully.

My neck cracks as I turn my head. I want to roll it out so badly, but I resist. There's no way I'll admit to feeling off in front of him. The bottoms of my feet are sore from all the walking I did yesterday, and my shoulders are tight. It's like every part of my body is paying the price for my hot date with Paris. Maybe I shouldn't have stayed out so long at that café, letting the warm summer air brush my face, and hoping the waiter would come back to check on me. And when he did, twice, I told myself that it was a great opportunity to practice my French, but I may have been carried away by the excitement of being in the most romantic city in the world. I liked this idea of Mia Jenrow, *Parisienne*-in-training, engaging in witty banter with a cute guy on a gorgeous summer night. I felt grown-up, charming, daring, and totally unlike myself. Now I just feel tired.

"More turnout, Lucy. And by more, I mean *a lot more*. Your *maître de ballet* is going to be asking for more out of all of you, every day. More, more, *more*!"

I hear Lucy's deep inhale as she complies, her legs quivering as she fights with her thighs to increase the turnout of her fourth position. She winces for a split second only, but that's enough for Monsieur Dabrowski to catch it.

"Is there a problem?" he asks, stopping right in front of us, his posture perfect and his face stern.

Lucy doesn't respond, doesn't bat an eye. She knows he

doesn't expect an answer, only the correct execution of his orders.

"Anouk, where did you learn that *grand jeté*? You look like you're mopping the floor. Show a little grace! This is a ballet class, not a discotheque."

"Mellie, where is your pointe work? Did you leave it at home?"

He knows all of our names and studies us from top to bottom, but he doesn't say anything to me, which makes me nervous—is there something even more wrong with me than everyone else? I keep waiting for him to say, "Straight gaze, Mia, straight gaze!"

I swear he's still watching my every move, though. I wonder if he can see my muscles shake, and how tight my core is. Sweat prickles my forehead and drips down between my shoulder blades. Maybe Audrey was right to be surprised that I got into this program; maybe I'm not good enough for this.

When the class ends, I'm so disappointed in myself that I don't even feel the cramps in my legs. Tears sting at the corners of my eyes as Lucy, Anouk, and I sit on the bench to take off our shoes. I focus on the pink silk ribbons, wrapping them neatly before unbinding my toes.

"Mademoiselle Jenrow." My heads jerks up to Monsieur Dabrowski, waving me over from the other side of the studio. Another rumor about him turns out to be true: he only calls us by our first names during class. Otherwise he prefers the formality of *Mademoiselle* and *Monsieur*. "A moment, please," he adds.

My heart sinks. It's worse than I thought.

He waits until all the students have left. Some of them gave me looks of pity as they walked out, confirming my instinct that this is not normal.

"I've been observing you," Monsieur Dabrowski starts.

I hold my breath. Should I beg? Plead my case? I try to think of the right words, but my mind goes blank.

"And I've decided that level four is not right for you."

He takes a seat and points to a chair beside him, but I couldn't move even if I wanted to. Do not cry, I repeat to myself. Do not cry.

"You're a talented dancer," Monsieur Dabrowski continues, clearly oblivious to the tornado going on inside my heart.

I nod. I know I'm a good dancer. I work hard. I never give up. I practice for hours until my body molds itself to my will. I strive to move through the air in a way that makes me feel something. But I know that Monsieur Dabrowski doesn't mean to praise me. He's just trying to soften the blow. Somehow that makes it worse.

"This summer is going to be challenging. But what I saw today made me think that your skills do not match this level. It might be too hard on you, I'm not sure."

My chin begins to quiver. I need to sit down after all. My legs are about to give out as I take the seat next to him. To think that just last night I felt like I owned the world. He's going to tell me I'm being bumped down to level three, isn't he? Or that there was a mistake, and that I should have never been accepted into the program. Maybe Mom was right all along.

"I've decided to move you up to level five." Monsieur Dabrowski eyes me, waiting for my reaction.

"You . . . What?" is all I can say. I can't have heard him correctly.

"You will be in level five starting tomorrow. Make sure you go to the office to get your new schedule and be ready to work harder than ever before."

Level five! Oh. My. God. This isn't really happening. My face breaks into a huge smile. "*Merci* so much! Thank you. *Beaucoup, beaucoup.*"

"I'm not doing you a favor," Monsieur Dabrowski says, one eyebrow raised at my excited rambling. "And I reserve the right to change my mind if it turns out that you are dragging the class down."

I nod, willing myself to stop beaming. He needs to see that I'm taking this seriously.

He's silent for a moment, and I wonder if this is my cue to leave. I perch on the edge of my chair.

Monsieur Dabrowski gets up, shuffles the papers resting on top of the piano, and then turns around to face me again.

"You may go now, but make sure you have the correct attire for tomorrow," he adds, pointing his chin in my direction. I look down at my outfit. I'm wearing the knitted leg warmers I usually slip over my pink tights at the end of class, and my gray leotard, of course. I was so proud to put it on this morning. I wanted to FaceTime Grandma when I was dressed, but then I remembered it was the middle of the night at home.

"I'm sorry?" I have no idea what he's talking about. My pointe shoes are brand-new; I bought four more pairs just for my trip.

Monsieur Dabrowski lets out a frustrated sigh. "Level five students wear the classic leotard from Repetto, white and sleeveless. It's a tradition at our school."

"I don't have a white leotard," I say in a whisper. "I'm not sure if I can get one tonight—" I'm about to say more when the look of contempt on his face stops me.

"The rules apply to all, Mademoiselle Jenrow. There will be no exceptions. Being assigned to level five is a badge of honor."

"I *am* honored! Very, very honored. It's just that . . ."

"That what?"

I look down, but I can feel his gaze burning through the top of my head. "I swear I'll do my best," I add, desperate.

For a brief moment I think that I could borrow one from Audrey, but aside from the fact that we're not the same size, I can't imagine she'd be so generous as to save my butt.

Monsieur Dabrowski clicks his tongue. "It sounds like your best might not be good enough. Please don't make me regret my decision."

"I won't, Monsieur Dabrowski. I promise."

And to keep this promise, I'm going to scour this city for as long as I have to, until I get my hands on that mythical leotard. *Ready, steady . . .*

CHAPTER FIVE

GO. THE MAP on my phone says that it will take approx-imately twenty-four minutes to get to the Repetto store, which closes in half an hour. Now is probably a good time to start panicking. I type in a few more searches, sweat coating my palms. There's another location a few blocks away from school, but it's already closed for the day.

I take one more look at the map, stumble down the main stairs, and rush to the exit. I jerk the front door open, but don't see the leather satchel on the steps until my foot slips over it. I catch myself just in time—any ballerina worth her tutu has perfect balance—but the contents of the bag go flying.

"Aargh!" I cry out.

"Enfin!" a boy shouts. *Finally.*

The shout belongs to a guy about my age who's standing at the bottom of the steps, staring at his stuff, which has now gone everywhere.

I do not have time for this.

"Oh, c'est pas toi," the boy mutters to himself when he looks up and sees me. *It's not you.*

He's not very tall, probably average height—but that's the only average thing about him. He has a lanky frame, his creased linen shirt billowing around him; thick, dark brown hair falling over one eye; and a mesmerizing dimple, even as he frowns.

I stare at him blankly, so he switches to English. "You're not . . . Never mind."

To be clear, my total state of confusion is not about his French. Okay, it's a little bit about the French, but it's mainly because he might be the most beautiful, no, cute, no, charming, no, sexy, no, gorgeous guy I have ever laid eyes on.

Ever.

Yes, that's a bold statement, but he is. Enough to freeze me in space. Enough to render me speechless. Enough to make me forget what I'm supposed to be doing.

"British?" the boy asks, coming up the school steps. He glances at the objects scattered on the ground—his keys, a phone charger, sunglasses—and I realize that I should stop staring and help him pick them up. I kneel down beside him, and our hands almost touch as we both reach for his keys.

"American," I answer. My throat catches, and it comes out in a raspy, barely audible, totally not attractive way. To top it off, I'm pretty sure that I've turned bright red, and I can't blame that solely on my talk with Monsieur Dabrowski and my race down the stairs.

"Américaine," I correct myself. *"Mon français . . . pas très bon."* I cringe. I must sound like a child. Surely the first rule of learning the language is that you should be able to say in proper French that you don't speak French properly.

"It's good enough," he responds in perfect English, his accent slick and not too pronounced. "Most girls here still can't speak a word of French by the time they leave."

The boy jams his belongings in the satchel and hangs it over his shoulder. As he stands up, he glances behind me to the front door, squinting to see through the glass.

"Je prends des leçons sur . . . umm, I have an app," I say, attempting a cute smile as I stand up, too. A few other things I should be taking lessons in: how to sound *charmante* on any occasion, and how to get to the other side of Paris while staying right here, smiling at this mysterious boy. Oh, and how to figure out if I'll see him again without sounding like a creep. So, basically, learning charm, teleportation, and mind reading. French may be easier after all.

"I'm Louis, by the way," the boy says with a little wave.

He pronounces it Loo-ee, the French way. *Obviously.* It's so unbearably cute that I wish he would say it one more time.

"I'm . . . ," I begin, getting lost in his smile for a second. Everything about my mad dash to Repetto comes crashing back. "I'm late, I'm so super mega late!"

Still, I can't move. Fun fact about this street: it was absolutely, definitely, one hundred percent designed to make people fall in love, with its lush plants and flowerpots hanging from windowsills, the old-fashioned lampposts, the notes of a violin coming from a nearby apartment, and the stacks of bicycles with wire baskets. It's almost *too* romantic.

"Then I should let you go. . . . I'm waiting for . . . a friend," Louis explains.

He's waiting for a girl. Of course. *Le* sigh.

"I think everyone's gone," I say. I didn't come across anyone on my way out.

"I should probably call. . . ." He trails off, looking a little sad.

"Okay, then . . ." I edge down the stairs.

He ignores his phone though and keeps staring at me. I can't walk away from him; that would be extremely rude. But I also can't break my promise to Monsieur Dabrowski. "I have to get this leotard or I won't be allowed back tomorrow. My instructor, he's . . . Well, let's just say that my life is pretty much over if I don't make it to the shop in time."

This puts a smile back on Louis's face, and I stop wondering why I even told him all that. It's not like he asked.

"A true ballet emergency," he replies. "You're going to the Repetto on Rue de la Paix, right?" He follows me down the steps and pauses in front of a Vespa that I've only just noticed.

I nod. Nodding is so great. It's the same in every language.

Louis starts undoing a lock that holds two helmets in place. "It looks like my evening just freed up." He offers me one of them with a smile.

My arms suddenly feel like noodles. No way he's suggesting what I think he's suggesting.

Louis puts on his helmet, straddles the scooter, and kicks it into gear. "Are you coming? We don't have much time."

I bite my lip. Well played, Paris. Well played.

• • •

We zip through the Marais, past the rows and rows of chic boutiques, then turn onto a large boulevard (so many other scooters!) and ride along the picture-perfect Canal Saint-Martin for a while. Even though it's all breathtaking, I can only really think about my hands around this boy's waist. Am I squeezing too hard? I am, I'm totally squeezing too hard. Maybe I'll just say that I was scared, that I've never been on the back of a scooter before. Right, and then he'll think of me as the silly American girl who's afraid of everything. I force my hands to relax, which only gives me a better sense of his firm abs under his thin shirt. My heartbeat quickens.

Louis is an expert, zigzagging between cars and buses, avoiding cyclists, and even glancing in his rearview mirror long enough to give me a smile *and* a wink. What am I doing, going off with a guy I don't know? I think Paris has messed with my head. Scratch that. I *know* Paris has messed with my head.

I catch a glimpse of Opéra Garnier—*the* Opéra Garnier!—just before we turn onto Rue de la Paix, and I crane my neck to get a better look at the ornate building through the visor. Louis zooms up to the curb in front of the Repetto store, and I'm already removing my helmet as he parks. There isn't even time for a hair check, or to admire the intricately beaded ballet costume in the window. I rush off before I realize that I forgot one major thing.

"Thank you, thank you, thank you," I call back. "*Merci,* I mean."

Louis gives me a dimpled smile in response.

But that's when my luck runs out.

"*Désolée, nous sommes fermés,*" the shopkeeper announces as soon as I walk in. *Sorry, we're closed.* Her black bob frames a face full of sharp edges. When I don't respond, she waves the keys in her hands to show me that she was just about to lock the door. I muster all the French I know to explain my problem and convey the state of emergency, but the woman keeps shrugging and telling me that they'll be open tomorrow.

"But it'll be too late! *J'ai besoin d'un, non . . . deux, non . . . trois . . .* umm . . . leotards *blancs, maintenant!*" I say just as the chime of the door rings. It's Louis. I'd assumed he'd left already, and the last thing I want is for him to hear me beg in lousy French, my cheeks flush, my words stumbling over each other as the shopkeeper looks on sternly. He did me a huge favor by driving me here, but I can't ask for his help again—I don't even know him.

"Louis!" the shopkeeper says, with a smile.

"Christine, comment ça va?" Christine, how are you?

He comes closer to give her *la bise*. One kiss on each cheek.

I look from one to the other, flustered. Louis is not a student at the school; I would have noticed him. He mentioned a friend, but that doesn't explain why he's on a first-name basis with the staff of this famous ballet store. They chat for a few moments, but they speak so quickly, I don't catch what they say.

"Everything okay?" Louis asks me. "You look . . . confused."

Confusion doesn't even begin to cover how I feel right now.

The woman looks from me to Louis and pouts. "Fine, I'll get them for you," she says in French, to him.

To me, she just points at the plush velvet seats in the middle of the shop. As soon as she's gone into the back, I exhale. "You just saved my life."

"I hear that a lot," Louis responds seriously.

I let out a nervous laugh.

"I'm kidding," he says. "I don't solve ballet crises for just anyone."

I let myself fall back on the soft pink seat and shake my head. "You have no idea how much trouble I was in. Our instructor is super strict. I mean, they all are, but he's next level. He says things like 'I will not tolerate anything less than absolute perfection from my students,'" I say, mimicking Monsieur Dabrowski's harsh tone.

Louis sits down next to me with an amused smirk. I should probably take this as a hint and stop talking, but I don't.

"I know he's supposed to be the best of the best," I continue, stress untwisting my tongue and letting all the words fall out, "but he's so scary. Seriously, honest-to-God scary. I bet he's going to say that my leotard is not the right shade of white and then kick me out anyway."

Louis bites his lip. "You still haven't told me your name, by the way."

My face drops. "I'm sorry!"

"*Salut,* Mademoiselle Sorry."

My cheeks grow hot for about the tenth time, and Louis laughs. "Mia! *Je m'appelle* Mia."

"Nice to meet you, Mia."

I'm about to speak again, but Louis cuts in. "And I haven't told you mine. I probably should."

"It's not Louis?" I ask. It comes out louder than I intended.

He chuckles. "No, I mean my full name. I'm Louis Dabrowski. And your *maître de ballet,* that scary man who's already giving you nightmares . . . he's my father."

"Oh," I say, my mouth hanging open. There's no way to fix this. I mean, unless I just happen to find a time machine,

like, right now, but I don't think that's a realistic expecta-
tion. Unfortunately.

"Yeah," Louis says with an apologetic look.

I swear he wants to laugh, but I really can't see what's
funny. Heat crawls up the back of my neck.

Have I just been flirting with the son of the toughest ballet teacher in all of Paris? Oh, Mia, no. *Non!* I don't care how
cute he is—*very* cute, *so* cute—that is just not a good idea.
Maybe next time don't jump on the back of a total stranger's
Vespa?

I've made so many mistakes already that I'm not sure I'm
going to last a whole week. And, let's be honest, if Monsieur
Dabrowski ever finds out what I said about him, I'm going
to be on the next flight back to New York faster than I can
do a *saut de chat*.

CHAPTER SIX

THESE WERE MOM'S exact words when I told her about being moved up to level five:

"Hmm, that sounds like a lot of hard work."

I think it was the "hmm" that really made my heart sink. Like, she couldn't find a single good thing to say about the fact that I've been recognized as one of the top dancers in the entire program.

"I'm probably just stating the obvious," she added after a while.

"Yep," I answered curtly.

We were FaceTiming. She was in the kitchen, and there was a baking dish next to her full of brownies just out of the oven. I wanted one. But it was fine. I'm in Paris. I can't have everything. No one has *everything*.

"I'm happy for you, Mia."

Are you? I wanted to ask. I didn't, but she must have read it on my face.

"I am. It sounds great. Congratulations."

"Hmm," I responded, feeling my throat tighten.

We hung up soon after. I didn't know what else to say, and Mom was running late to Grandma's house.

Like Mom predicted, level five is hard work. So hard that I have to focus solely on ballet, which is why I don't think about Louis for the rest of the week. I don't picture his smile in the middle of pointe class, or remember the feeling of wrapping my arms around him as I learn to improve my form during an *arabesque*. I don't replay our conversation in my head during lunch with Lucy and Anouk. I don't wonder where he is every time I pass a neat row of scooters parked on a sidewalk. I don't hope that he'll be waiting at the front of the school every evening as I head back to the dorm with the girls after a long day.

Seriously. I don't. I swear. I *do* cringe at the memory of my silly rant about his dad, of my broken French as I tried to plead my case to the shopkeeper. I was so ashamed afterward that I just muttered a thank-you and ran out of the store, ditching him right then and there. I was terrified that he would tell his dad about all the stupid things I'd said, but thankfully I don't think he has. Monsieur Dabrowski is a tough instructor, but he doesn't seem to hate me, at least. When I showed up in my white leotard to my first class— early, of course—he gave me a quick nod, and that was that.

"Kenza, you're losing focus," Monsieur Dabrowski now calls out to the girl on my left. She's from Senegal, subtly toned from head to toe, the body of a true ballerina. "I can see it in your eyes. Your mind is not here. Does it have any-where better to be?"

Kenza straightens up right away, her entire body coming back into its own, sharp and determined.

He stands in front of her at the barre, placing his hand on it.

"*Dégagé devant, deux, trois, quatre.* Two to the side, *coupé développé,*" he says, demonstrating the moves. He's dressed in his usual all-black and seems to have more grace in his raised pinky than the rest of us put together. "Reverse, *plié, soutenu.* Other side."

We all start again, not daring to take our eyes off the bun on the head of the dancer in front of us.

"*Rond de jambe, et deux, et trois, et quatre, passé, dével-oppé, rond de jambe en l'air, piqué, battement tendu,* close to fifth. Reverse. Repeat in *relevé,*" he explains, finishing the combination. "Again, Kenza. Everyone, please observe her."

A flicker of anguish passes across Kenza's face, but she gets into fifth position with a confident smile and goes through the sequence seamlessly. At least that's how it looks to me.

"*Non!*" Monsieur Dabrowski says. "Your *rond de jambe* is too wooden. And your leg needs to be one hundred percent straight during *piqué. Encore une fois!*" *One more time!*

Kenza starts over, but our *maître* interrupts her almost immediately. "*Non, non, non. Regarde-moi.*" *Look at me.*

He and Kenza take turns for the next five minutes. Kenza never wavers, never lets her emotions get in the way.

"This isn't just about the physicality, about the technique," Monsieur Dabrowski says, interrupting her once again. "Your mind *must* be in one place, and one place only."

I'm half-convinced he's talking about me. The girl who spends her time flirting with adorable French boys and can't stop thinking about them. Well, him.

Now Monsieur Dabrowski turns to face the rest of the class, his eyes meeting mine for a brief second. The fire behind his eyes is so different from his son's relaxed, friendly gaze. "What are you all thinking about right now? And what will you think about when this class is over?"

No one responds, of course.

"Ballet isn't something you can do halfway. It has to be inside you, deep in your bones. Or else you will fail."

I didn't come this far to fail. I set my shoulders back and push Louis out of my mind. *For real.*

• • •

I've been doing ballet for most of my life, but this is the first time I've danced all day long, day after day after day. My arms and back feel so sore that I can barely hold my fork at dinner. My leg muscles tremble long after I get into bed. No amount of stretching makes me feel like I'm fully recovered. My feet are raw, a permanent shade of bright red. My first pair of new pointe shoes look like I feel, stained and crushed and as exhausted as I am. One week in, and I'm going to have to break in the next pair already.

Every morning I'm not sure how I will even stand upright at the barre, let alone move. But when I get there, something happens in my mind, in my heart, and I feel brand-new. Ballet is everything to me. Always will be.

The only really tricky thing is that I have to share it with others. And not just any other, a certain someone in particular. Monsieur Dabrowski paired us up to demonstrate a duet version of the "Dance of the Little Swans," and guess who he assigned as my combination partner?

I thought Audrey was going to faint with rage when she found out. After my adventurous trip to Repetto, I'd gleefully announced at dinner that I was being moved up. Lucy had given me a high five, and many others had congratulated me. Audrey had just shoved more salad in her mouth and looked away as she chewed noisily. Now we're stuck with each other in every possible way.

"You have to be kidding me!" she fumed on the way out of the studio after Monsieur Dabrowski told us we'd be dancing together.

The "Dance of the Little Swans," or *pas de quatre,* is one of the most well-known sequences in *Swan Lake,* in the middle of Act Two. It's both technical and ethereal, and these four roles are the next best thing to Odette. Monsieur Dabrowski is having us perform this dance to help make his decision about the roles in the famous ballet.

Finally it's Friday: audition day. Like every other duo, Audrey and I stayed an extra hour after class, watching and correcting each other's form. I asked her for tips on how to improve my *attitude*—the ballet step, not my mood. And in return, I reminded her to widen her collarbone without clenching her jaw.

I won't go as far as saying I'm glad we're in this together, but Audrey has great technique, and I'll take any help I can get. Right before it's our turn, I check the mirror to make sure no hair has escaped from my bun. I know Monsieur Dabrowski will notice even the tiniest detail.

We take our positions side by side in the center of the room. All eyes are on us as the rest of the class hovers at the edge of the mirrors. Monsieur Dabrowski gives the nod to the pianist and as the music starts, so do we, our arms linked and our steps mirroring each other.

At the end, we stand still right where we started, waiting for him to call up the next group. But that's not what happens.

Instead, Monsieur Dabrowski asks me one of the worst questions I've ever had to answer. "Mademoiselle Jenrow, tell me about Mademoiselle Chapman's weaknesses. What could make her a better dancer?"

Audrey's eyes go wide. She's as taken aback as I am, but she's not the one who has to answer.

"Audrey is a great dancer!"

Monsieur Dabrowski sighs. "That is not my question."

I watch Audrey, the panic in her eyes, as total silence blankets the room. She knows I have to say something; she's just scared of what it might be.

"Well . . ."

"This isn't just about her," Monsieur Dabrowski says. "If you can't tell what she needs to improve, then how are *you* supposed to improve?"

I take a deep breath. Audrey is basically perfect . . . almost too perfect. I've seen her dance dozens of times, and sometimes it feels like I'm watching a battery-powered ballerina. I try to ignore our classmates as I say, "Audrey doesn't know how to have fun with it."

Audrey's mouth drops open, but our instructor nods approvingly, so I continue. "Ballet is not a science, it's an art. You have to make people feel something, and you can only do that if you feel it yourself."

The moment I stop talking, she jumps in. "Maybe I don't have enough emotion, but Mia has too much. Way too much."

I let out a quiet gasp. It's not an unfair comment, and that's probably why it hurts.

"All right," Monsieur Dabrowski says to her. "Continue."

"She needs to work on her precision," Audrey adds with a smile, like the dutiful student she is. "She can't expect that the steps will just unfold on their own. Mia needs to learn complete control over her body. Over everything."

"*Très bien,* girls. I've seen everything I need to see."

Audrey and I both perk up, along with every other student in the room.

He doesn't say anything else. Still, we know he's talking about the roles in *Swan Lake.* He's been quiet on the topic all week, and no one has dared ask any questions about how and when, exactly, he will assign them.

Audrey hesitates for a moment before blurting out, "When will we find out the roles?"

"Good things come to those who wait," he finally says before moving on to the next group. We'll have to hope, pray, and dream for a few more days at least.

For now, Audrey and I stare at each other coldly. She's wrong about me, anyway. I *am* in control, but that doesn't mean I can't enjoy it, too. It's a waste of Paris not to drink in the spirit of this place, its history, the art, the culture, the boys. Well, fine, not the boys.

Ugh, maybe I have been distracted by my emotions. Paris is not about dreamy French guys and impromptu trips on the backs of their Vespas. Paris is not about Louis's gorgeous brown eyes; the dimple in his left cheek that made me want to rub my hand against his soft skin; or the sweet, musky scent that wafted back to me as I held him in my arms. Now I just wish our ride around the city had lasted all night, because it can't happen again.

So, fine. Paris is not about falling in love, not for me. It's about *dancing*. The whole reason I came here is to learn from the best and to one day get into the American Ballet Theatre. Maybe even one day soon, as long as I don't forget why I came here in the first place.

CHAPTER SEVEN

THE MUSÉE D'ORSAY might be one of the most beautiful of all the Parisian landmarks. There's a lot of competition, but to me, the contemporary art museum along the Seine river is even more swoon-worthy than the Louvre or the Pompidou. Before the Musée d'Orsay housed world-famous works of art, it was a train station. You can tell by the large clocks on the side of the building, underneath which the old train routes are still engraved. Inside, the high curved glass ceiling with intricate moldings is a masterpiece in its own right. It's a grand hall, one that's packed with black-and-white statues of all sizes.

I've never seen anything like it, and my heart fills with delight as I look all around me. Is this what it's always like to discover a foreign place? Experiencing not just new sights, sounds, and smells, but feeling every moment differently, like your life started anew? Or is it just the Paris effect? In any case, there's a reason why Musée d'Orsay has been on my must-visit list: I read in my guidebook that it hosts the biggest collection of Degas paintings in the world.

After some much-needed rest on Saturday, I'm excited to be officially out on the town. This excursion was optional, and surprisingly few people from my dorm signed up.

"Hard pass" was Audrey's answer when I asked if she was going. Anouk is off catching up with friends she made last year, and Lucy's parents are in town from Manchester for the weekend. So the field trip is just me and a few other students I don't know.

We walked along the riverbank to get here, mingling with the weekend crowds and tourists, to the tune of an enchanting melody played by an accordionist, an older man wearing a vest and a khaki beret. There were little green kiosks all along the way, and I peeked at the vintage books and antique posters in the stalls, which gave off a delicious whiff of old printed paper.

Inside, we're led toward the Impressionists floor by Max and Émilie, two of the student instructors at school, who are only a couple of years older than me. I wonder if they actually wanted to join us or just got stuck with chaperoning duties. It doesn't matter anyway; as soon as we arrive in the Degas area, everyone scatters to explore at their own pace.

When I was little, Grandma Joan, Mom, and I would make annual trips to the Met in New York City, and we'd always stop by to admire *The Little Fourteen-Year-Old Dancer*, Degas's famous sculpture of Marie van Goethem, a Belgian ballerina. The sculpture was reproduced after his death, and the different versions are exhibited around the world, but, from what I've heard, the original wax one is right here in the Musée d'Orsay. If the family legend about my great-great-great-grandmother is true, she and Marie van Goethem would have been around the same age. They probably danced in the same ballet, or posed for the same paintings. Isn't that wild? I know, I know. *If* it's true.

I make my way through the collection, stopping at each painting for several minutes, taking in every detail: Degas's ethereal combination of pastel colors, the delicate grace he conveys with just a few quick lines, and the spirited movement of his dancers—which proves he was drawing right there in the same room. I snap a picture of each with my phone, so I can look at them again later. After *Dancers in Blue,* I move on to *The Star,* then to *Seated Dancer.* I lean forward to scrutinize the dancer's face when I sense a presence behind me.

"Excuse me, Mademoiselle. You're not supposed to get so close to the art. Please step back."

My heart leaps to my throat and I jerk away, ready to apologize, when I realize I know that voice and that oh-so-cute accent.

"Louis?" I say, turning to face him.

"Salut," he says with a wide smile.

Louis leans in to give me *la bise,* and for one crazed moment I think he is going to kiss me, like *really* kiss me. I want it to happen more than I would ever admit out loud. My eyes grow wide and a grin takes over my face, until I realize that he's just greeting me like he would anyone else. I'm only slightly awkward as we touch cheeks and pull back.

"Are you following me?" I mean it as a joke, of course, but it comes out totally tongue-tied.

Louis shakes his head. "That's my best friend, over there." He points his chin toward Max, the student instructor. "He's been working nonstop since the start of the program, so I figured I'd come by to hang out with him."

"Oh!" I say, probably sounding too excited. "So that's who you were waiting for the other day?"

"Well, hmm . . ." Louis looks over to Max and Émilie. She frowns back at us. "I didn't know his girlfriend would be here," Louis says, pulling away. "Maybe I should leave them alone."

I take it to mean that he's not staying. "So, I'll see you around?" I ask, trying to sound upbeat.

Louis pauses, then says, "I feel like I should stay with you, just in case you get in trouble."

"In trouble for what?"

"I don't know. . . . You looked like you were very close to stealing this painting."

"True. I *am* going to need your help if I get arrested and thrown in jail for extra art appreciation."

"Exactement," Louis says seriously. "So, shall we?"

I look back and notice that our chaperones have moved on to another room. They told us at the start that we were free to do whatever we wanted, and leave whenever, so I'm going to take them up on it. Louis and I methodically make our way to each painting and sculpture, and I stop to read the explanation card every time.

"You're really into this guy, huh," Louis comments as we get near the end. "I guess you kind of have to be."

"What do you mean?" I ask, frowning. I haven't told him anything about my family. I haven't told anyone, in fact.

Louis shrugs. "You're a dancer. Degas painted dancers."

"How come you speak English so well?" I ask, not just to change the subject, but also because I've wondered about that since we met. Louis speaks English with such fluidity that I almost forget that I'm in France.

He rubs at the back of his neck, as though he's embarrassed at the compliment. "My mom is half-French, half-English, and she travels a lot for work. And my dad . . ." He pauses.

"Yup, definitely know your dad."

"Right. Well, they liked talking to me in English when I was little. I even went to an international school in Switzerland, but I wanted to come home for high school. I can speak English in Paris. I mean, I can speak English anywhere, but Paris is the only place I want to be."

"I think I understand why." I glance through the window, across the Seine. I spot the Sacré-Cœur, the famous basilica towering over the city in the distance. It seems like it's hovering on the horizon wherever you look, like when you're driving and the moon follows you. I can't wait to see it up close. With Louis. Or not. Whatever.

We keep walking, and I don't know why I notice this, but our steps are in sync.

I recognize the next piece along the wall immediately, and my heart nearly stops: *Ballet Rehearsal on Stage.*

"Oh. My. God." I say with a gasp, "It's here!"

I can't contain my giddiness as I shuffle in front of a large group so I can get closer to my favorite painting ever. There's a similar version of this painting at the Met in New York City, but this is the one I love the most. It's so surreal to finally see the original. Paris really is a magical city: so far it's making all my dreams come true.

"It's *soooo* incredible," I whisper. Louis walks closer, stepping up next to me.

"I've never seen anyone so excited about a painting," Louis says, gently nudging me. My mind flashes back to when I was sitting on the back of his Vespa, and how I'd wanted to rest my head on his shoulder. Deep down a little voice tells me that it can't be a coincidence that we bumped into each other twice in a week. I don't want to shut it down.

I force myself to focus on the painting again, and grin. "I have a poster of it in my room," I say. "It's my favorite."

Louis smiles. "Give me your phone," he says.

I hand it to him, and he waits until the large group has moved on to take my picture in front of it.

"Parfait," he says after he gives me my phone back.

"I'm going to sound like a total nerd, but I'm really excited to have this."

Louis chuckles. "I like art nerds."

I beam, and probably blush, but mostly his words make me feel bold enough to grab his arm and pull him close to me. "You should be in the picture, too," I say, bringing my phone up to our faces. He presses his cheek against mine, and it sends shivers down my spine as I click on the button. Afterward I itch to look at the picture but hold myself back. I can gaze at it all night if I want to. And I already know I'll want to.

"And what gets *you* excited?" I ask, hoping my cheeks are getting back to a normal color.

He takes a moment to think about it. "Taking trips with friends across France. Not knowing what tomorrow will bring. Really good food. In fact"—he checks his watch—"one of my favorite cafés is not far from here, in Saint-Germain, and it's almost lunchtime. . . . Do you have plans?" Louis asks. "We could go. I mean, after you've finished studying every Degas with a magnifying glass, obviously."

I can't go. I mean, I *shouldn't* go. I need to stay focused on why I'm here, on dancing and knocking the socks off ABT, and it's pretty obvious that Louis is . . . distracting. Distractingly cute. So cute. But I *do* need to eat, so . . .

"I guess I have time for that," I say, trying to keep my face straight.

• • •

We walk down the twisty streets of the sixth *arrondisse-ment,* but just as we arrive at the place Louis mentioned, he has another idea. "Café de Flore is just around the corner. Do you know it?"

"It rings a bell," I say, trying to figure out where I've heard the name before.

Louis smiles, like he's about to let me in on a secret. "It's one of the oldest cafés in Paris. It's always been *the* meeting place of the most famous Parisians: authors, journalists, actors, and all kinds of celebrities. It even has its own literary prize."

"But I'm not famous," I say jokingly.

"Not *yet,*" Louis says with a glimmer in his eye.

A few minutes later, we're seated at the corner terrace of this famous café, alongside many chic Parisians. The white cursive lettering announcing *Café de Flore* is almost covered by the lush plants hanging from the balcony above. I sneak glances around, wondering if I'll recognize anyone, but, except for dancers, I'm not too familiar with the French art scene. The older couple next to us eats their steak frites in silence, white cloth napkins neatly placed on their laps. Their glasses of red wine barely fit on the tiny table and clink against each other with every move.

"I live not too far, with my dad," Louis says, pointing to his left. "It's a few streets away, off the Jardin du Luxembourg."

"Wow" is all I can come up with. I try to picture what it would have been like to grow up around here, just off a gorgeously manicured park, wandering past centuries-old monuments on your way to school, peeking inside elegant boutiques and stopping by a star-studded café in the afternoons. It sounds like a pretty good life.

He blushes a little. "It's not as fancy as around here. I swear," he says, then adds, "my mom's in London. Well, when she's not traveling. She's a director, so she's always off filming somewhere."

Louis goes on to talk about his mom's latest film, a dark drama set in various parts of Europe, which is coming out in theaters later this summer. He says it like it's no big deal, and when he starts asking me questions, I hesitate to tell him about my way-more-average American family.

"My mom is not a famous director, but she works in marketing at a beauty company, so I get a lot of free makeup." I shrug. "My dad and my little brother don't get so excited about that, but it's a pretty good perk for a ballerina."

Our salads arrive, bursting with colorful *crudités* (aka raw vegetables), and we switch topics to his favorite things about Paris: the Canal Saint-Martin, where he goes to hang out with his friends; the outdoor concerts in summer, and the crêpes slathered with Nutella, for sale on many street corners. Apparently I'm not allowed to leave Paris without having at least one.

It feels oddly comfortable between us, like we've done this many times before, even though I didn't even know Louis existed a few days ago. We're sitting close together, and I can feel the vibration of his knee bouncing, almost like he's nervous. I don't know why he would be; Louis is way too cool to be nervous about anything or anyone. Especially me.

"Why ballet?" Louis asks me, tearing into his second piece of baguette, which he smears with salted butter.

"It's in my blood." The words come out before I can stop them.

Louis raises an eyebrow.

"I'm kidding. Sort of. I just fell into it when I was little, and that was it. I love being transported by music from hundreds of years ago. It's like I belong to a different era."

"Like you belong in those paintings we just saw?"

"Yeah." I feel myself blush. "You're going to think it's stupid," I say, leaning back in my chair.

"Try me."

"There's this story my grandmother told me. . . ."

I tell him what I've kept to myself all these years. How the women of my family have been dancing for generations, and how my grandmother even believes that our ancestor was one of the Degas dancers. That it's supposed to be a sign that being a ballerina is my destiny.

"I told you, it's stupid," I say when I've finished.

Louis just stares at me with wide eyes. I've said too much. I don't understand what happens to me when I'm with him. "I think you and I have a different definition of *stupid*," Louis finally says. "What else did your grandmother say?"

"Not much. She gave me the phone number of her aunt who lives outside Paris."

Louis starts playing with the bread crumbs on the table, crushing them with his index finger one by one. He frowns as he does this, like he's completing a very important task. Even his frowns are cute. "And you think that this aunt would know something more?" he asks.

"I don't know, maybe?"

The white-aproned waiter interrupts us to take our plates, and we order two *cafés,* which arrive a few minutes later in microscopic cups branded with the café's name. A square of chocolate wrapped in foil sits on each saucer next to a sugar cube. I like how the French do coffee: strong and sweet.

Louis seems deep in thought, and I'm still processing the fact that I just confessed this entire story to a boy I hardly know. But maybe time is not the only indicator of knowing someone, or feeling close to them.

"Seems like there's only one way to find out about this dancer," Louis says. "Do you have this aunt's address?"

I laugh, certain he's just kidding, but he looks at me deadpan. So I nod and pull up the photo on my phone. "I looked it up. It's this tiny little village about an hour south of Paris. There's no easy way to get there. . . ."

"Easy isn't what makes it fun," Louis says, checking the map on his phone.

"I should give her a call, but she doesn't speak English." I don't think Louis is even listening to me anymore.

After we split the bill, he pushes his chair back and gets up. "We have to go."

I get up as well. "Go where?"

"If I tell you, you're not going to come."

"I still want to know."

"Why?" Louis asks with the most charming crooked smile. Okay, by now we've established that *all* his smiles are charming—when they're not gorgeous—but some hit me harder than others.

"We're going on an adventure."

He's joking, right? "What kind of adventure?" I ask as I follow him down the street, back in the direction of the Musée d'Orsay.

Louis stops and stares deep into my eyes. "You ask too many questions."

I cross my arms against my chest. "You don't have enough answers."

Louis bursts out laughing. It sounds like a magic spell, in the best possible way. And maybe it is, because just yesterday I swore off boys for the rest of the summer and promised myself I would give ballet all my attention. That's the reason I'm here. Of course, I still feel that way. And yet, I know I'm in trouble. . . . Because let's be honest, I'm going to follow that sound anywhere.

CHAPTER EIGHT

FOR THE SECOND time this week, we're zigzagging through the streets of Paris, and I can't believe that it's me on the back of this Vespa, my hands wrapped around his waist again, like this is where they belong. My heart knocks against my chest and my fingers tingle with excitement. I force myself to come to my senses when we turn onto a little street off a busy boulevard, passing by an entrance to a train station called the RER. Louis stops in front of a white building with large double windows and the same wrought-iron window guards I've seen all over Paris.

"Unfortunately, we can't drive all the way there," he says, locking his Vespa in place.

"We are *not* going to my great-great-aunt's house," I say, meaning it.

Louis purses his lips. "Don't you want to know if this whole thing about your ancestor and Degas is real?"

I let out a sigh. I could say that I don't even know my

great-great-aunt, that I should go home and get some rest for the week ahead, that I didn't come here to flirt with anyone, no matter how cute they are. . . .

"We can't just turn up there," I say, but Louis starts heading toward the station.

"Pourquoi pas?" Why not?

We walk past a couple with two large dogs on a leash, which is too many people and animals for the narrow sidewalk. We have to veer onto the street just to avoid them.

"Because I don't know this woman. I can't just show up. I have to plan a visit."

"That sounds extremely boring," Louis says, taking the stairs down to the RER two at a time.

"It's the normal thing to do." Feeling like a seasoned pro at the public transportation system already, I scan my métro pass in order to keep following him, and soon we're on the platform, waiting for the train.

Louis shrugs. "Normal, boring. Same difference."

"What if she's a serial killer?" I ask a little too loudly. A few heads turn to give me a weird look.

"If she is," he whispers in my ear, "then it's going to be one hell of an adventure."

I shake my head, and his shaggy hair brushes my face. It smells lovely and feels so soft. I want to shake my head again. And again, and again.

"Look, you're in Paris for what, six weeks?" Louis asks.

"Yes, to dance. Only to dance," I say, more to remind myself than anything else.

"Fine, so you'll leave at the end of the summer without knowing your true family history. You'll spend the rest of your life wondering if your grandmother was right, and if maybe your great-great-aunt knew something she could have told you. And then she'll die, and you'll never know."

"Uh . . . morbid much?" I say.

"Morbid but true."

Touché.

I glance at the electronic countdown board. The next train leaves in six minutes.

"We have to call her first," I say, pulling up the photo of Grandma Joan's note. I dial the number and hand it to him.

A moment later, I hear someone pick up. Louis winks at me. *"Bonjour, Madame,"* he starts. Obviously that's not all he says, but I only follow little snippets of the conversation in French. "Mia Jenrow . . . *Train. Aujourd'hui. Merci beaucoup."*

When he hangs up, Louis has the most mischievous grin on his face. "She can't wait to meet you."

• • •

We get off the train an hour later, and two elderly ladies are waiting for us at the station. I recognize them from Grandma's pictures. The older one is obviously my great-great-aunt Vivienne, who does indeed look pretty great for her early nineties.

She lights up when she sees me. *"Tu dois être Mia!"* You must be Mia!

She gives me *la bise,* then wipes what I assume is a lipstick stain off my cheek. She continues speaking in French, and I glance at Louis, desperate.

He starts translating right away. "She says that you look exactly like your grandmother."

"*C'est vrai!*" I say extra-enthusiastically. *It's true!*

The other woman is her eldest daughter, Madeleine. Since Vivienne is my grandmother's aunt—my great-grandmother's sister—I'm pretty sure that means Madeleine and I are cousins a few times removed. I should have asked Grandma to run me through the family tree one more time before I left.

Madeleine has very short, bright red hair, and wears wide-legged pants with a white tunic. She looks about the same age as Grandma Joan. I'd guess late sixties. She also speaks some English, which makes me feel better right away.

"*Maman* was, uh, very happy . . . when your *petit copain,* uh, boyfriend, called," Madeleine tells me over her shoulder as we get into her car and she starts driving. She pauses every few words, searching for the right ones. I can't imagine she gets to practice her English all that often. She speaks again before I have time to correct her. *Sorry,* I mouth to Louis about the whole boyfriend misunderstanding, but he just smiles back. "*Maman* doesn't drive anymore, but I live nearby, so I visit her often."

"Thank you, Madeleine. It's so nice to meet you." Then I lean forward to my great-great-aunt. "Vivienne . . . Grandma

Joan is going to be very happy to know I came here." Louis translates for me, and Vivienne responds with a big grin.

We pass villages and fields where cows happily graze, before Madeleine parks the car on the side of a little square, by a row of stone houses. On the other side of it, and I swear this is true, is the entrance to a castle, or as the French say, *château*. The building itself is at the end of a long, tree-lined alleyway and is about the size of ten houses put together.

Vivienne catches me staring and says something I don't understand.

Louis explains. "She said: 'The owners are lovely, but we almost never see them. It would be nice to know what it looks like inside, wouldn't it?' "

I let out a sigh of relief. I'd think Grandma Joan would have told me if we were descendants of French royalty. Instead, Aunt Vivienne and Madeleine take us inside one of the cozy houses on the square. A tiled corridor goes straight through the whole length of the house, with small, dark doors on either side. There are plants and framed photographs everywhere, and a staircase going to the second floor. I take a peek at the photos as we walk by, but they all seem like your typical family portraits. No tutu in sight.

Aunt Vivienne leads Louis and me to a veranda, and then outside to a walled garden. The three of us sit under a wide, leafy tree, sheltered from the bright afternoon sun.

"I thought Joan would have taught you French," my great-great-aunt says through Louis.

"She did, when I was younger. But then my parents insisted I take Spanish in school."

Louis repeats my words in French. Vivienne nods, somewhat disappointed. Right now I feel the same, and wish I'd worked harder to learn the language.

"Spanish is very useful, too," Madeleine says, bringing over a jug of orange juice and a plate of biscuits from the kitchen. The word *beurre* is stamped on them, just in case you can't tell from their golden color that they're full of butter.

"*Maman* is very proud that you're dancing at the Institut de l'Opéra de Paris," Madeleine says to me.

Aunt Vivienne beams at the mention of the prestigious school. I wish my own mother felt the same way, but I brush the thought away.

"She wanted me to be a . . . you know, a *danseuse,* too. But I was not good," Madeleine says with a laugh.

Vivienne presses her hand on Louis's arm, silently asking him to translate. Once he does, Vivienne opens her mouth wide. *"Ne l'écoute pas!"* she says to me. *Don't listen to her.*

"My daughter was very talented. She just gave up too soon. All the women in this family are made for ballet. Like you, Mia." Louis smiles as he tells me this, and I feel myself blush.

"That's what Mia wants to talk to you about," Louis says in French. The more I listen to him, the more words I pick up.

"J'ai des questions," I add tentatively. I do have questions,

but I feel a bit silly asking them. Even though they're family, I don't know these women. Vivienne nods at me with a bright smile.

"You stay to eat *ce soir,* yes? To talk more?" Madeleine asks, though it sounds more like a statement.

I shake my head. "We shouldn't," I answer at the same time Louis says, "We'd love to."

"We have to get the train back," I whisper to him.

Louis shrugs. "The trains run until late. C'mon—live a little. Let's have a wild night with your elderly relatives."

He smiles. How could I resist that?

We go back inside when dinnertime approaches. Even though it's still bright out, the air has gotten just cool enough to remind us that the day is coming to an end. Madeleine heads to the kitchen to prepare dinner while the rest of us make our way to Vivienne's dining room. It's covered in floral wallpaper, which is yellowing in places. A rustic wooden table and matching chairs fill up most of the tiny space. Compared to the rest of the house, the walls seem very bare, except for an ornate frame hanging on the wall.

Vivienne catches me looking and grabs my hand, taking me closer.

Inside the frame is a sketch of a young girl from the waist up, done in soft black charcoal and green pastel. She's looking off to the left, her eyes unfocused. Her braided hair rests on her shoulder, tied in a large bow at the end. Her shoulders are back, her posture perfect. The thin paper is ripped in one corner, and it's only a few sharp but faded lines.

Maybe it's because I studied Degas's sketches all morning, but the style and color are unmistakable.

The look on Louis's face tells me that he's thinking the same thing. "This is a beautiful drawing," he says to Vivienne in French.

There's an immediate spark in my great-great-aunt's eyes. *"Tu aimes Degas?" You like Degas?*

My heart starts to beat faster. "This is a real Degas? Grandma Joan told me the story," I say in broken French, my voice full of excitement.

Aunt Vivienne runs her hand along my cheek. *"C'est une belle histoire,"* she says softly. *It's a lovely story.* I hold my breath, waiting for more, but she just motions for us to sit down.

Madeleine comes in with a potato salad and a crisp-looking baguette that I can smell across the room. My mouth waters instantly.

"Du vin?" Madeleine asks once we've all helped ourselves. She doesn't wait for an answer and leaves the room. A moment later, she's back with a chilled bottle of rosé. Louis nods, raising his glass, and I hesitate for a moment. I've never had wine before, but Madeleine is already pouring me a glass.

"You'll like it," he whispers in my ear.

This week has brought so many firsts already, and I feel a twinge of trepidation at tasting what I've always thought of as grown-up juice. Or maybe it's just the sweet smell of Louis's breath that is making me feel . . . *quelque chose.*

Aunt Vivienne raises her glass, and we all follow. *"À Mia!, ma petite-nièce!"* To Mia, my great-grand-niece!

"Bon appétit!" Vivienne chimes, bringing me back to reality.

I wait awhile to bring up the drawing again. I don't want to make it sound like it's the only reason I came here. Instead, I spend most of the meal catching up Aunt Vivienne on Grandma Joan and Mom, whom she's only met a couple of times, before I was born. I also learn that Madeleine has two sons who are in their late thirties. One of them just had a second child with his wife, and Madeleine is thrilled to be a grandmother again. She pulls out her phone to show me a picture and puts a hand on her heart.

Then, noticing my empty glass, she refills it. I'm feeling a little tipsy already, but I nod anyway. This is the French way, and I shouldn't pass up an opportunity to learn about the culture.

"This drawing," I begin, after taking a small sip. I turn to Aunt Vivienne. "You said something about Degas?" I don't want to ask outright if she has an extremely valuable piece of art hanging in her living room.

Before Louis has time to translate my question, Madeleine shakes her head at her mother. *"Maman! Qu'est-ce que tu as dit à Mia?"* Mom! What did you tell Mia?

Mother and daughter bicker in French for a while. They speak pretty fast, so Louis gives me only the highlights. "Madeleine is annoyed because she thinks Vivienne told you the drawing is a Degas, when everyone knows that's not true. Vivienne said you wanted to know about the drawing because it's so lovely, and that it doesn't matter what she said."

"So is it a Degas or not?" I ask Louis, realizing that I care about this a lot more than I thought.

Louis shrugs, and continues to listen in to the conversation, but Madeleine heard my question. She looks at me across the table and says, "It is not real. Don't listen to *Maman*. She just . . . How do you say? Her grandfather bought it at an . . . *antiquaire*—an old store. He joked that it was real, and then people forgot that it was a joke."

Even though Madeleine was speaking in English, Aunt Vivienne looks like she understood Madeleine's speech. She shakes her head and puts her hand on Louis's arm. "It *is* real. Tell Mia it's our ancestor, the *danseuse étoile*."

"*N'importe quoi,*" Madeleine says, rolling her eyes. *Rubbish.*

Louis looks over to check if I got that, and I nod. I'm still confused, though. Mom's words resonate inside me. How she said that some people have chosen to believe the legend, some have chosen not to. That the truth is irrelevant, because we'll never know. I try to smile, to hide how disappointed I am. I don't want this to be some nice little story. I want ballet to really be in my blood, in my ancestry.

Madeleine asks me to help her with dessert, so I follow her into the kitchen.

"*Tu es triste* . . . uh, you're sad," she says. "I see it on your face."

I shake my head, looking away. I feel tears coming, which is silly, I know. I can't let this get to me. There's more to life—that's what Mom would say.

Madeleine washes a handful of strawberries and places them in a glass bowl. Meanwhile, I fill up the dishwasher.

"I am sorry," she says. Her English is basic, but at least it's clear, and it's still better than my French. "That thing is not real. I took it to a person, how do you say, to have proof, many years ago, to make *Maman* happy. He, uh . . . what's the word, laughed. He said there are a lot of people who copy art, and some are very good. Nobody can know if this was done by Degas."

I nod, trying to take it all in. There's no way to prove it, so that's it. If an expert couldn't figure it out, then we'll never know for sure if my ancestor was one of Degas's ballerinas. My shoulders slump.

"I . . . ," I start, but I'm not sure what to say. And Madeleine probably wouldn't understand me anyway.

"Dis-moi," she says. *Talk to me.* "We are family."

I gulp, feelings bubbling up my throat. "Being a ballet dancer is my dream," I say slowly, checking that she follows. She encourages me with a nod. "I want it more than anything else. But it's so hard, so competitive. This legend . . . it helps me believe that I can do this, you know? That it will happen for me. It gives me hope. I . . . *need* it to be true." I look down at my feet. I've never thought about it like that before, but, now that I'm saying it out loud, I realize that this is how I've always felt about Grandma Joan's story.

"Mia, *regarde-moi*," Madeleine says, lifting my chin up with two fingers and forcing me to look up. "You should believe what *you* want to believe. If this legend inspires you when you dance, then believe. If it makes you feel something, then that's what's important."

I wipe a tear with the back of my hand. I hadn't even noticed it was making its way down my cheek.

• • •

It's almost dark outside after dinner. I realize we've been here a long time and pull out my phone to look at the train schedule. "The last one leaves at 11:05 p.m.," I tell Louis.

He checks his watch. "Vivienne just said she wants to show you some family photos." He must notice the anxious look on my face. I should go home and rest. Will Monsieur Dabrowski announce the roles first thing in the morning, or will he make us wait all day? "It's fine, Mia," Louis says, pushing my thoughts away. "We have plenty of time."

Luckily, there's no curfew at our dorm. I was surprised when I learned that students over sixteen can pretty much do whatever they want. Maybe it's a French thing, or a big-city thing, to treat teenagers like adults. As long as we show up to class on time—and perform well—we're the masters of our own destinies outside of school.

Still, an uneasy feeling gnaws at me as my great-great-aunt gets up and opens the imposing wardrobe in the corner to retrieve a few thick albums. I hesitate for a moment, but

Vivienne looks so delighted, and I don't want to disappoint her. I help Madeleine make tea, and we settle down in the adjacent living room, where the four of us can't even fit on the sofa. Louis stands next to it as Madeleine and I sit on each side of Vivienne. I force myself to forget about the drawing and smile. I'm still glad I came here today.

• • •

We kiss Vivienne goodbye an hour and three albums later, and Madeleine drives us to the station. But as soon as we arrive, before she has even parked the car, I know something's wrong. It's dark and very quiet. *Too* quiet.

Louis and I rush out of the car and run up to the station door. It's locked.

"It's not possible," I say, my heart beating loudly in my chest. "I checked the schedule! There's a train at 11:05 p.m., I'm sure of it."

Louis runs his finger along the timetable taped behind the glass. "That's on weekdays. The last weekend train back to Paris left twenty minutes ago."

My stomach drops. Louis and I stare at each other in silence. What on earth are we going to do now?

CHAPTER NINE

"PLEASE DON'T LOOK at me."

I walk into the bedroom dressed in a pink fluffy meringue masquerading as a very old floor-length nightgown. It's big and frilly, with a dozen cutesy little buttons. It would be way too much even for a girl who likes cutesy things, which I do not. Outside of ballet, my style is pretty pared down: black or white tops with skinny jeans or a skirt. I did buy a couple of striped tees before my trip, because it seemed like the obvious thing to wear in France, but candy pink nighties? *Non merci.* Oh, and the smell of it. My guess is that it's been sitting on a moth-repellent stick in a dusty drawer for about a millennium. I know, at least I'm not sleeping on the streets tonight, but still.

"That thing is . . . I don't know how to say it in English," Louis says, shaking his head with dismay. "In French we say a *tue-l'amour.*"

"*A love killer?*" I ask, pulling it up my legs and doing

a few dance steps. I spin around and throw my head back with a laugh.

Louis folds over laughing, too. He's much better off than me: Vivienne found him a faded lime-green T-shirt to wear with his boxer shorts.

Normally I would feel silly and embarrassed at being dressed like this in front of a dreamy boy (or any boy, really), but mostly I'm just relieved. Goofing around with Louis feels so right. I don't know how he does it, but he makes everything—strolling through a museum, catching the train to the countryside, taking a few sips of chilled rosé—feel like the most thrilling experience.

After the shock of the missed train had worn off, Madeleine took us right back to her mother's house and told us not to worry at all. I was mortified by my mistake, but she and Louis seemed to find it funny more than anything else.

Luckily, trains start early in the morning, so I keep telling myself that it will all work out in the end: I'll have plenty of spare time to get back to the dorm, grab my things for school, and make it to class ready to bring my best ballet game. I texted Lucy that I was staying with family, and figured she would pass on the message to the others if anyone wondered where I was. Although, I'm guessing Audrey couldn't care less.

"What are your parents going to say?" I'd asked Louis on the way back. "Please don't tell your dad it was all my fault."

I've been trying hard to forget about that all day, but of course it's been hovering in the back of my mind: Monsieur Dabrowski—the great scary teacher who holds my fate in his hands—is Louis's dad.

"It *is* all your fault, Mia," he'd responded deadpan. I felt my face grow hot. "Don't worry," he'd added with a smile. "I've been going out at night alone since I was fourteen. I'll send my dad a text, but he might not even notice I'm gone."

Aunt Vivienne had already been in bed when we got back. In her sleepy state, she led us to her guest bedroom on the second floor.

"You're in luck. I have two single beds in here for when my great-grandchildren come to stay. But, wait. Would your parents let you sleep in the same room?" She may have been half-asleep, but she was still a ninety-year-old great-grandma with principles.

Louis just laughed it off and told her that our parents should feel lucky we even have a roof over our heads to-night. I'm not sure my dad would agree with that, but I smile and nod. Hopefully he'll never know about this.

"I need to ask you something," I say to Louis when he stops laughing. I turn the light off, and the room is plunged into total darkness. He must have closed the outside wooden shutters while I was in the bathroom. I take a few tenta-tive steps forward until my shins reach the edge of the bed. "Why are you helping me?" I continue, sliding under the covers. We've been joking around all day, and maybe it's because we're so close right now, but I can't help it. I need to know more.

"Because it's fun. I told you, I'm all about going on adventures. If you'd told me this morning that I'd end the night with a smart, pretty girl . . ."

I smile a big bright smile, even though he can't see me, or maybe *because* he can't see me.

There's something else I want to ask. Was he *really* waiting for his friend Max that day we met on the steps? I guess it's not really my business, but I'm having trouble believing that Louis doesn't have . . . someone else to go on adventures with. I picture that someone with shiny hair, chiseled cheekbones, and the innate chic air that I've observed in some of the French girls my age. My heart twists with a pinch—okay, more than a pinch—of jealousy. Stop it, Mia. This would never work anyway. You're going to be kind of busy over the next few weeks, remember?

I let out a silent sigh and decide to change the subject. "I had a great day," I say, "but I . . . well, I didn't realize it before, but I really hoped all of this was true. I still do. I know how naive it must sound, but the idea that my ancestor was so special that one of the greatest painters in history used her as a model, that a painting of her might be in a museum somewhere . . . it sounded like a fairy tale. I'd love to find out more, but I have way too many things on my mind already. I need to focus on the program and getting a role in *Swan Lake*. This legend will just have to wait."

I pause, expecting Louis to respond, but the room, the entire house, is completely silent.

"Louis?"

More silence, then "Hmm?"

"Were you asleep?"

"Hmm," he whispers from his bed across the room.

Seriously? I just bared my soul to him and he fell asleep?

There are a few minutes of silence before Louis speaks in a mumble. "You're so passionate. It makes me feel like . . ."

"What?"

"I don't know. Like I'm missing something."

"I'm sure you have your own passion," I say, but it hits me that today has been all about me. Louis is still a mystery. "So what is it?" I ask. "Your passion?"

"Hmm," he says, sounding both a little sad and sleepy. "I dunno. Maybe I don't want one."

"You don't mean that," I say, joking.

"What if I do? I grew up with two parents who were so passionate about their jobs that nothing else ever seemed to matter."

"But . . . ," I start. I don't know what to say, though. I couldn't imagine not having a passion, something that makes me want to jump out of bed every morning. To me it sounds pretty amazing to have grown up with two artistic parents who went after their dreams and became very successful. But what do I know about Louis's family life?

He's silent for a while, and I wonder if he's fallen asleep.

"Mia?" he says at last. "I didn't really come to the Musée d'Orsay to hang out with Max this morning. I saw your name on the list at school. I wanted to see you again. . . ."

I grin into the darkness. My ears fill up with the drumming of my heartbeat, and it sounds like pointe shoes thundering across the stage. I close my eyes. Ballerinas dance all around me, their arms fluttering as they twirl and whisper, Maybe you don't have to pick between love and ballet, Mia. Maybe you can have both.

I look across the room, where Louis is, just inches away from me, listening to his soft breathing. Today was . . . perfect. Well, maybe not perfect. I picture Louis's full lips, how pink and bright they look when he's laughing. They seem so soft, too. I grunt in my head. Alone with my thoughts, I can finally admit it: I wish he'd kissed me. That should be part of the French experience, right? Yes, I know he's my teacher's son. I can't deny that it could look pretty bad if anyone from school found out what Louis and I did today, even though we didn't *do* anything. . . . All right, Mia, enough. You need to rest for the big day tomorrow. But, as I fall asleep, I think, yes, maybe I can have it all. With Louis, everything feels possible.

CHAPTER TEN

"WAKE UP! *WAKE up!* WAKE UP!"

There's a moment this morning, after I open my eyes in a dark and unfamiliar place, when I think I'm going to have to leave without Louis. It takes clicking my fingers many times, shaking him gently, then not so gently, and finally screaming in his ear to get him to join the living again. Not to mention the blaring alarm on my phone that woke *me* up in the first place.

As we make our way downstairs, we're greeted with the two most distinctive smells of France: coffee and fresh croissants. Louis's whole face lights up as Vivienne invites us to sit down and eat before Madeleine drives us back to the station.

But as Louis is about to do just that, I put my hand on his arm. "We have to go."

"Tu devrais manger quelque chose," Vivienne says to me as she pours coffee into a bowl. Like, a cereal bowl.

You should eat something. She says a few more things, so Louis translates. "Madeleine went to the *boulangerie* especially for us."

I don't need to respond; the look on my face says it all.

"Thank you so much, but we have to take these to go," Louis explains to Vivienne in French. She looks a little disappointed but doesn't protest as she wraps the pastries in the paper bag they came in. Just as I'm about to step out of the kitchen, Louis holds up his index finger, asking me to wait. He grabs the bowl of coffee and gulps it down in one go.

"Didn't you burn your tongue?" I ask.

Louis nods, his face scrunched up. "Worth it," he says, his voice coarse.

Kisses, croissants, and promises to see Vivienne and Madeleine again are exchanged, but my shoulders remain tense until Louis and I are sitting on a moving train, back to Paris, and back to reality.

He immediately tucks into the croissants, offering me one. "We're finding out about the roles in *Swan Lake* today," I say, shaking my head. The weekend has been a fun escape, but now my stomach is in a knot. All I can think is that, by the end of the day, I will either be delirious with joy or crushed with disappointment. All my hope of ABT hinges on today.

"I know," Louis says between mouthfuls, half his face covered in buttery flakes. His tone is completely neutral, but my mind starts spinning anyway. Does he know something

I don't? What if his dad had shared his picks for the roles? Monsieur Dabrowski carries a notebook everywhere—a black leather-bound one in which he writes notes at the end of every class. Maybe he left it open on the dining-room table, and Louis just happened to see it?

Oh my God, I think. He knows.

I turn to Louis, who's suppressing a yawn. "So you *do* know?" I ask, my eyes growing wide with fear.

Louis raises an eyebrow and yawns once more.

I try to remain calm. It doesn't work. "You do!" I say, too loudly.

Louis raises the other eyebrow. "Hmm . . . one thing *you* might need to know about me is that I really need my eight—or preferably nine or ten—hours of sleep a night. Right now I'm extremely sleep deprived, so you're going to have to be a little clearer about what you think I know."

Part of me wants to just ask him and get it over with. But what if he tells me I haven't even snagged a role as a page girl? I might burst into tears or yelp in rage. Given the choice, I'd rather look like a complete mess in front of my entire class *and* Monsieur Dabrowski than in front of Louis. "It's nothing," I reply, trying to play it cool. It will have to wait.

"It sounds like something."

I eye the pastry bag on his lap. "You know what? I think I *am* hungry," I say, helping myself to the remaining croissant and ignoring the strange look he's giving me.

"Okay, then I'm just going to close my eyes for a minute," Louis says, leaning his head against the window.

He sleeps the whole way, leaving me to wonder if I will soon receive my wings or be cursed for the rest of the summer. At least the croissant is great company. For the two minutes it lasts, anyway.

...

I knew my summer in Paris would be physical. There was no doubt that my body would be put to all kinds of tests. But I could never have guessed that my time here would involve so . . . much . . . running. A week ago I raced through the airport after my flight was delayed, sweaty and breathless. Soon after I dashed to Repetto on the Great White Leotard Chase, and now I'm sprinting through the Gare de Lyon terminal, down the stairs to the métro, then back up after the short train ride, along Boulevard Saint-Germain, and finally, to the front door of my dorm. *Phew.* The second week of the program hasn't started yet, and I'm already spent.

I take a second to catch my breath before going in. The sound of showers running trickles down from above, but mostly it seems like everyone is just waking up. I tiptoe up the stairs, crossing my fingers that no one will see me. I made it; everything's fine. I can relax now. I take a deep breath in front of my room, and, as I'm about to grab the handle, the door bursts open. Of course, Audrey Chapman looks put-together from the moment she steps out of bed. Her braided hair is smooth, her eyes have that wide-awake look, her skin is dewy . . . even her pajamas seem like they've just been ironed.

She looks me up and down. "Isn't that what you were wearing yesterday?"

I gulp, heat flooding into my ears, as I wonder what to say.

Then she shuffles past me and heads off to the showers without waiting for an answer. Let's look on the bright side: Audrey remembers my outfit from yesterday, when I left for the Musée d'Orsay. Who knew she paid any attention to me?

• • •

"He's going to make us wait the whole day," Audrey mutters to me as we get dressed in the locker room. I put on my puffy warm-up slippers—the ones I got last month for my birthday—over my leg warmers, and wrap my cream mohair cardigan around my leotard. It might be the height of summer, with temperatures to match, but I still need to keep extra toasty until the moment we start dancing. Dancer fashion is weird, but it makes me feel like I'm in a cocoon and helps my muscles stay relaxed.

Audrey and I haven't spoken since I arrived back at the dorm, but we didn't need to. It was obvious we were thinking about the same thing all along. To be fair, none of our morning classes are with Monsieur Dabrowski that day:

first up is contemporary, then jazz. Even if ballet is all you want to do, classical training requires that you learn many different types of dancing. It expands your repertoire and teaches you to move in different ways. Then, before lunch, we have a session with a well-known choreographer for the Paris Ballet, who has us try out a piece he's creating for an upcoming show.

It's one of the many great things about this program: you get to meet renowned artists who work with some of the top ballet dancers in the world.

I do my best to focus on the steps, but the tension in the air makes it extra hard. Looks are exchanged. Sighs are let out as quietly as possible. Jaws are clenched, but no one breaks the silence or betrays the slightest hint of impatience. Deep down we're all just young girls, and three boys, having traveled from far corners of the world with hope and fear constantly tangled up inside us. But, on the outside, we'll do whatever it takes to appear like soon-to-be professional dancers, willing to deal with whatever is thrown at us, as long as it gets us closer to where we want to be.

And then the afternoon comes. Just like Audrey suspected, Monsieur Dabrowski gives us the entire class without a word about the roles. As is tradition, we end with *reverence:* our *maître de ballet* bows to us, and we respond with a curtsy. Then we give ourselves a round of applause. It's not until the clapping begins to die down that Monsieur Dabrowski holds up a hand, ready to deliver the news.

"Gather around," he instructs us as he brings a chair to

the center of the room for himself. The air feels charged. The twenty of us form a half circle around him, sitting cross-legged on the floor as gracefully as we can. My mind has been all over the place today: one minute I can hear the applause at the end of my triumph as the White Swan, the next I can feel the tear in my heart if I'm not even invited to perform. My body is bone-tired after eight hours of classes, but it's the mental exhaustion that's starting to get to me. I wish I had Lucy's or Anouk's friendly face nearby, but, aside from lunch, I only occasionally pass by them in the hallways.

"As you know," our instructor says, "the final perfor-mance of the summer is an important event for our school. It gives our dancers a chance to prove that they have been worthy of this experience."

No one moves. We're all well aware of the stakes, and, at this point, we just want him to get it over with.

"Every dancer in this room will be part of the swan *corps de ballet*," he says.

A delighted gasp escapes someone's lips. My heart is rac-ing a hundred miles a minute.

"Unless," he continues, "I call out your name."

Then he opens the infamous leather-bound notebook. "The role of Prince Siegfried will be played by Fernando," Monsieur Dabrowski announces, turning to him. I don't think anyone is surprised, least of all Fernando, who clutches his fists with delight. A seventeen-year-old from Brazil, Fernando has been one of the most talked-about students around our lunch table. Some of it has to do with his bright green eyes and tousled black hair, but he's also an amazing dancer. He has incredible strength and an ability to bring intention to every move.

"Ishani, Gabriela, Anna, and Yuang, you will perform the 'Dance of the Little Swans.'"

I glance at Audrey and can practically see her shoulders melting. I try to tell myself that it's okay if I'm just a swan. That I'm unlikely to be one of the names on the list. I already managed to be accepted into this extremely competitive program. Then, I impressed Monsieur Dabrowski enough to be moved up to the next level. It should be enough.

Monsieur Dabrowski lists a few more roles: Rothbart, the Queen. Some of them will have gone to students in level four, too. Just as I'm waiting to hear my fate, I know Lucy and Anouk are crossing their fingers, too.

Finally, our *maître* clears his throat. This is the moment we've been waiting for. "And for our Princess, our graceful and delicate White Swan, I have chosen . . ."

I hold my breath. In fact, the entire room stops breathing. I remind myself that whatever happens next has already been decided.

". . . Audrey Chapman."

Someone just slapped me really hard across the face. At least that's how it feels. It has suddenly turned hot, and I can hear my heart hammering in my ears. I hadn't realized until this moment just how much I wanted it to be me. You can try to manage your expectations and remind yourself that you're competing against a dozen other girls, all very talented, all as eager as you are. You know your odds are very low. It's simple math. And numbers don't care for feelings, for all the hopes, irrational as they may be, that you put into something. But still, the fact that it's Audrey feels like a personal blow.

When her name is announced, Audrey grins widely. A few seconds later, she snaps back to her usual composed self. "Thank you," she says to Monsieur Dabrowski. I would probably have jumped up and given him a hug. That's why Audrey gets the lead role and I don't: she's the master of her emotions.

For the rest of us, it's like the tension has been switched off. Life can go on now that we know where we stand. A few students make a move to get up, but Monsieur Dabrowski frowns at them. "A moment, please," he says. "Have you forgotten about the Black Swan?"

Audrey grimaces. As is the case in most productions, she'd assumed that she was getting the part of Odile, too. She takes a deep breath, and then asks the question that's on all our lips. "Won't *I* be the Black Swan?"

Monsieur Dabrowski smiles politely. "You could. And you would do a splendid job." Audrey smiles and looks around to make sure we all heard him. "But," our instructor continues, "this program should offer opportunities to as many students as possible. That is why you're here, isn't it?"

A few of us nod, but you could hear a pin drop.

"So, the role of Odile, the seductive, deceiving Black Swan, will be danced by Mia Jenrow."

My eyes pop wide open. For a split second I wonder if I'm imagining it, if I only heard my name because I wanted to. But a couple of the girls smile at me, while a few others can't even look me in the eyes.

Of course, the White Swan is the role I've been pining for all along. She's the star of the show, the one everyone came to see. But the Black Swan? She's the underdog. She comes out of nowhere to disrupt the peace and immediately commands everyone's attention. She brings darkness to the stage and steals the spotlight. No one wants her to win, and no one expects her to. Yet, she's the only swan left standing at the end.

This is a chance to step out of my comfort zone, to show off my skills, a real opportunity to shine in front of ABT. I didn't get what I wanted. I got something even better.

CHAPTER ELEVEN

I CAN'T COME down from my beautiful black cloud. I'm going to be performing one of the most technically challenging roles in front of the apprentice program directors of the best ballet companies in the world. They will come to watch my performance, and then possibly change my life forever. Max, the student teacher, spent a few hours with Audrey, Fernando, and me yesterday afternoon to set the pieces, meaning that he taught us the choreography so we can begin practicing on our own before rehearsals with Monsieur Dabrowski. I kept looking for a sign in Max's behavior that he knew about my escapade with his best friend, but I didn't see any.

Now that I'm back at school, I can't stop thinking about what would happen if anyone here found out about our little trip. Maybe that's why Louis pulled away from the group at the museum; he understood before I did how bad it would make me look if people knew that I'm sort of seeing my teacher's son. At least the pressure of dancing Odile hasn't fully hit me yet. I'm too deliriously happy to think about the many hurdles that lie ahead.

Lucy and Anouk both snagged roles in the *corps de ballet,* so the mood at breakfast two days later is still higher than high. That is until Audrey Chapman comes storming into the dining room.

"We should go," she tells me, like there's no one else in the room. She's carrying her dance bag on her shoulder, looking annoyed.

I check my watch, which confirms that class doesn't start for another hour and a half, as evidenced by the fact that everyone here is still pouring themselves orange juice, buttering *tartines*, and deciding between apricot and strawberry jam to spread on top of said *tartines* (I'm Team Apricot, by the way).

I tell Audrey just that, and she shakes her head in disapproval. "You're not seriously thinking about getting to school *on time,* are you?"

I pause before answering what is obviously a trick question. On the one hand, I don't want to go anywhere yet. Yesterday was a bit of a post-announcement blur, so Lucy and Anouk were just now filling me in on their weekend adventures. It turns out that while I was off chasing family legends with a cute French guy, my friends were off chasing . . . other cute French guys. Anouk invited Lucy to join her and her French friends for a picnic on Champ de Mars, the park in front of the Tour Eiffel. The girls had spent hours devouring delicious cheese and that incredible view, chatting and sunbathing. Lucy spent most of the afternoon ogling a boy named Charles, who is in Paris for the summer for an internship at an advertising agency.

"Aww," I said, bummed that I missed it. I pictured the sun warming up my face as I admired the iron structure glistening in front of me, my head resting on Louis's bent legs while he read poems aloud from a book. We would have stayed until sunset, lying on a gingham blanket and sipping rosé. Louis would have taught me French phrases, and I would have stared, mesmerized, at his beautiful lips making shapes and sounds and looking extremely kissable. The world around us would have ceased to exist. No one but Louis and me. Louis and me. Louis and me.

But there was no Louis and me at the Champ de Mars.

I was just about to ask how Lucy and Charles had left things—was there a date coming up? Did he kiss her? Did somebody *at least* get her dream French kiss?—when Audrey came in.

On the other hand, if Audrey thinks we both need to get there early, I don't want to look like a slacker.

Audrey lets out a loud sigh. "I didn't want to say this in front of everyone, but . . ." She sighs again. Then she adds, at a normal level, so that in fact everyone *will* hear her, "Your *fouettés* are just not good enough."

Her tone is definitive. It's more statement than criticism, something that can't be argued. So I don't. Even though I feel my cheeks grow hot and would prefer to hear the rest of

Lucy's story and lazily stroll to school, deep down, I know she's right. I get up, wipe the bread crumbs off the sides of my mouth, mutter a "see you later" to the girls, and follow Audrey, ready to whip my legs into oblivion.

• • •

Once we arrive at the still-empty school, Audrey chooses a studio on the top floor, "to get the best natural light." We immediately put on our pointe shoes and start to work. As we warm up—stretching calves, circling arms, rolling necks—I'm struck all over again by the beauty of the space. The soft, early morning glow shines through the long panes of glass that open like shutters to the cool summer air. Looking out onto a cluster of grayish-blue roofs lined with dormers fills me with glee. Paris is so full of heart and history; it's no wonder artists thrive here. Even the air smells sweeter.

Here's a fun fact about the Black Swan: she might only be onstage for a short amount of time, but hers is also the most technical part in the whole ballet. When, encouraged by her father, Von Rothbart, Odile tries to seduce Prince Siegfried in Act Three, she executes an elaborate and sensuous sequence that includes thirty-two *fouettés,* one of the most famous, and famously hard, turns of all time.

Fouetté is French for "whipped," a circular movement done with one leg in the air while turning on the other, popping onto the tip of your pointe shoe in the exact same spot every time. It's a struggle even for very experienced ballerinas, as it's almost physically impossible to accomplish the turn flawlessly thirty-two times in a row. I've done *fouettés* before, obviously. But until now, I've felt really nervous about attempting the Black Swan sequence. I'm scared I won't be able to do it perfectly, but time is ticking. I better get started.

Audrey and I agree that we'll each practice by ourselves for half an hour first, before watching each other's variations—aka solos—for feedback. She takes up the farthest corner of the room while I stand at the barre near the entrance, starting with a few stretches to prepare my calves for what's about to hit them. And off we go: two little swans, two gigantic dreams.

We've been dancing for twenty minutes when I hear a muffled beeping sound. I ignore it, focusing instead on my arm work: up and down in a sweeping, seamless motion, just like a swan taking flight. The beeping sound continues once, twice, three times, before I realize it's coming from my bag, which I left on the bench by the door. I stop and glance at Audrey, who appears to be about halfway through her Act Two solo. *Phew.* She didn't hear it. I decide it's best to pretend that I didn't, either.

But as soon as she finishes her sequence, she glares at me, hands clenched on her hips, and says, "Are you going to turn that thing off?"

"Sorry!" I say, skipping to my bag. "I thought I had it on mute."

"Well, you didn't," she quips, shooting daggers at me as I fish out my phone.

Here's what I should do: turn my phone off, zip up my bag, and get back to business. But curiosity gets the better of me, and I can't resist a quick glance at the screen. I know Audrey is watching, but when I see that Louis has sent me not one but *five* text messages on WhatsApp, I grin.

I glance up to see that Audrey's arms are crossed against her chest. I've seen her look annoyed before, but now she's mad. Really mad.

"Is there some kind of emergency?" Audrey asks.

"Um, no. Sorry. I'm turning it off!" I say, doing just that and jumping back into position. But that's not enough to keep the peace.

"This isn't a game to me!" she snaps, taking quick strides toward the bench. "We have less than five weeks to rehearse our roles, and I'm not going to do it while you're texting your friends."

"I'm sorry. You're right."

But my apology doesn't work. She just grabs her bag and heads for the door. Without looking back, she says, "I know."

I cringe, unsure what to do. Of course I can practice my *fouettés* by myself, and, when I'm ready for someone's opinion, Lucy and Anouk or any one of my classmates will be more than happy to help. Still, I feel guilty for ruining Audrey's practice time. And even guiltier about letting Louis filter into my ballet practice. So I get back to work, making a pact with myself to dance for another half hour before I allow myself to read his messages.

Then, I sit on the bench and, still panting, savor them all at once.

> Wanna meet for lunch today?
>
> I know a great place next to school. Your school I mean.
>
> By now, you've probably noticed that school cafeterias suck everywhere in the world.
>
> I mean, it's not that bad, but I wouldn't want you to think that this is the best Paris has to offer.
>
> Okay, I feel like I'm just talking to myself now. Let me know!

I smile, and smile again, as I read and reread the messages. Would I like to pop out of school to meet Louis for a delicious meal? Yes, I would. I look down the hallway to where I assume Audrey is practicing on her own, and my shoulders sink.

I'm sorry, I type, but delete it immediately. How can I explain? I can't do this over text, so I call Louis. He picks up right away.

"Bonjour!"

"Bonjour," I reply, my heart beating a little faster at the sound of his voice. Then I switch to English, because I'm

starting to realize that, in my few weeks in Paris, I can focus on my dancing *or* my language skills, but not both at once. "I got Odile," I say.

"That's fantastic! I'm so happy for you, Mia!" He sounds genuine, and I feel embarrassed remembering my mini meltdown in the train on Monday. In hindsight, I can't imagine that Monsieur Dabrowski would share the details of his work with Louis. "We'll celebrate over lunch," he continues.

Yes, please! I'm dying to say. But, no. I must be firm. No lunches. No escapades. No. More. Fun. Argh! Who comes to Paris to not have fun? Me, I guess. And every other student in the program who would do anything to take my spot.

"I can't have lunch with you today," I say.

"Tomorrow, then?" Louis asks, just as cheerful.

"Louis," I say, in the softest possible voice. "I can't do this."

He chuckles, but it sounds a little awkward. "You can't do what? Eat?"

I sigh. I'm not sure, exactly. Come on, Mia, what is it? I can't waste an hour of school time when I could be practicing my solo. I can't take the risk that anyone might think that I'm getting preferential treatment because I know Monsieur Dabrowski's son, or that I'm not taking the program seriously. For a brief moment, I picture my instructor telling me that I don't deserve Odile, after all. It sends shivers down my spine, and not the good kind.

"When we missed the train on Sunday," I say, lowering my voice, "I could have gotten into a lot of trouble if I hadn't made it back on time." Through the glass windows, I see a few students walk past me in the hallway and file into the next studio, a sign that classes are about to begin. "And now that I'm dancing Odile . . ."

"You need to practice for hours a day, I get it," Louis says, "but you're still going to eat lunch, right?"

"Well . . . yes."

"And, if eating is going to happen no matter what, do you really think the geographical location of said meal will affect your dancing skills?"

"Louis . . ."

How can anyone be this cute all the time?

"It's a genuine question."

"I only get an hour break for lunch. . . ." I can feel my resolve weakening. Saying no to Louis might be the hardest thing I've ever tried to do, and that includes all the *fouettés* I've just practiced.

A woman walks into the room, probably an instructor for another level, and gives me a strange look. I need to hang up.

"I get it," Louis continues, his tone suddenly serious. "This is probably not a good idea anyway. I can't get between you and your passion."

This jolts me. "No one could ever get between me and ballet."

I hear him sigh, but he doesn't respond. My heart crunches. Our conversation at Aunt Vivienne's house about his feelings on passions comes back to me, and I worry that I've said the wrong thing. "I have to go," I say, checking the clock on the wall.

"Okay. Well, bye, Mia."

I take a deep breath, my finger already hovering over the "End Call" button. But something stops me.

"Louis?"

"Yes?" he says quickly.

"Can you promise me something?" I feel a grin spread across my face. "It's just lunch. Tomorrow, for one hour only. And, no matter what happens, we're not taking a trip to the French countryside."

He laughs. It's the most beautiful sound I've heard in all of Paris. "I promise, Mia. But just this once."

Can't stop, won't stop smiling.

CHAPTER TWELVE

IT'S NOT UNTIL the end of my morning classes the next day that I fully appreciate it: I'm going on a date with Louis. An *actual* date. Sure, we've had lunch and explored Paris together before, but this feels more real. Maybe it's because you usually go on a few dates with someone before introducing them to your great-great-aunt.

I put on the outfit I planned out this morning: a white skirt, a black tank top, and a gold bracelet. Then I use a liberal amount of dry shampoo on my hair, apply concealer under my eyes and my favorite rose-tinted lip balm on my lips. I smile at my reflection in the mirror. I wanted to look nice, but not like I *tried* to look nice.

I peek outside the locker rooms before I exit, feeling totally silly doing it. Usually I have lunch with Lucy, Anouk, and a few other girls from their class. Audrey will only mingle with girls from level five, but there's no love lost there. I prefer taking a break with people who can relax a little.

"I have some errands to run during lunch," I told Lucy at breakfast. "Don't wait for me, I'll just grab a sandwich on the way."

She gave me a quizzical look. "What kind of errands?"

"Just . . . stuff," I said, wishing I had prepared a better story.

It's not like me to keep secrets. In fact, I've always been an open book: I started dancing at two years old and instantly decided that that's all I ever wanted to do. Since then, I've told anyone who would listen that I would become a professional ballet dancer. I never lied to my parents about having a sleepover at a friend's house when we actually went out to party. I never said I'd finished my homework when I hadn't. In fact, I rushed to do it so I could spend my evenings and weekends dancing. I didn't need to make things up; everyone around me always knew what I was up to.

"Stuff?" Lucy asked in a slightly mocking tone. And then, like something clicked in her head: "Do you need tampons?" she whispered. "Because I have some."

"No—I . . ." I almost blurted out everything, but I stopped myself. I couldn't tell Lucy that I was meeting a guy for lunch in the middle of a school day, because I wasn't prepared to admit it to myself.

Instead, I sheepishly told her that I needed to get some allergy medicine. From Lucy's expression, I could tell it worked. *Bingo*.

When I arrive at our meeting spot, I realize that Louis didn't give me the address of a café or a restaurant. In fact, as I stand halfway down a nondescript street, I check on my phone that I'm where I'm supposed to be. There are a couple of tall, glass-walled office buildings behind me, and cars parked along the street. A bus drives past and stops just a few feet away. People get on, others get off, and I'm starting to have doubts about this date. But then I spot Louis walking toward me and I smile.

He smiles back, and any concern I had about slipping out of school is gone. I take in his outfit—his signature creased linen shirt, light blue chinos, and floppy hair. By now it feels both totally familiar and still kind of . . . sexy. He's also carrying a wicker basket. White cloth napkins and a bottle of sparkling water peek out of it, but it's the baguette I zoom in on, my mouth already watering. When I'm back home, I'm going to find a way to import these to Westchester. Now that I've gotten a taste of straight-out-of-the-oven baguettes, I'm not living without them for another day.

For the first time, I don't flinch when Louis leans in to kiss me on the cheeks. I'm cool. I'm your totally blasé *Parisienne* who's meeting her handsome date for a romantic lunch like it's no big deal. And now that I've mastered *la bise,* I try to go as slowly as possible to feel the warmth of Louis's skin against mine. He smells like the outdoors. Like sunshine and sweat and something woodsy I can't place.

"I was kind of hoping you'd be wearing a pink leotard, maybe even a tutu," he says with a sparkle in his eyes.

I blush. "Oh yeah?"

My reddening cheeks only make him tease me harder.

"Yeah. I bet you look totally . . ." He pauses and looks into my eyes. I'm yearning for him to finish his sentence. "Like a ballerina," he adds mischievously.

I laugh to hide my slight disappointment. "I can confirm that I definitely look like a ballerina in my leotard."

"Good," he says, still staring at me. "I guess I'll just have to keep imagining."

The world around us comes to a halt. Everything goes quiet. Sometimes I think I'm imagining Louis. Because I had no idea a guy could make me feel like this. I never want it to stop.

"Mademoiselle," Louis says, offering me his arm. Fine, I'll come back to earth, I think, hooking mine through it.

Then he points at a green metal stairwell off to the side, behind me. *"Par ici,"* he says, leading me up the steps. *Right this way.*

"What is this?" I ask when we get to the top. We're at the start of a narrow pathway, lined by many plants, trees, and benches. Above us, an archway covered in greenery makes it feel like an oasis in the middle of the city.

"This," Louis says as we walk along, "is the French ancestor to—"

"The Highline in New York!" I finish for him, remembering the elevated pedestrian walkway going through downtown Manhattan.

"Yep. I went there with my mom when she had to go for work, and I must have walked up and down the Highline three times. French people like all things American, but I think the feeling is mutual. We're always stealing each other's ideas."

A sign informs me that the Parisian version is called "Promenade plantée" (Planted Promenade), which sounds more poetic. Louis tells me that it goes on for miles—well, kilometers—but we don't need to go very far to find an empty bench by a patch of grass.

"I love a good terrace," Louis says, unwrapping goodies from his basket—cheese, charcuterie, a carrot and beet salad from his local deli, and a pint of cherry tomatoes—"but since it had to be close to school, and cool enough to impress you, I thought this would tick both boxes."

"It's perfect," I say, ripping off a piece of baguette with my hands. I like how the hard crust snaps to reveal the soft-as-a-cloud flesh.

Conversation is easy with Louis. He tells me that his mom is coming from London next week. From the way he talks about her, I suspect that, even though she moved away to pursue her career, he's closer to her than to his dad. It's hard to imagine Monsieur Dabrowski doing anything else besides shouting "Higher! Lower! Faster! Slower!" I wonder what their relationship is like. Immediately, I feel the twitch of uneasiness at the thought of my *maître de ballet*. Louis's dad has the power to make or break my career—I'm sure the ABT apprentice program director values his opinion more than anyone else's—and going out with Louis is at best risky, and at worst totally wrong. So wrong. But so good.

After we polish off most of the food, I check my watch.

"See," Louis says as we get up to leave. "Quick, easy, delicious lunch, as promised."

"Thank you, this was wonderful."

You *are wonderful,* I want to say as we pack up cups and utensils. I can't believe I said yes to this, but I also can't believe I almost said no. I find myself wishing that I could stay with Louis all afternoon, wandering around Paris and discovering all his favorite spots.

"Mia," Louis says, leaning forward so close I can smell the sweet taste of tomatoes on his breath. He stares at my mouth, his eyes sparkling, and my heart drops. I know what he's about to do, and I freeze, scared of disrupting the moment. He inches closer, and I think, this is torture, but the best kind of torture, and I would like more of it, please and *merci.*

"You . . . ," he says softly, "have bread crumbs all over your face." I think he brushes them off with his thumb, but in truth I'm not sure what happens.

When I've recovered, we head down the stairs, walk along Rue de Lyon and back toward Place de la Bastille. But just as we arrive at the main square, I stop in my tracks right in front of the modern opera building. Fernando, my classmate and future dance partner, is standing there, talking with a girl I recognize as one of the student teachers: Sasha, a graceful redhead who always looks very tough and serious for her eighteen years. If I walk any farther, they'll see me. And Louis.

I don't have time to think: I duck behind the bus stop we just passed and hide behind an advertisement. I peek through the glass partition, checking on Fernando and Sasha, who haven't moved.

This . . . is not my proudest moment. It's even less so when Louis rushes to join me behind the billboard, the look on his face a cocktail of adrenaline and amusement. I'm pretty sure the look on mine reads something like "mortified." I give him an embarrassed smile.

"Are you hiding from that guy?" Louis asks, looking to the side behind me. "Because he's gone."

"Oh," I say, relief flooding me. "I wasn't hiding from *him* . . . ," I say, my cheeks growing hot. I should just stop talking.

"You just didn't want him to see you." He bites his bottom lip, suppressing a laugh.

"No. I mean, yes. I mean . . . it's complicated."

"He's from your program, right?"

"It's not what you think," I reply right away. Could Louis actually be jealous? I mean, Fernando is totally cute, but he's not Louis. No one is Louis.

"What I think is that you don't want people from school to see you out having lunch," he says. "Because it's your business what you do outside ballet."

"Oh," I say, my eyes opening wide. "Well, then it's *exactly* what you think."

We both let out a laugh, and I immediately feel better.

But then I think of Odile. How ecstatic I was when Monsieur Dabrowski called my name. He gave me the opportunity of a lifetime. I cannot forget that.

"You're allowed to have a private life. No one has to know about us."

It takes my heart a second to recover from that "us." You'd think waiting to find out about the roles in *Swan Lake* was nerve-racking, but the meaning of that "us" will probably keep the wheels turning in my mind all day and night. "I'm taking the program very seriously, and . . ."

"You don't have to explain yourself to me," he says seriously. "And I won't tell anyone."

I let out a sigh of relief. "Not even Max?"

Louis shakes his head, like this is a silly question. "No way." He glances at his watch, then adds, "So I really shouldn't walk you back to school."

"No, I'm just going to . . ."

We stare at each other for what feels like a long, loaded moment. His brown eyes search mine, like he's trying to say something important but can't find the words. Ultimately, Louis sighs and just grabs my hand instead. His feels warm and soft, and mine fits neatly inside it. They seem right together.

"You need to go," he says, his voice soft and raspy, but instead of releasing my hand, he tightens his grip and pulls me a little closer.

"I do," I reply, following his lead and closing the gap

between us. Our faces are just a few inches from each other, and my legs feel like jelly.

"So, umm, bye?" I say, but it sounds more like a question. He leans forward, and instead of heading straight for my cheek, his face hovers over mine. I just stand there and hold my breath. Nervous. Hopeful. Excited, and totally panicked at the same time. It feels as if we're just suspended like this for so long that everyone has stopped to stare.

I glance to the side. No one is gawking or even batting an eye. It is the City of Love, after all. I've seen so many couples—young and old—kissing on the streets, embracing on the tiny sidewalks, or just staring deep into each other's eyes on a busy corner, right in the way of foot traffic. Every day it seems like you're walking through dozens of love stories, getting a glimpse into these intimate moments. *L'amour est dans l'air.* It's easy to get swept up in it.

Suddenly it hits me: If I really want something, I can't just wait for Prince Charming to make it happen. So I stand on my toes, look up to him, and, just as I tilt my face to one side, he does as well, so that his lips, wherever they may have been headed, hit just to the right of my mouth.

Almost touching it, but not quite.

And I may not know all about French customs yet, but this is definitely not any kind of kiss. Not a friendly *bise*. Not a *kiss* kiss. Just a weird in-between that means nothing and everything at the same time.

Have I just missed my first chance at a French kiss,

original edition? I wish I could be brave enough to lean back in and smack my mouth on top of his, but afternoon classes start in a few minutes, and I still have to get changed. I'm going to have to make a run for it, *again*. I can't leave things like this, but the truth is, if something is going to happen between me and Louis—despite all the reasons why it shouldn't—what I want is a *real* kiss. Not a quick little whatever hidden behind a bus stop, next to an old lady chewing loudly on a piece of gum. This is not a Paris moment, not how I picture it, anyway. And my time here is far from over.

"Louis," I say.

"Mia," he replies sweetly.

"Can I see you this weekend?"

He smiles. "The weekend is really soon, right?"

Not soon enough. Absolutely, one hundred percent not soon enough.

CHAPTER THIRTEEN

AS WE CLOSE up week two of the program, Monsieur Dabrowski announces a change to the schedule: for the next four weeks, afternoons will be devoted to *Swan Lake* rehearsals. He will meet with the *corps de ballet* first, and then with the leads: Odette, Odile (that's me!), and Prince Siegfried. Since Max taught us the choreography, I've practiced little bits every chance I get: before and after class, of course, but also around lunch, right before bed, and even in the shower. For the record, I don't recommend trying to *pirouette* on a wet surface.

"Mia, Fernando, let's see the *entrée* and *adage* from your Act Three *pas de deux*," Monsieur Dabrowski says when it's just the four of us in the studio. A pianist has stayed back as well, but they're all so good at making themselves discreet that they usually just blend in behind their music.

I take a deep breath as Fernando and I get in position at opposite ends of the room. Until now, it didn't even occur to me to suggest that we practice before our session with Monsieur Dabrowski. I bet Audrey did, and that, when it's time for their duet, they'll dance seamlessly together. I glance at Fernando, and my stomach ties in a knot. Louis's face pops up in my mind, and I shake my head to make it go away. Not now, Mia. If Monsieur Dabrowski knew what or who you're thinking about . . . I don't feel prepared enough for our *maître de ballet*'s tough judgment, but then again, I never will. He nods at the pianist, and the music starts. Fernando and I make our way toward each other, and my concerns melt away with every step. We can do this. We *are* doing this.

"You need more intent here!" he calls to Fernando as my dance partner lifts me into the air. "Watch your leg, Mia; a little faster there, Fernando."

As our sequence ends, he tells us to go again, and again.

"Softer on the *port de bras,* Mademoiselle Jenrow. Round out your arms!"

None of his comments surprise me, especially not the one about my *port de bras.* It's been giving me so much grief. Getting it right is particularly important in *Swan Lake,* because while real swans have strong and graceful wings, we mere humans have to try to achieve the same movement with fleshy sticks also known as arms. And while it doesn't *look* hard, it does make your muscles burn so intensely that you feel like you will never be able to raise your hands again. Put simply, if you can still rip up a piece of baguette, then your *port de bras* practice has gone very wrong. I guess that's why Audrey was wincing and grumbling as she ate her ratatouille last night. She's been avoiding me since the phone-beeping incident, which is fine by me: I don't have the mental capacity to deal with anyone's bad mood.

"Let's stop here," Monsieur Dabrowski says after maybe our tenth round.

Sweat drips down the front of my chest. I try to catch my breath silently as he recaps our performance.

He addresses Fernando first. "You have to be more in control when you lift her up. She has to be able to trust you one hundred percent so she can focus on her steps. If she feels like your arms are weak, then you're impeding not only your dancing, but hers, too." Fernando nods at every word, taking it all in. I've noticed before that he seems so good at accepting feedback. He doesn't show any sign of nervousness or irritation, and just listens carefully.

Then it's my turn. I take a deep breath and tell myself that, whatever is coming, everything will be fine. I will make it so.

"A little bit faster, Mia. You were out of sync with him a couple of times. He should never have to wait for you."

"Of course," I say, serious. But inside, I'm leaping with relief. Of all the challenges ahead as I learn to become Odile, this is totally in the realm of achievable.

"And that *port de bras,*" he adds, shaking his head. "I'm not going to repeat it again, but next time I want to see a better flow. No stiffness. No straight arms, are we clear?"

"Yes, absolutely," I reply, bracing myself for more. The next thing he says floors me.

"Audrey, let's give these two a rest and see your Act Two variation."

Wait, that's it? I almost want to ask if he forgot something. I was prepared for a sermon on how I'm nowhere near Black Swan material or, at the very least, a laundry list of criticism on my *grand jeté* or my *pirouettes*. But our instructor has moved on. He's now focused on Audrey as she takes center stage. Fernando and I sit on the bench, both still panting, as we watch her.

She is flawless. Every one of her steps is so carefully executed. And her *port de bras* is definitely on point, pun intended. Her face relaxes as soon as the music stops. She doesn't quite smile, but I can tell she's pleased with herself.

Monsieur Dabrowski paces around the room for a minute, like he's considering what to say. Finally, he stops and purses his lips. "How did you feel, when you were dancing?"

Audrey frowns. "Uh, good . . ."

He nods. "What were you thinking about?"

"During my routine?" Audrey plays with her fingers, looking confused. I would be, too. "About the steps . . . whichever one was coming next." She doesn't sound so sure.

Our *maître* nods again, his face impassive. This man is a puzzle. A very hard one to solve. "Can you tell me the story of *Swan Lake*? What is Odette's story?"

Audrey perks up a little. That answer we all know. "She's cursed. A swan by day and a young woman by night. She can only be free if a man promises to love her, and her alone."

"And how do you think she feels about that?"

Audrey's chest rises and falls slowly. She's still catching her breath, and probably praying that she'll get off the hook very soon. "She's sad . . . and confused. Angry?"

"You don't know," Monsieur Dabrowski says sharply. It's not a question. "You have memorized the steps; you perform them extremely well. But you don't understand how Odette feels. You're not in her skin, in her heart, or her mind. You're not the White Swan. You're just Audrey Chapman, pretending to be."

Audrey's eyes grow wider as he speaks. Mine do, too. I can't believe he just said that. She's the best dancer I know.

We rehearse for a while longer, but I can tell Audrey is elsewhere. The minute Monsieur Dabrowski leaves the room, she rushes to the bench; jams her arms through the sleeves of her cardigan; and wipes her sweaty forehead, along with the corners of her eyes (which are filling with tears), with the back of her hand. Then she snags her bag before running out. I call out after her, but she's determined to get away as fast as possible. I don't blame her.

• • •

On my way home, I almost fall asleep on the shoulder of the businesswoman sitting next to me on the métro. In the subway car, a young man croons a song in French a cappella, looking for tips, and the music begins to lull me to sleep. I'm not just tired. I'm drained, wiped, completely done in. In fact, I don't think I understood the true meaning of exhaustion until this week. Sure, I've taken my fair share of Epsom baths, I've used ice packs on every part of my body, and I've spent hours stretching while watching videos of the greatest ballerinas performing in the classics. But I have never felt like the shoulder of a total stranger would be an appropriate place to rest my head. Until now.

I get to the dorm, take a long hot shower, slip into track-suit pants and a T-shirt, and lie on my bed. I have an hour before dinner, and though my pillow is whispering my name, there's something even more urgent than sleep right now.

Mom is the first to pick up the family landline.

"Hi!" I say, trying to sound chipper, but it comes out a little coarse.

"Mia, finally!"

"Hi, sweetie," my dad says, joining the call. "Don't worry about us. If I'd been in Paris for the summer at your age, I probably wouldn't have even called my parents once."

"Well, we're happy to hear from you, whenever you do call, Mia," Mom adds. I can practically see her shaking her head at him. We've exchanged a few texts over the last two weeks, but this is only the second time that we've managed to speak on the phone. Between school, their work schedule, and the time difference, keeping in touch is harder than I thought.

"I had my first official rehearsal today, and it went well," I say.

"Just well?" Dad asks.

I shuffle a bit, readjusting the pillow behind my back.

"Well is good, Dad. Well is excellent, in fact. I got a few notes, but it could have been much worse than that." I could have been running out of there crying like Audrey, I think. I glance at her bed. Her dance bag is on it, but I haven't seen her since I got back.

"You sound tired," Mom says flatly.

Not a word about my rehearsal, not a question about how things are going. I want to grunt, but I don't want her to hear it. "I am."

"Are you sleeping well over there?" Dad asks.

"Yes, it's just—"

"It's just that she's working too hard," Mom finishes for me. There's irritation in her voice; she's not even trying to hide it.

"I'm only working as hard as I need to."

I don't add that I'm feeling a little homesick. Being in Paris is exciting, but it's also very different. I miss Dad's pancakes; waking up in my own bed, wrapped in soft sheets that haven't been used by hundreds of students before me; and hearing nothing but silence from my room, instead of the continuous honking of cars and ambulance sirens. Their melody, if you can call it that, is completely different over here, with two tones alternating. The first few times I woke up in panic, wondering what was going on.

"I'm sure she's looking after herself," Dad says, but he sounds dubious, too.

I close my eyes. They feel heavy, a little swollen. "I try. I'm just so happy I get to dance Odile, you know?" But just as I ask the question, I realize that they *can't* know. They don't understand that this intensity is how things have to be.

We talk a little more. Mom asks where I've visited in Paris, what I'm eating for breakfast, what my plans are for the weekend. I answer them all, trying not to sound too annoyed. Because I know what she's really asking: are you doing something other than ballet?

I mention that I've made good friends here—Lucy, Anouk—and that we sometimes take a walk around the neighborhood after dinner. Last night we stopped at a *fromagerie*, bought the stinkiest cheese they had, and dared each other to finish our slice first. It wasn't as disgusting as I'd imagined, but my breath still tasted foul this morning, even after I brushed my teeth twice. All I could think was: never, ever eat cheese before seeing Louis.

"I'm jealous," Dad says with a laugh. "Sounds fun."

But then I let out a loud yawn, and Mom sighs. "Mia."

"Yes?"

"Just . . ."

"What, Mom?"

"You don't have to push yourself to the limits. Remember that we'll still be proud of you, no matter what."

My throat tightens. I want to hang up and erase her words from my memory. Because maybe she'll still love and respect me if I fail, but I certainly won't.

CHAPTER FOURTEEN

THE WEEKEND ROLLS around and I'm ecstatic to sleep in. I enjoy a late breakfast at the dorm with my friends before I leave to meet Louis for . . . well, I don't know. He texted me that he had a great idea for our afternoon together, but when I asked questions, he would only say that it's a surprise.

At the breakfast table, everyone shares their plans for the day. Picnics. Sightseeing. Shopping. I nod and smile, but mostly I just focus on my *tartines* in silence.

"You're coming with us to the beach?" Lucy asks with a laugh after Anouk mentions Paris-Plages, the city "beach" set up on the banks of the Seine for summer.

"I can't," I reply, looking sideways. "My aunts are in town today."

Lucy frowns at me, and I catch an inquisitive glance from Audrey. I'm *such* a bad liar.

"What are you going to do?" Anouk asks, leaning over me to grab a yogurt.

"It's . . . a surprise." I probably blush, but at least that part is true.

"Okay," Lucy says tentatively, "but you're not ditching us tomorrow."

Tomorrow is Bastille Day, the French national holiday. We've been talking all week about what we'll do, and where we'll watch the fireworks from. Lucy even started a group chat with everyone from the dorm so we could share ideas. Going to Champ de Mars near the Tour Eiffel is the current winning option, but we'll have to be there very early if we want a good viewing spot.

I try to look offended. "Of course not!"

There's no chance of me running off with Louis tomorrow. He told me he always spends *le quatorze juillet*—as the French call it—with his dad and some extended family.

"What time are you meeting your aunts?" Lucy asks. She pops a bright red strawberry in her mouth but doesn't take her eyes off me. "And where?"

I stare at her for a moment, wondering if she's just being curious or . . . Wait a minute. It's Lucy we're talking about. Curiosity is her middle name.

I check my watch. "Very soon, actually." In fact, I'm not meeting Louis until the afternoon, but I won't be able to keep up my lie for much longer. As I feel my cheeks grow hot, I realize that I should get out of here before I come clean and blurt out Louis's name. "We're meeting near Opéra Garnier."

Lucy, Anouk, and Audrey all look at me at the same time, and I think I'm about to get caught. Deny everything, Mia. It's for your own good.

"Well, have fun," Anouk says, elbowing Lucy.

Audrey shrugs and . . . that's it. I'm off the hook. Still, I'm not going to push my luck. I get up, clear out my breakfast, and say a quick goodbye before rushing upstairs to finish getting ready.

Once on the street, I decide that—though my blistered feet may disagree—the best way to kill time is to just wander the streets of Paris in the direction of Opéra Garnier. A few minutes in, I cross the bridge in front of Cathédrale Notre-Dame, finally taking the time to admire it face on. It was struck by a terrible fire a few years ago, and parts of it are still covered in scaffolding, but I can't imagine it looked more majestic than this. I take a deep breath, feeling a little woozy at how lucky I am that I get to discover a city that so many people dream of seeing. One day, when I'm a professional dancer, I hope to travel all over the world to dance, but I'm not sure it will ever feel as special as it does right now.

When I'm on the other side of the Seine, I check the map on my phone and realize that my route will take me right past Le Louvre. On the way, I try to listen in to the conversations around me, and catch little bits of French.

For a while I follow a group of girls my age, who are laughing hard and regularly tapping each other on the arm in a teasing way, as they keep mentioning *"ce mec."* Intrigued, I edge closer to them as I search the word in my app. It's slang and means *that guy*. They're talking about boy troubles. I feel a pang of guilt as I think back to breakfast. I haven't told a soul about Louis, not even my friends back home. I know it makes me sound paranoid, but I'm afraid that if I even put it in a text, one of the girls at the dorm will find out, and my life will be over: the program, performing Odile, and my chances with ABT.

The crowd around the Pyramide du Louvre is even thicker than in front of Notre-Dame. The contrast between the striking triangular glass structure and the traditional building is fascinating, and I spend some time doing what everyone else seems to be doing—taking selfies. I wish I had someone to share this with, because it's so much more beautiful in real life than on my phone screen.

I mosey over to Rue Saint-Honoré, a street lined with gorgeous boutiques.

Looking around, it seems every girl on the sidewalk is dressed like she has just stepped out of a magazine. Silk dresses, elaborate strappy sandals, and designer handbags seem to be the norm around these parts. I feel more self-conscious with every step.

It was fine for Louis to be all mysterious, and I have nothing against surprises, but they do present one big problem: what do you wear when you don't know what you're going to do? In the end, I decided to play it safe and settled on a black sleeveless cotton jumpsuit, brown wedge sandals, and a ponytail.

By the time I arrive close to Opéra Garnier, I've come to the conclusion that my outfit is all kinds of wrong. When I left the dorm, I felt like I could almost pass for a true *Parisienne,* but now it's clear that I don't even qualify as a pale imitation.

Before I have a full-on panic attack, I tell myself two things: I'm an hour early for our date, and I just happen to be right around the corner from some of the world's best department stores. Grandma Joan gave me special "Paris money" before I left and made me promise I would treat myself. Now seems like a perfect time to do just that.

Galeries Lafayette is bustling with people, and my head quickly spins. There are so many corners with various brands—most of which I've never heard of—and I don't even know where to start. After I check the directory, I go up the escalators, past a floor dedicated to luxury jewelry, and another for high-end designers. Finally I come to a section that looks more my style, and my budget. I'm not much of a shopper—unless we take my large collection of non-white leotards into consideration—and I quickly realize that I have no idea what I'm doing.

I've been browsing, overwhelmed, for ten minutes when a salesgirl in her early twenties—with bleached blond hair, rings on every finger, and a name tag labeled *Kim*—approaches me.

"Je peux vous aider?" she asks with a kind smile. *Can I help you?*

"Non," I say quickly. I don't know what else to say.

But she smiles even deeper. *"Vous cherchez quelque chose de particulier?"* *Are you looking for something specific?*

"Well, uh," I start. I look down at my outfit and picture Louis. How do you say, *I want his jaw to drop all the way to the ground* in French? *"J'ai un* 'date.' "

She chuckles and switches to English. "You have a romantic rendezvous with a guy?" She smiles, like she's excited for the challenge.

I nod. *"Oui,* and I . . . kind of want to impress him." Even though she's a total stranger, it's nice to finally tell someone about Louis.

"Come with me," she says, leading me through a few racks. "I have some ideas."

I watch in awe as she pulls out half a dozen items in quick and precise moves. The way her hands flick the hangers off and hook them on her arms, and how she twirls around the space she clearly knows so well, it almost looks like a dance.

Moments later, she sets me up in a changing room with her loot.

"I'll come back to check on you in a minute," she says.

I take a deep breath and start scanning the pieces she picked out. There's a black dress with tiny polka dots, a short-sleeved white shirt, slim pink pants, a silky floral blouse that feels as light as air, among others. They all look really nice, but I'm not sure any of them are my style. Maybe that's the point?

"How are you doing in here?" Kim suddenly asks from behind the curtain.

I pop my head out, and she notices that I'm still dressed in my boring black jumpsuit.

"I don't know where to start," I say with a laugh.

She smiles and slips inside the changing room with me. She studies each piece carefully, and pouts. "The real question is, how do you want him to see you? This dress is flirty and romantic, but this shirt would look great with the buttons half-undone for a kind of sexy look."

She pauses, waiting for me to weigh in.

"Sexy sounds good, but not *too* sexy, right?"

She looks almost offended. "Of course not! Sexy the French way. Suggestive, sensual, but never too much."

I chuckle. "I want that."

"Wait!" she says, struck by an idea.

She runs off and comes back a moment later with a slinky, no-frills navy dress with a V-neck *décolleté* and spaghetti straps. It looks almost like lingerie, but the fabric seems so luscious that I can't help but immediately stroke it. It's buttery soft, and I don't want to take my hands off it.

"Trust me," the salesgirl says firmly.

I do, and even before I exit the changing room, I feel like there's not enough fabric on my body. I step outside, feeling like I should use my arms to cover the rest of the bare skin.

"I feel kind of naked," I say, staring at myself in the mirror.

Kim says nothing, just studies me from top to bottom. I spin around, thinking that of course I can't wear this out, but also, it feels good. *I* feel good.

"Can I be honest with you?" Kim asks.

I nod, not taking my eyes off my reflection in the mirror.

"You have amazing legs, so I would definitely show them off. And look at the fit around your butt."

It's true—the smooth fabric flows perfectly around my curves.

"But . . . ," I say.

She raises her index finger, silently telling me to hold that thought. Then she steps inside the changing room, retrieves the white shirt, and helps me slip into it. She does up just two of the buttons, ties the ends in a knot at my waist, and then pulls on the dress a little to adjust the whole look.

"There," she says, stepping back to admire her handiwork. "How do you feel?"

I stare in the mirror. "Is it wrong if I say that I feel kind of hot?"

She laughs and retrieves a shoebox that I'm only just noticing. "And now, my favorite trick: sexy outfit, casual shoes. It's the best way to look like you just threw an outfit on, even if you're wearing a ball gown."

She opens the box to reveal a pair of navy espadrilles. I've seen girls wearing these all over town with everything from fancy dresses to smart pants.

I slip them on—she guessed my size correctly—and feel immediately at ease, like I'm standing on sand.

"One last thing," she says, reaching behind me. She pulls on my hair tie, and my waves cascade around my shoulders.

As I study my reflection, my stomach fills with butterflies. I know I'm supposed to dress for myself. This is about me, not about what a boy might think. But Louis always seems so confident that I sometimes wonder why he's hanging out with me. Today I want to feel like he looks: dashing, irresistible, and like Paris is my oyster. I cannot wait for him to see me like this.

CHAPTER FIFTEEN

"WOW," LOUIS SAYS when I meet him at the corner of Boulevard Haussmann and rue Drouot, a few minutes away from Opéra Garnier. His eyes sparkle as he keeps taking me in. "Did you do something to your hair?"

"Not really," I say, giving myself a mental high five.

"Oh. Well, you look great," Louis says. "*Really* great." He lingers on me for another moment, his lips pursing. That look alone was worth breaking the bank.

"Thank you," I say with a casual shrug. My old outfit is tucked inside a tote bag swinging from my shoulder, but there's no way I'm admitting to the sartorial crisis I just went through.

"So what are we doing here?" I ask.

Not that I want to switch the topic from how good I look, but I *am* curious. I did some Googling when Louis gave me our meeting point, but it didn't give me too many clues.

Louis starts walking down the smaller street, and I follow.

"I've been thinking a lot about your family legend," he says.

"Really?" I ask, intrigued.

We stop in front of a modern glass building covered in red flags stamped with DROUOT AUCTION HOUSE. A few older people, holding catalogues with the same color and lettering, walk past us and go inside.

"Come," Louis says, following them.

"Are you going to tell me why we're here?" I ask.

"We," he whispers, grabbing my hand and leading me through the hall, which is packed with well-to-do gray-haired people, "are at an auction house, the most famous one in Paris."

"That first part I figured out," I say with a laugh. "But why?" We must be the youngest people here by about thirty years.

Louis stops in the middle of the crowd, and his whole face brightens as he says, "Today's auction is about Impressionist paintings that haven't been seen for decades, or even longer. Art experts didn't even know some of these pieces existed."

My heart starts to race. "Are you trying to tell me there's a lost Degas here?"

"*Oui,*" Louis says, clearly enjoying the look on my face. "Wanna see it?"

I beam. I haven't had a minute to think about the drawing in Vivienne's dining room, my ancestor, or the Degas legend. But Louis remembered, and even did his research. If he's trying to impress me, it's working.

We arrive at the front of the exhibition room, and through the open door, I see bright red walls covered from top to bottom in paintings, small and large, framed and unframed. Several people pace the room, looking from the catalogue to the paintings on the walls, pointing and talking with serious faces on. The security guard checks my bag, mutters a few rules about not touching anything, and then asks something about an invitation.

Louis frowns. *"On n'a pas d'invitation,"* he says. *We don't have an invitation.*

The security guard shakes his head. *"Je suis désolé."* He goes on talking, and Louis's face grows more concerned with every word.

"Non, non," Louis says, becoming agitated. *"On en a pour deux minutes."* *We'll just be two minutes.*

The man shakes his head again, and they keep talking for a while.

"He's not letting us in?" I ask Louis as soon as there's a lull in the conversation. He turns to me, looking stricken. "I'm so sorry, Mia. I had no idea some auctions are by invitation only."

I feel my whole body deflate, and not just because Louis seems so disappointed. For the last few minutes, I've been replaying Grandma Joan's stories in my head, my heart filling with excitement at the idea that I could be about to uncover my family's great mystery. I'm starting to accept that it's not going to happen when the security guard sneaks a glance behind him. Then he looks from Louis to me and sighs.

"*Trente secondes,*" he says in a whisper. *Thirty seconds.* "*C'est tout.*" *That's it.*

Louis's eyes open wide with shock as the man steps aside, deliberately ignoring the both of us.

I grab Louis's hand and we rush inside, my heart beating faster with the thrill of it all. Pastel colors, creative brushstrokes, and soft lines abound on the walls in front of us. Many feel familiar, but there's only one artist I recognize for certain: a small painting of a dancer dressed in a bright blue costume, sitting on a bench, bending over to tie her shoes. The work is so precise that I find myself wishing I could run my fingers on the silk of the ribbons.

Unfortunately, you can't see her face, only the top of her dark brown hair in a neat bun. I read the small placard next to it:

EDGAR DEGAS

ENVIRON 1879

ORIGINE INCONNUE

TITRE INCONNU

LIEU INCONNU

Circa 1879. Origin, title, and location unknown.

I let out a sigh. It seems like every time I allow myself to hope that this legend is true, something comes along to remind me that dreams are just that: something nice to think about between large stretches of reality. I study the painting again, searching inside me. What do I feel? Is this the one? But before I can even begin to form answers in my head, the security guard clears his throat loudly in our direction. Louis and I share a nervous glance. The man looks scary enough that we don't even attempt to argue. I sneak one last look at the painting before Louis drags me away.

Back out on the street, we stand on the sidewalk facing each other for a moment.

Louis is the first to break the silence. "I really hoped this would be . . . something."

"It was a long shot." I act like it's no big deal, but I know I'm lying to him, and to myself. Louis seems genuinely bummed, so why can't I admit that I am, too?

"I'm sorry, Mia. I shouldn't have gotten your hopes up. I just thought . . . maybe your great-great-great-grandmother's painting has been sitting in an attic for a century, and that's why your family is still looking for it. I was being naive."

"I guess we both are," I say with a sad laugh, but he just shrugs as he looks down at his shoes. "But we shouldn't let this ruin our afternoon."

"No . . . It's just . . . ," Louis says, but then he trails off.

"Hey, I have an idea!" I say, feeling the need to cheer us

up. "We might not find the painting, but we can at least relive it."

"Oh!" he says, perking up. He grabs my hand and starts to walk. I love that we both know where we're heading without having to say it.

• • •

Half an hour later, we're first in line at the cashier of Opéra Garnier. Doing my best to enunciate, I say, *"Deux tickets, s'il vous plaît."* Two tickets, please.

But when I pull out my wallet, Louis puts a firm hand on my arm. "It's on me," he says. "To make up for our aborted mission at Drouot."

I shake my head. "It's not your fault."

He shrugs, clearly feeling responsible, and pays before I have time to do it.

As soon as we begin exploring the building, my mind twirls with thoughts of my great-great-great-grandmother who, *maybe,* danced here. From the grand double staircase punctuated by bronze statues, to the colorful ceiling of the main stage and the never-ending ballroom covered in gold detailing, everything in this magnificent space makes me yearn to become a ballerina even more so I can perform here one day.

"It means a lot that you took me to see the painting," I say as we reach the end of the main ballroom. It's quieter in this part of the building. The tour groups we saw at the bottom of the stairs are clearly moving at a slower pace. "You really . . . get me. I can't say that about many people." I look away as I finish my sentence, almost regretting it.

Louis inches closer to me. "Why? I'm sure you have many friends back home."

Sigh. Here's the ugly truth about having an "impossible dream," as Mom calls it. Very often, you're alone with it. Your passion fills up all the space inside and around you, making it hard for anyone to get through.

"I have ballet friends, yes, but the rest of them . . . they don't understand," I explain. "Like my mom."

"She doesn't like ballet?"

I ponder this for a moment. "I think she does. At least, she used to. She was a dancer, and then she stopped. I'm not sure why. But she acts like I should do the same: have fun with it for a while, and then get on with real life."

"Is that the worst thing that could happen?" Louis asks, serious.

"Umm, yes!" I stare at him, wondering if he's messing with me.

"I'm sorry, Mia," he says, raising his hands in defense. "I didn't mean to . . . I just believe that you can love doing something, but it doesn't have to become your whole life."

"It does for me," I say, unable to hide the hint of sadness in my voice. "I *want* ballet to be my whole life."

He looks stung for a moment, but shakes it off before

speaking again. "So what's the problem? You want your mom to share your dream?"

I shrug. "I've been working so hard for so long, and she just acts like I'm not making the right choices, or something. A little support would be nice."

"I get that," he says. "My parents are the opposite of yours. They want me to have a passion, like they did at my age. They're always pushing me to apply myself, to have more focus. But, honestly, I'm not sure I want to be like them."

"Of course you have to forge your own path, but they love what they do and they just want you to feel the same way. . . ."

"Maybe, but growing up, I sometimes felt like there wasn't enough room for me. My mom used to call ballet my dad's 'real wife.' Dad was always dancing, Mom was gone on film shoots for weeks at a time, and me . . . well . . ." He looks down sadly as he trails off.

"I'm sorry," I say, rubbing his hand with mine. "That doesn't sound fun."

"I'm sorry, too, about your mom. We're just being true to ourselves, but they don't see it that way."

"No," I say, shaking my head and thinking back to the many conversations I've had with Mom. "I've told her so many times. This is what I want."

"Then she shouldn't try to change your mind," Louis says, his eyes full of compassion. "Besides, you look like you have plenty of fun already."

He smiles at me, and I bite my lower lip, feeling charming and understood all at once.

"And your parents should get that one day you'll find your true passion."

"Maybe," Louis says with a heavy heart. "Maybe one day I'll find something that makes me want to jump out of bed in the morning, like you have."

I laugh. "At the moment it's more limping out of bed, because I'm so sore, but yeah. And I feel like if my mom were here, if she could see me perform, maybe she'd finally get it."

"Hmm," Louis says, a twinkle in his eye. "I think I need to see it for myself."

"What?"

"You. Dancing."

"You can't!" I start. I'm about to go on a rant about how no one can know about us at school, that it could get me in all sorts of trouble, when the amused look on his face stops me.

"Here, I mean," he says.

I frown. "Now?"

Louis grins. "Why not?"

We both look around. There are a few people at the far end of the room, but then again, a small audience doesn't scare me.

"There's no music," I say.

"I bet you know the *Swan Lake* songs by heart. And all

the other classics," he says, making a cute face. I mean *even* cuter than usual.

I'm out of arguments, so I put my bag down against the wall, walk back a few steps, and turn to face Louis. He looks gleeful as he watches me get in position. My new dress clings to my thighs as I turn out my feet, and I catch him glancing at my legs. I smirk on the inside. This outfit might not be as comfortable as a leotard, but it's pretty perfect otherwise.

I perform a short sequence I practiced over the last few days for the upcoming showcase, not taking my eyes off Louis's, whose face brightens with each move. I *piqué* turn once, then twice, and, when there's no more space between us, I wrap my arms around his neck. His own arms find my waist and pull me so close I can feel my heart beat against his chest.

"You're so beautiful," Louis whispers into my ear.

I take a deep breath, scared that if I say or do anything, I might disrupt this moment.

His lips find my neck and slowly travel upward. I shiver, and soon I feel like I'm watching us from above. Am I really nestled in a gorgeous French boy's arms in a centuries-old room ornate with floor-to-ceiling gold? How did this even happen?

When his lips reach my ear, Louis pulls back just a little to look me in the eyes.

"Louis . . . ," I start.

"Mia . . ."

Louis sighs deeply, which lets me know that maybe I'm not the only one feeling beyond nervous. I feel like my legs are about to give out. Lucky he's holding me.

"Ahem," someone says next to us.

We don't move at first—I definitely don't want to—but a loud clearing of a throat tells us that we don't have a choice.

Finally we pull away from each other, just a smidge, and slowly look to the side. A group of older Chinese tourists—maybe thirty of them—stare at us with a mix of annoyance and amusement. A short lady with bright red hair shakes her head while her companion looks on grumpily. I glance around and realize what the problem is. We're blocking the way to the next room. Louis and I look back at each other and chuckle, both of our cheeks growing hot. Then we shuffle to the side, still in each other's arms, not ready to let go of the moment.

CHAPTER SIXTEEN

"YOU KNOW, MY dad has meetings here sometimes," Louis says when another horde of tourists interrupts us for good.

My heart skips a beat as my head whips around as I look across the room for Monsieur Dabrowski's white mane.

"I'm sure it's fine," Louis adds, but now there's panic in his eyes. He searches the room as well, and I grow more and more uncomfortable.

"Let's get out of here," I say, feeling like all romance has gone out of the window.

We leave Opéra Garnier and walk to where Louis has parked his Vespa.

"Maybe this Degas thing was a bust," Louis says on the way, "but there's one thing that can't go wrong on a hot summer day."

"What's that?" I ask with a flirty smile.

"Ice cream."

"Oh!" I say, excited. I'm still full from my late break-fast, but I always have room for ice cream. "Is there a place nearby?"

Louis grimaces with mock outrage. "You can't just get ice cream from anywhere. There's only one place in Paris for ice cream. Trust me, even their vanilla is extraordinary."

"I trust you," I say with a laugh.

So off on the Vespa we go. As we drive across half of the city, most of it along the Seine, I remember a conversation we had at the dorm about the best food places in Paris. Best *crêpes*, best desserts, best café, best traditional *bistrot* . . . we've been swapping addresses on our WhatsApp group, and I'm pretty sure an ice cream place was mentioned.

It comes back to me as soon as we park near two wooden-clad shop fronts facing each other on a narrow street, with "Berthillon" written in gothic lettering at the top. A dozen people wait in line outside, and many more snake around the corner. That's it. Lucy, Anouk, and I tried to come here one night—it's a short walk from the dorm—but we were too tired to wait.

Today the line moves surprisingly quickly. Once it's our turn, we have a hard time choosing between the wide range of flavors. Louis opts for a raspberry and peach sor-bet, while I decide to pair the aforementioned vanilla with salted caramel.

Afterward, we walk around Île Saint-Louis, licking our already melting scoops as fast as we can. We stop off to the side of the bridge—Pont de la Tournelle—to enjoy the view of the water.

I point at the cone in my hand. "You were right, by the way—this is the least 'vanilla' vanilla ice cream I've ever tasted."

Louis frowns.

"You know," I explain, "it's not vanilla at all? It's flavorful and distinct."

More frowning.

"I don't get it," Louis says, looking from me to my ice cream. "It *is* vanilla, so it should *taste* like vanilla, *non*?"

We stare at each other for a beat, and then it finally hits me. "We call something 'vanilla' when it's kind of bland. Boring. Basic."

Louis nods. "Ha! So you're like, the opposite of vanilla."

"Very funny," I say, gently hitting him on the arm.

"I mean it," Louis replies, taking hold of the hand that just touched him. He rubs his fingers along my palm, and I shiver.

Then he leans toward me, just as his phone beeps.

I sigh. He mentioned that he's meeting Max later, but I don't want him to go yet.

Louis bites his bottom lip. "It's Max," he says, checking his phone. "Hmm, maybe I can meet him tonight instead. I'll call him."

He takes a few steps away as he begins to talk. I decide to check my own phone. Our group text has blown up with dozens of new messages since this morning. I flick through to the end, and my heart drops to my stomach.

Anyone here at the dorm? Lucy said fifteen minutes ago. *We're walking over to Berthillon now, if you want to join.*

I look around, spinning to get a good view of all the people walking by. Louis has disappeared off in the crowded space, and I take a few steps left and right, reassuring myself that everything is fine. Île Saint-Louis is a pretty small island, but what are the chances that my friends saw Louis and me?

I guess I'm about to find out, because here they are—Lucy, Anouk, Audrey, and a few others from the dorm, each holding an ice cream cone—right on the other side of the street. I consider hiding behind a group, but it's too late. Lucy's eyes dart in my direction. She waves at me, tentatively at first, and then, certain it's really me, her face brightens.

I jog toward the group, away from Louis, who, last I saw, was still on the phone.

"That's a gorgeous outfit," Lucy says, studying me head to toe. Then her gaze stops at the paper napkin stamped "Berthillon" in my hand.

"They're delicious, right? I had the vanilla and salted caramel. So amazing! I could have another one," I say quickly, not catching my breath.

"Where are your aunts?" Anouk asks, looking around me. I follow her gaze, but Louis is nowhere to be seen.

"I—I just left them. We had an ice cream and then—"

"They disappeared," Anouk finishes for me, her tone slightly mocking.

"I was actually on my way back to the dorm," I say.

We all start wandering off in that direction, and I force myself not to glance back. I don't know what Louis saw, but I can explain to him later.

"So you're going to tell us where you went today?" Audrey asks.

I frown at her, wondering what her game is. This might be the first personal question she has ever asked me. Usually it's ballet or bust, as far as she's concerned.

But now she, Lucy, and Anouk are looking at me, waiting for my answer. "We went to this famous auction house to see a Degas painting."

Audrey's eyes narrow, but I hold firm. I'm telling the truth. *Ish.*

Anouk makes a funny face. "So, you spend your entire week dancing, then, on the weekend, you go look at paintings of other girls dancing?"

"It was my aunt's idea," I say. "She thought I would like it. Besides, Audrey was watching ballet videos during breakfast this morning, and nobody found *that* strange." I do my best to pull a joking face, thinking that maybe I should give up dance and take drama classes. I'm getting good at this acting thing.

Audrey shrugs. Anouk and Lucy exchange a nod. Checkmate.

Lucy finishes another bite of her ice cream and turns to

me, an excited smile on her face. "Did you read all our messages from today?"

"Umm, not yet," I say, pulling out my phone. I was kind of busy waiting for Louis to kiss me, but of course I don't add that.

Lucy does a little jump. "We have an amazing idea for tomorrow!"

Anouk laughs. "More dancing!"

"But the fun, no-pressure kind," Lucy adds.

They take turns giving me a quick summary of the group exchanges. Students from another dorm heard about a nightclub on a houseboat that sails on the Seine. The perfect spot to watch the Bastille Day fireworks.

"Some famous DJ is performing," Anouk says.

"And we get to go past all the most magical Paris spots and live our best life!" Lucy adds.

And I hate to do it, really I do, but I have to rain on their parade. "We'll never get into a nightclub."

"Of course we will," Anouk says. "My friends do it all the time."

"They have fake IDs?" I ask, trying to keep any judgment out of my tone. I have nothing against people who skirt rules to do what they want, but I'd probably dissolve in shame if I got caught, so I've never tried, well . . . anything.

Lucy jumps in. "We don't need fake IDs."

Anouk nods. "Just walk in with confidence, smile at

the bouncer like you've known him or her for years, and you're in."

I try to contain my surprise and turn to Audrey, convinced she'll try to talk them out of this plan.

"I know," she says. "The legal age is eighteen, but apparently it's not that big a deal here."

My eyes grow wide, but all of them just shrug. Lucy nods enthusiastically, waiting for me to get on board. Am I really that uptight? Oh my God, am I more uptight than Audrey Chapman? That changes now.

CHAPTER SEVENTEEN

EVEN MORE SHOCKING: Audrey decides to join us on our party boat. Sure, it was only after Lucy presented her with endless arguments: it would be a crime against Paris to spend Bastille Day inside; we were all responsible enough to get a good night's sleep on a school night so we would be fresh and ready tomorrow morning; and many of our classmates were coming—it was almost like an official outing. Audrey pouted and shrugged as she listened to Lucy, but deep down I think she actually wanted to come. There are only so many ballet videos on YouTube, after all. I would know.

We spend most of the afternoon getting ready. There are many debates regarding outfit choices. Sleek and black or bright and fun? We swap our makeup—I love red lipstick and have several options to share. And, of course, shoes.

Here's a thing no one tells you when you want to do ballet: after years of dancing, your feet are going to look . . . terrible. Tortured, blistered, raw, and lumpy. When you buy new summer shoes, you'll zero in on styles that hide most of the damage, which is why none of us own any of those trendy minimalist sandals. We have to hide the not-so-pretty part of ballet so we can perpetuate the dream for everyone else. My new espadrilles are perfect for tonight.

Once we're all dressed up, the four of us head out to a well-known *crêperie* a few streets away. We'll meet the rest of the crew on the boat. This area is a favorite of college students and tourists of all stripes, so it's packed with cheap eateries serving cuisines from all around the world. Tonight we opt for classic French. We get a table, and I cast a glance around to see what others are eating before settling on a *complète* (ham, sunny-side-up egg, and Gruyère). As we wait for our meals, Lucy and Anouk fill us in on what's been going on in level four: who's great, who's a bit of a drama queen, and who likes whom.

"You have time for that kind of stuff?" Audrey asks, shaking her head in disapproval.

Anouk scoffs. "To notice which boys are cute? Um, yeah . . ."

Audrey sighs like she can't believe it.

"Don't tell me you've never looked at Fernando," Lucy asks Audrey.

"Of course I've looked at him. He's my dance partner, remember?"

Audrey's tone is condescending, but it takes more to put off Lucy. She just rolls her eyes, and she and Anouk start laughing.

"Come on, Mia," Lucy says, "tell us the gossip about level five."

I shrug. "There's not much to tell. We just work really hard."

Audrey lets out a deep exhale. "Yep. We give everything we can and then, no matter how perfect we are, Monsieur Dabrowski complains that the look on our face isn't quite right."

"Nobody's perfect," Anouk says.

"Except for Audrey." I mean it as a joke, but it's kind of true. I glance at her, checking her reaction, and she answers with a small smile.

"It's still not enough," she says sadly.

We all fall silent. I would never trade my spot in a million years, but, yeah, being in level five is a lot to deal with sometimes. I look at Audrey's sloped shoulders as she rubs her cloth napkin mindlessly. She can seem so tough, unaffected. I guess that's what Monsieur Dabrowski meant about her Odette solo. It's strange to see her looking vulnerable now.

As we finish eating, we change the topic to the *crêpes* we just had. Mine was perfect, but Lucy positively gushes about hers, which was full of *crème fraîche* and mushrooms.

Then we head straight to the boat. A nightclub on the water. Anouk was right. No IDs, no questions, just four ballerinas grabbing drinks and marching onto the dance floor.

There are lots of trendy-looking young people: girls in dresses and high heels, boys in crisp white shirts and hipster sneakers. I recognize many students from school: Fernando is here along with a few others from level five, and Lucy and Anouk take us straight to where their classmates are hanging. The DJ blasts the latest hits over the speakers, and there are purple lights near the floor, making everyone look like they're floating. The music pulses through my body. It's so loud that I can't hear my own thoughts. It's just music and sweat and bodies and drinks sloshing everywhere. It's so fantastically the opposite of everything about ballet that I feel my entire body relax. I love it.

The boat departs, and the city begins drifting by. Lucy grabs my hand in excitement. "Let's go outside," she says.

I wave at Anouk and Audrey, who follow us to the back of the boat. When we arrive, we can see the most epic view of Notre-Dame lit up against the night sky in all its glory. Pinch me. Seriously.

"I love it here!" Lucy screams into the wind in front of us. "Let's ditch school and just do this every night."

Anouk laughs, but I can feel Audrey tense up next to me.

"The only problem," Anouk adds, "is that we're rehearsing *Swan Lake* all of tomorrow. Madame Millet will be teaching us the choreography, so we can't miss that."

I shoot Audrey a glance. Madame Millet is the *maître de ballet* for level four, but the rest confuses us both equally.

"You're still learning the choreography?" I ask, slightly amazed. "We're supposed to have memorized it all by now."

"Memorized? That's crazy!" Lucy says.

Anouk spins around on demi-pointe and laughs. "But that means you get to spend more one-on-one rehearsal time with Fernando."

I lean over the balustrade, breathing in the fresh air of a sweet summer night. "Yeah, it's not really like that." Our boat passes under Pont-Royal, away from Notre-Dame.

"Get the hint, Mia," Lucy says, gently kicking her elbow in my side. "Anouk is trying to ask if anyone in your class has eyes on Fernando. Or, more importantly, if Fernando has eyes on anyone."

Anouk blushes slightly but perks up as she awaits my answer.

I'm sorry to disappoint her. "I honestly have no idea. I haven't paid attention to the guys in class."

Audrey gives me the side-eye. "That's true. Mia has only been paying attention *outside* of class."

Lucy's and Anouk's faces light up, thirsty for gossip.

"Ooh, Mia," Anouk says in a singsong voice.

"She keeps getting all these text messages," Audrey adds.

"It's just . . . ," I start.

But Audrey acts like she didn't hear me. "Is your ninety-year-old aunt texting you late at night?"

"Tell us everything," Lucy adds, hooking her arm over my shoulder.

"I don't think Fernando likes girls," I mumble, trying to change the topic.

Lucy will not let me get away with it. "Tell us, Mia! Did you meet a cute French guy?"

"Oh!" Anouk says like she just figured out something important. "Is that why you looked so chic yesterday afternoon?"

"And why you didn't come home last Sunday?" Audrey adds.

The girls surround me now. There's no escaping. "I *really* went to visit my great-great-aunt, and I stayed over—"

"But you didn't pack a bag," Lucy cuts in.

"I missed the last train. I told you all that."

"And no one believed you," Audrey answers.

The other two just laugh. Clearly, it's true. I'm starting to wonder if they even bought my excuse yesterday, or if they've been suspecting me all along.

"Come on, Mia, what's his name?" Lucy asks.

This is such an unfair fight, three against one.

"Paul," Audrey says, her lips pursed and her accent perfect.

"Martin!" Anouk says.

Lucy pouts, giving the question some serious thought. "It's got to be a classic French name. Mia did not come to Paris to fall for an American. Pierre?"

I shake my head. "You're all completely wrong."

"Pierrrrrre," Anouk says in an exaggerated French accent.

"*Paul, je t'aime,*" Lucy adds in a raspy voice.

Audrey turns to me, more serious than the other two. "Come on, it's not fun to keep secrets."

The boat passes by the Musée d'Orsay, but I'm the only one who looks up at its giant clocks and curved windows. No one will care about the view until I've dished.

"I—I . . . ," I start, but I can't say anything. The minute I lie about Louis, my cheeks will for sure turn fire-engine red. But if I admit that there is, indeed, a *very* cute French guy, Audrey will give me hell for thinking about anything other than Odile. And if they ever discover who it is . . . I love Lucy, but I don't think she can keep this to herself. By lunchtime tomorrow, everyone at school will think that I only got a lead role because of Louis. I can't let that happen.

"You have that glow," Lucy says, pointing at my cheeks.

"The glow of luvvvv," Anouk adds.

Just as I'm racking my brain to change the topic, Audrey raises an eyebrow as she looks behind me.

"Crap!" she says. "Did you know they were going to be here?" she asks Lucy and Anouk.

I turn around to see who she means, and my mouth drops open. Max, Émilie, Sasha—our student teachers—are standing on the other side of the boat.

Louis is with them.

"What if Monsieur Dabrowski finds out about this?" Audrey asks, her voice shaking a little.

For once I agree with her.

Lucy shrugs. "Half the school is here."

Before we can debate any further, the Tour Eiffel comes

into view. A nearby church strikes ten loud, resounding chimes. The grand iron tower lights up from top to bottom and sparkles in the night. This is the first time I've been out late enough to see it.

I sneak a glance at Louis and can't help but break into a smile when I notice he's looking at me, too. Many people squeeze between us, all jockeying for a view, but for a moment, we're the only two people on the boat. Yesterday, I texted him as soon as I got back to the dorm, explaining why I'd ditched him after our ice cream. It turns out that he saw me talking to the girls and put two and two together.

Suddenly fireworks light up the whole sky. The three girls and I link arms, holding our breaths in awe as they sparkle and fizz. I turn toward the embankment and see that people young and old have gathered, their wine bottles and blankets spread all along the Seine to take in the spectacular view. The wind blows my hair away, and my heart is full of love. For this summer. For this city. For dance. All of it. This moment is nearly perfect.

And then I feel a very light touch on my lower back. It's almost imperceptible, but I'm certain Louis is standing right behind me. There are enough people around that I hope no one will notice. Every part of my body comes alive, and all I can think about is his hand on my back and the space between us. It sends shivers down my spine, in the best possible way. The fireworks explode in a blur, but I barely notice. This moment lasts forever, but also not nearly long enough.

When the final sparkle goes up in smoke, leaving nothing but a cloudy haze in the sky, his hand disappears. I unlink my arms from the other girls and turn around. No Louis.

"Let's dance!" I say over the blasting music. I swear it's gotten even louder after the fireworks. Lucy lets out a "woo!" and they all follow me to the dance floor.

Before long, Anouk has disappeared off with some of her friends who also came out tonight; Lucy has found Charles—her crush—and they're dancing together at the other end of the dance floor. I'm pretty sure Audrey is sulking somewhere, regretting her decision to come. As for me, I jump and twirl, soaking in the music, my heart pounding and my breath ragged. But I can't stop looking for Louis. Finally I see him in the back corner of the bar. I take my chances and make my way over. There's a dark corridor behind him, a decent enough hiding spot.

"What are you doing here?" I ask, resisting the urge to wrap my arms around him.

"I was coming home from my family thing, and Max texted me about this party. . . ." He takes a gulp of his beer while his other hand takes mine. He manages to do this without getting closer to me. I shiver at this forbidden gesture.

"Did you know I'd be here?" I scan the room to make sure that no one is looking at us, but the crowd is too thick, and this part of the boat too dark. I think we're safe.

"I hoped you would," Louis says. "I kind of thought maybe we could be alone for a few minutes."

Next to us, a couple is full-on making out on the edge of the dance floor, standing still right by all the moving bodies, like the rest of the world doesn't matter. I'm jealous.

"Maybe," I start. . . . But dozens of my classmates are all over this party, not to mention the student teachers. Still, I scan the space for an even quieter corner—just for a moment, just for one kiss—when I see Audrey pushing through the crowd toward me.

I take my hand back and turn away from Louis immediately. Even before she arrives in front of me, I can see the stricken look on her face.

"We have to go," she yells over the music. "Now."

I don't protest. Something in her demeanor tells me not to.

The boat has already returned to the dock, but the party is far from over. We don't say a word until we're back on firm land. Lucy and Anouk look like they're having way too much fun, so we leave them behind. Even at this hour, every street is still bustling with people. It's such a beautiful night; I think we're all a bit electrified by the summer heat and celebration. Except for Audrey, who looks charged by another feeling entirely.

"What if the student teachers tell Monsieur Dabrowski we were out so late?" she asks.

"I'm sure it would be fine," I reply, though I'm not actually *that* sure. I can't imagine Monsieur Dabrowski would give us his blessing to go out and party on a school night, but we didn't do anything wrong.

"We're the leads!" Audrey spits out. "Different rules apply to us. I should never have come."

"Fernando was there, too," I say, trying to remain calm.

Audrey shakes her head. "Boys get treated differently."

She has a point. There are so few boys in the ballet world that it's easier for them to feel special, and for their talent to stand out. There are fewer male roles, but also much less competition. Or maybe it's just that boys can get away with more, in general.

We arrive at the front of our dorm, and I fish inside my bag for my keys. Audrey hovers near me, still fuming.

"Why are you like that?" she asks.

For a moment I wonder if she can read on my face what I was doing before she came to find me, but I don't think that's what she means.

"Like what?" I ask, frowning.

To be honest, I'm not mad that we came home early. This weekend has been exhausting in many ways. As much as I wanted to stay out and sneak away with Louis, the right thing to do is to get as much sleep as possible before another grueling week of classes and rehearsals.

"Tell me you're putting the program—and the show— first," she says, ignoring my question.

I sigh as I unlock the door.

"This is too important, for both of us," she adds.

"I promise," I say quietly. The hall inside is silent. "I want this to go perfectly as much as you do."

"No one wants this as much as I do."

She goes up the stairs two at a time and disappears off in front of me. As I follow her slowly, I wonder if she's right. I've always wanted to be a dancer more than anything else, but something feels different now.

Is it me? Is it Louis—his gorgeous eyes and devastating, distracting smile? Or is Paris sweeping me off my feet? I squeeze my eyes tight, trying to shake the sleepiness from them. Whatever it is, there's only one way this summer can end for me: by winning ABT's heart and returning home triumphant.

CHAPTER EIGHTEEN

I'VE BEEN WORRYING about so many things that I almost forget that today is not a regular class day. Instead, to mark the halfway point of the program, we're showcasing some of the dances we've practiced over the last two weeks. I've performed in front of an audience for so many years that it all feels natural to me: fighting for mirror space backstage to do my hair and apply a thick layer of makeup, slipping on my white tutu, and struggling to find a spot in the cramped space to tie up my pointe shoes.

"Girls in *Paquita*!" Monsieur Dabrowski calls out. "You're starting in two minutes!"

Audrey checks her reflection in the mirror and gets up to join the other girls she's dancing with. We're only doing group dances today: no solos, no stakes, just an occasion for our *maîtres de ballet* to observe our progress in a more formal setting. Each of us gets to perform twice, and our outfits reflect the simplicity of the day: all white for level fives, all black for everyone else.

The clock edges closer to showtime, and I take a deep breath as my stomach begins to tie in a knot. I've been expecting it. In fact, I welcome it. No ballerina dreams of dancing in front of a mirror at the barre. We only put up with months of practice so we can get a chance to dance onstage for a few minutes. So give me a bundle of nerves and a showcase any day. Give me a darkened room full of mostly strangers, and I'll skitter out in front of them, determined and focused on the outside, full of pride and joy on the inside.

But before I head to the wings, I unlock my phone and glance for the millionth time at the message Louis sent me this morning.

Good luck at the showcase! 🐦

I haven't seen him since Sunday, two days ago. I considered asking him if he would be here, and then reality called and set me straight. As much as I want to be with Louis, Odile and my dreams of ABT have to come first. Still, I miss him. We've exchanged a few texts, but he hasn't suggested another date yet. And I probably shouldn't, for all the reasons that have been blaring warning signs in the back of my mind. I push Louis out of my thoughts as Audrey's group takes the stage.

A few students are gathered in the wings to watch, and I join them. The girls are dancing a piece from *Giselle*. As they get into position, I glance around at the room. *Maîtres de ballet* and staff occupy the first two rows, while the rest of the audience is half-filled with unfamiliar faces: the family and friends of the few local students who were able to pop by on a Tuesday afternoon. I'm about to turn my attention back to the stage when I spot them.

My eyes narrow, trying to make sure I'm really seeing Aunt Vivienne and Madeleine in the third row. Vivienne is wearing a bright floral dress, her white bag placed neatly on her lap, while Madeleine is chic in all navy with a large gold pendant. I can't believe they're here! I didn't tell them about the showcase; in fact, I didn't even know what day it would be when I last saw them.

I search my memory, trying to figure it out. I told Mom I'd be performing today, but she didn't sound too interested in the details. Come to think of it, Grandma Joan was at our house when I called. I don't think I mentioned what time it was, but maybe she figured it out and asked them to come?

When it's my turn, I run to center stage to take my starting position along with several other girls from level five. I risk a glance down toward Madeleine and Vivienne. Madeleine notices and gives me a small wave. She leans over to her mom, and then Vivienne is waving, too, so enthusiastically that a few people start to notice. It's the kind of thing that would drive me nuts at home—as snobbish as it sounds, everyone should know that you do not distract a dancer when she's about to take the stage—but coming from my elderly aunt, it makes me smile. She barely knows me, and yet she seems so excited to be here. The flutters in my stomach double. By the end of my performance, I want my great-great-aunt to know that I'm destined to become a professional ballet dancer.

I may not know much about her at all, but my great-great-great-grandmother, the infamous *danseuse étoile,* is behind my every step. Her destiny is mine, too, and carries me across the stage. *Bourrée, waltz turn, piqué, arabesque* . . . and on we go, across and around the stage, to the tune of "The Waltz of the Snowflakes" from *The Nutcracker.*

My feet float off the ground with great energy, and my movements come together almost effortlessly. Still, I wish Louis were here. It's annoying to admit, but maybe I should have asked him to come. It's not until we finish up that I realize that I've landed slightly in front of the other girls. We should be in one straight line, but I'm about half a foot forward. I shuffle backward, slowly and discreetly, as the room erupts in applause. Looking up to see all the delighted faces makes me forget everything else. We take a bow, and when we come up again, everyone in the audience is standing. I smile brightly as I catch my breath. Nothing is more rewarding than sending a room full of people into a frenzy of rapturous delight. I'm going to chase after this feeling performance after performance, for the rest of my life.

• • •

Vivienne and Madeleine are waiting for me in the main hall of the school.

"Ma Mia!" Vivienne says, cupping my face with her hands. She plants a wet kiss on each of my cheeks.

"Merci!" I say. Then I search my words for a moment and gather up every bit of French I know to say how touched I am that they came all this way. *"Merci beaucoup d'être là! C'est tellement gentil d'être venues."*

Vivienne beams back at me, clearly impressed with my progress. I turn to Madeleine. "How did you know?" I ask in French, still giddy from the show.

"Louis called us," Madeleine says slowly. Vivienne's face lights up even more at the mention of Louis, and I'm pretty sure mine does, too.

"Louis?" I say, louder than I intended.

The hall is packed with students, instructors, and all the audience members. Everyone is chatting happily; only Audrey hangs back by herself nearby. I smile at her and give her a nod that I hope is saying, *You were great.* She shoots me a funny look back. I wonder if that's because Vivienne and Madeleine are here—proof that I do spend time with my family. I don't have time to think about it more because behind her, talking with Max, Émilie, and Sasha—is Louis. He senses me looking and catches my eye, but only for a brief moment. "Thank you," I mouth. He smiles discreetly, and then turns back to his friends. My heart skips a beat. I'd love to go ask him what he thought of my performance right now, but these secret encounters have a thrilling romantic flair about them.

Between Madeleine's basic English and my broken French, I gather the rest of the story. A few days ago, Louis called Vivienne to thank her again for dinner. She told him she hoped I'd visit again, but Louis reminded her that I might not have time. He mentioned the showcase, and that I'd be so happy if they came to see me dance. Louis even went as far as picking up my two relatives from Gare de Lyon.

"Mom really likes Louis," Madeleine says with a suggestive smile.

Me too, I think. But I don't need to say it out loud; I'm pretty sure they can tell from the look on my face. I turn around to see if he's still there, but the hall has emptied out, and there are only a handful of students left.

"We will go soon," Madeleine explains. "Mom is worried about missing the train home," she adds with a laugh. It takes me a second to get what she means. It feels like a lifetime ago that I ran out of her car to find the train station locked.

"Oh!" Vivienne says, placing her hand on my arm and squeezing it. I can tell she has something important to say. Once again, I curse my terrible French. Instead, she fishes inside her bag, pulls out a small envelope, and hands it to me. Her eyes sparkle with anticipation as I open it to find two grainy, sepia-toned photographs with frayed edges.

They both feature the same dark-haired young woman. In one, she is standing on a cobblestoned street, posing in front of a building with two other girls. The next is a portrait of her standing in first position and wearing a ballet costume—pointe shoes, a short cardigan, and a long, stiff tulle skirt.

Vivienne starts to speak quickly with grand arm gestures, but then she realizes that I don't understand much. I need Louis. It's so much less fun to do this without him. Giving up, Vivienne turns to her daughter and says, *"Dis à Mia." Tell Mia.*

So Madeleine does. "We think, this is . . . the girl, hmm, you know, our ancestor." She doesn't sound quite as excited as her mom. Vivienne points to the back of the second photograph, and I flip it over. There's an inscription in beautiful cursive handwriting.

Élise Mercier,
Opéra de Paris, 2 février 1880

I gasp. *"C'est vraiment elle?"* I ask Vivienne. *Is that really her?*

She grins and nods at the same time. "Élise Mercier, *ton arrière-arrière-arrière grand-mère.*" She squeezes my hand, making sure I understand her. And I do. This is my great-great-great-grandmother: a ballerina standing in front of the Paris Opera. In this moment, it doesn't even really matter if she was painted by Degas. This photograph feels like a treasure of its own.

"Mom found this in the attic after your visit," Madeleine explains in French as Vivienne watches for my reaction. "She thought maybe it could help you find the Degas painting." She looks to her mom, and then quietly adds, "If there is one."

The thought warms me up inside. I want to call Mom and say *I told you!* Even more so, I want to let Grandma Joan know that she was right. But most of all, I want to push the crowd out of the way, throw myself in Louis's arms, and tell him to strap on his helmet. Because whatever crazy adventure we embarked on the day we met on the school steps is only just beginning.

CHAPTER NINETEEN

THE NEXT DAY, the showcase already feels like a distant memory. From now on, it's just one straight line to the final performance, and it's becoming very real. I'm feeling tenser in class, and it's obvious that my classmates are as well. There's less chatting before the instructor arrives, bigger circles under our eyes, and fewer smiles. And it's not just that the show is coming up in two short weeks: our first fitting with the costume team from the Institut de l'Opéra de Paris is today.

After class, I head to the lower level of the school, below reception, to the costume department. On my way, I do what I've done pretty much every time I'm in this part of the building. I stop by the information board and zoom in on the call sheet for the next day's rehearsals. I run my finger on the paper, my heart palpitating, though I know exactly what I'm going to find: Mia Jenrow—me, me, me!—next to the name of Odile. It never gets old. I gaze at the call sheet for a moment, my confidence boosted for another day.

A few minutes later, my hands tingle with anticipation as a woman named Valérie hands me a black beaded corset with a tutu attached at the waist. I immediately think of it as *my* costume, but it turns out I'm wrong. Excitingly so.

"Myriam Ayed wore this in the last production of *Swan Lake*," Valérie tells me, her eyes sparkling.

My jaw drops. "Myriam Ayed wore this exact costume?"

"Don't worry, it has been cleaned," Valérie says with a small laugh.

I squeal. "I'm going to wear Myriam Ayed's Black Swan costume!"

Next to me, Audrey is receiving the same careful consideration from one of Valérie's colleagues. She rolls her eyes at me. I gather that her White Swan costume was also worn by Myriam Ayed, but Audrey is too cool to get excited about that.

I return my attention back to the piece of black tulle in my hands. It's both stiff and soft under my fingers, and, while it needs a few repairs—some of the beads have come undone, and there's a small rip in the chest—it feels magical to hold. I put it on over my leotard and slip off my straps to get a better feel of the sweetheart neckline. This is seriously an out-of-body experience.

"Let's see," Valérie says once I'm dressed.

She studies me carefully and then grabs her sewing kit.

"Oops," she says, stabbing the top of my thigh lightly with a needle. "This tulle is so thick!" Is it weird if I tell her that she can stab me all she wants? Ballerinas are used to pain. We live with it every day, from our split toenails to our strained muscles. You can't be a dancer if you're not willing to make friends with pain.

Audrey spins around to accommodate her seamstress, who starts pinning the top in the back. Facing me now, she looks me up and down, her face impassive. "You were good earlier," she says flatly. "Your *fouettés* are coming along."

Before this, we had another rehearsal with Monsieur Dabrowski, and he was as hard on each of us as ever. "All that stomping around! You're swans, not horses!"

"Oh," I say, taken aback. An unsolicited compliment coming out of nowhere from Audrey Chapman. Paris, city of miracles.

"I'm impressed," she says, shrugging, like she could hear me think.

"Thank you," I reply. "You were really great. You're always great."

Audrey shrugs again, but even her shrugs are tired. Her shoulders slump as she looks away.

The truth is Monsieur Dabrowski has been especially hard on us leads. "Where is your heart, Audrey? You're a young woman in love with a prince who can deliver you from a curse. Does that mean nothing to you?" He will not let that go. "You need more intent in that leg, Mia. It has to carry you all the way! What are you going to do during the performance? Hop like a bunny?" He even called Fernando an Oompa Loompa. Which is actually pretty funny, considering how tall he is.

"How does it feel?" Valérie asks me as she leads me toward the floor-length mirror.

She stands behind me and smiles at my reflection, proud of her handiwork.

"It's perfect," I say. *"Merci."*

She pinches a bit of loose fabric at the waist. "I just need one small touch-up here."

A little while later, Audrey and I each remove our costumes, careful of all the pins still stuck in them. Valérie tells us that they'll come back next week for another fitting as they hang up our tutus. "Don't lose any weight between now and then," she adds. "We know how stressed you girls get."

"Our daily dose of croissants won't let that happen," I say with a smile.

Audrey chuckles a little. We make our way through the now-deserted school. I pause when we reach the front door. "I have something to do, actually. . . . I'll see you later," I say nervously.

"Oh," Audrey replies, sounding not so surprised. "You're going . . ."

"Out?" My voice sounds more on edge than I'd like it to be. But what else can I say?

"Hmm . . . ," she replies, arching one eyebrow.

"My aunt invited me to dinner," I add. I try to keep a straight face, but I can feel my cheeks flush.

Audrey looks at me deadpan. "Your aunt, right." Her tone is only a little snarky.

Note to self: never underestimate her. She's not easily fooled.

"She's . . ." I take a deep breath, ready to dig myself into a deeper lie, but something in Audrey's eyes stop me. "I won't be home late," I continue. "And I'll be just as ready to dance tomorrow morning."

Audrey nods. "Have fun."

Those might be the two strangest words Audrey has ever said to me.

"Really?" I ask her.

"Really," she says.

And, maybe for the first time, we smile at each other.

• • •

There was no surprise this time, from him or from me. I didn't feel nervous, and I refused to overthink it. I just finally found the courage to admit to myself what I wanted to do and simply texted Louis about taking him out on a date at his favorite restaurant. Which is why I'm standing on a hip street in the ninth arrondissement, underneath a neon sign that reads "Hôtel Amour." That's right, Louis chose a place called the "Love Hotel." You can't make that up. One thing I've learned about French people is that they're not afraid to get romantic. When Americans do it, it can feel over-the-top, but Paris is swarming with oh-so-cool Cinderellas in Breton striped tops, lips stained in red, their tousled sun-kissed hair bouncing as they casually stroll down the street toward their knights in shining armor. Or on a shiny Vespa, in my case.

"Mia!" Louis says as soon as he removes his helmet. I don't know if we're going for *la bise* or if we're kind of past that now, so I give him a hug, the American way.

"I'm sure no one has ever said this before," he tells me as we make our way to the table I reserved in the lush garden at the back, with vines climbing up the walls, "but you danced so beautifully yesterday. We should celebrate your triumph!"

I laugh, but he seems determined as the waitress comes over.

"Deux coupes de champagne," he orders. "My treat!" he says to me.

My eyes open wide. "Did you just order champagne?"

Louis shrugs. "You drank wine at your aunt's place."

While he has a good point, this feels different. It's one thing to take a few sips at a family dinner. It's quite another to be out on a date on a gorgeous terrace on a hot summer night, surrounded by Parisians, and drinking expensive sparkling wine. It seems a little too grown-up for me, like I'm playing the role of an older Mia Jenrow.

But then again, I feel like I've aged five years since I've been here. Until now, I had no idea how natural it would feel to take care of myself in a foreign city, but I've done okay so far. Better than okay, even.

The waitress comes back with two flutes that she fills with great ceremony after she places them in front of each of us.

"À toi!" Louis says, raising his.

I clink mine with it. "And to you," I say.

"Okay, then, to us," he adds, emphasizing the "us" and giving me a pointed look.

I hold his gaze, and he winks at me. I mentally pat myself on the back for not blushing. *I think*. After a small sip that tickles my tongue, I retrieve the photographs from my bag and slide them across the table. "I have something to tell you," I start, a little giddy.

"Let me guess," Louis replies. "Vivienne found pictures of your ancestor in her attic, and she gave them to you at the showcase so you could find the Degas painting."

Giddiness gone.

"Désolé," he says, laughing. "I couldn't help it."

That's when I put two and two together. "You had something to do with this, didn't you?"

Louis shrugs with innocence. "What can I say? Grandmas love me."

Not just grandmas, I think. And *now* I'm totally blushing.

The waitress comes back to take our order, but I'm not ready to look at the menu yet, so she leaves us to it.

I take a deep breath. "I have something to ask you. I don't have much spare time until I leave, but I'm prepared to go around Paris, rummage through every museum, interrogate every art collector, and maybe even break into a few attics if I have to. I want to find proof that Degas painted my ancestor. It would make me so happy if I could figure this out before I go home. Do you want to do this with me?"

Louis smiles. "Yes, Mia. I would love to make you happy."

This is a total code red on the blushing scale, but I don't care.

"I told my mom about you," he says, before taking another gulp of his champagne.

My eyes open wide. "You did?"

He nods. "I told her about a beautiful, talented ballerina with a legendary history." He pauses. "And then I mentioned you, too."

His tone is so flat that it takes me a second to get it. I roll my eyes. "And what did your mom have to say about this beautiful, talented ballerina?"

"She loved the story. She also knows tons of people in the arts in Paris. Some she's worked with, friends of friends . . . She gave me the details of a curator at the Musée d'Orsay."

I hold my breath, excited for what's to come. "And?"

"She has a PhD in Impressionist art, or something like that. Her name is Charlotte Ravier but I've been thinking of her as Dr. Pastels."

I giggle and pull out my phone to write her details, but Louis retrieves a notebook and a pencil from his satchel instead. He opens it to a blank page and scribbles her name, phone number, and email address. Then, in a few quick strokes, he doodles a twirling ballerina with her arms straight up in the air. I smile, impressed, as he rips off the page and hands it to me, but he just shrugs in response. We make plans to call Dr. Pastels the next day, and then we don't take our eyes off each other for the whole dinner. We order food, but I can't remember what. It may have been pasta. Or fish. Or even a cactus plant, for all the attention I paid. None of it is as important as the way Louis looks at me. We laugh and eat, share stories, and take more sips of our champagne.

Louis protests vehemently when I remind him I'm paying for dinner, but I hold my ground. *I* invited him for a date, and no matter how much he grumbles, I count my euros, place them on the table, and tell him he can repay me by helping me find this painting.

His hand finds mine the moment we exit the restaurant. At his touch, my whole arm tingles. A few girls walk past us on their way inside and give Louis a look. *Yeah, I know,* I want to tell them. *I can't believe it, either.* Because here's the thing: I can't. Since I've been in Paris, nothing has turned out how I imagined it would. I spent months dreaming of this summer here, but I could never have pictured anything like this, and I refuse to think about the fact that I'm leaving this all behind soon.

"I'd offer to take you home," Louis says as we stand in front of his Vespa, "but I don't think the night is over yet."

I shake my head; my mouth is too dry to say anything.

"Would it be really cheesy if I took you to the most touristy neighborhood in Paris?" Louis asks with a bright smile. "We're close by."

No matter how nervous I get around him, he always has a way to put me at ease. "I like cheese. Especially French cheese."

Countless stairs later, we find ourselves at the front of the Basilique du Sacré-Cœur, in the heart of Montmartre. We're still panting after the climb up here, but it's the view of the entire city that really takes my breath away. The sun is just setting on all the slate rooftops. I scan the endless horizon, and Louis must guess what I'm looking for, because he pulls on my hand and silently points toward the right, in the direction of the Tour Eiffel, which is just visible in the distance.

"Is this for real?" I ask.

Louis stands behind me and wraps his arms around my waist as we keep admiring the view. "I hope so," he whispers in my ear.

I feel his heart beat against my back, and breathe him in as he leans closer. He rests his head on my shoulder, and I could stay like this all night. Actually, that's not true: I want to turn around and kiss him, but there are so many people here that we barely have elbow room.

"Come on," he says, breaking the spell of the moment.

He leads me down the twisted little streets of Montmartre, lined with restaurants, art galleries, and tourist shops. I notice *crêperies* on almost every corner. But the main attraction is a cobblestoned square called Place du Tertre, where many artists are exhibiting their work. It's bustling with people, so we have to slow down and admire the pieces— some modern and abstract, others classic depictions of our surroundings. But something else catches my eye.

"What's that about?" I ask Louis, pointing at an artist drawing a caricaturist portrait of a young girl sitting in front of him. Her parents look on proudly as he sketches gigantic ears and extra long teeth. We've already passed by several other people getting their portraits done in various styles, but caricatures seem to be the most popular.

Louis shrugs. "It's just the thing to do around here."

"Let's get one!" I say, suddenly excited. I look around for the perfect artist, and notice a woman who's just finishing up a portrait.

"What? No," Louis says, blushing slightly. "It's for tourists." But when I pull his hand, he doesn't resist.

"*I'm* a tourist," I say, pointing at the now-empty stool in front of the artist, and asking her if we can be next. "And I told you, I'm all about the *fromage*."

Louis chuckles and rolls his eyes at the same time.

"*Comme ça*," the artist says as she positions us, sitting me down slightly angled, and Louis kneeling behind me.

The woman frowns deeply as she looks from us to the pad in front of her, the black charcoal making swooshing sounds as it brushes the paper, and I have to force myself not to look back at Louis.

"*Et voilà*," she says a while later as she puts on the finishing touch. She looks up, smiling, and I practically leap off my stool to see the result. For me, she drew a bun so large that it almost looks like a halo around my head, and very full dark lips, to mimic my red pout. Louis got very thick eyebrows that practically cover his eyes, and a razor-sharp jawline.

"You look beautiful," Louis says, looking at it over my shoulder.

"You're not too bad yourself," I reply.

Louis pays for the sketch before I have time to pull out my wallet.

"A gift for you," he says, handing me the now-wrapped sketch. "A memory of your time in Paris."

"*Merci,*" I say, to both him and the woman, as I tuck it into my bag.

We walk away, and Louis lets out a deep sigh as we turn onto a much quieter street. "I hope you'll remember me."

"Of course!" I say. "I don't think I could ever forget . . . this summer." I wanted to say *you,* but my heart has taken a life of its own.

"I don't know what to do . . . ," Louis says, looking down.

"About what?" I ask.

He purses his lips. "You. Me. You going home. Me being here."

I nod slowly, tears welling up in my eyes. Has he been thinking the same thing all along? It doesn't make sense for us to even start something. There are so many reasons not to. But, to me at least, the idea of not being together for as long as we still have is . . . ridiculous. Unacceptable. Something I'll regret forever.

"I wish I could stay," I say after we look at each other silently for a while.

"You don't mean that," Louis says sadly. "ABT is your dream. And ballet always comes first. You told me that."

"Yes, but . . . ," I start. He's right. But he's also wrong. If this summer has taught me something so far, it's not about ballet. Yes, I've learned that I have great potential and a real shot at ABT. Monsieur Dabrowski believed in me enough to give me Odile, and I'm so much less afraid of failing than I was when I got here. Being a dancer means everything to me, but my life is bigger than that. There's room in my heart for so much more, and definitely for Louis.

"Ballet is not first right now," I say, leaning closer to him. "Right now is about us."

Louis's eyes open wide as he pulls me to him. This moment feels different. Charged. Expectant. I wrap my arms around his neck. He brings his face and rests his forehead against mine.

I brush my nose against his and get another whiff of him, sunshine and cedar. I inhale deeply, trying to bottle it up in my memory. Everything about this moment feels right: the murmurs from the street around us, the warm air, the sweet taste of his breath. My heart can no longer handle the anticipation: I part my lips and close the tiny bit of space between us to go find his.

I'm sure you've had croissants before. You can get them pretty much anywhere. They usually taste fine, a little bland, maybe. But when you come to Paris, the croissants are unlike anything else you've eaten before. They're warm and soft, golden and buttery. Like baked clouds. Deliciously decadent clouds. They may *look* the same as the other croissants, but they are far superior in every single way. And why I am thinking about that right now? Because croissants are like kisses. You don't fully "get" them until you've had them in Paris. And now I know this: French kisses taste a million times better in France.

CHAPTER TWENTY

AS A DANCER, I'm uniquely qualified to understand how bodies work. If I do a hundred *relevés,* my calves will burn the next morning. It's completely normal, a sign that I did them correctly. So, naturally, the morning after my French-kissing lessons with Louis (numbers 1, 2, 3, and 4— let's just say it was an accelerated course), my lips feel swollen. I run my fingers over them a few times and check my face in the mirror of the locker room as I get ready for class. I can't *see* anything, but I don't need a visual reminder to think about what happened last night. Louis barely let us come up for air, and I was okay with that, because breathing felt totally optional. I'd say I'm walking on sunshine, but it's better than that: I'm *pirouetting* up and over a rainbow of happiness.

The rainbow disappears at approximately 8:50 a.m. as I come out of the locker room.

Monsieur Dabrowski is standing right there. "Mademoiselle Jenrow, please, I need to speak with you."

He points at the farthest studio along the hall, which is empty. As I walk inside, I start to wonder if I will make it out of there alive.

"Take a seat," Monsieur Dabrowski instructs me. I remember the day he told me I was going to be in level five. Same place, same two people, though this time there is no doubt in my mind: he's not here to deliver good news.

I take a seat on the bench, and he brings a chair over for himself. "I wanted to talk to you about the showcase."

My heart drops. I tried hard to get this out of my head, but of course he saw it. Why did I think that I could get away with it unnoticed?

"What happened during the showcase, Mademoiselle Jenrow?"

"Don't you know?" he asks when I fail to respond.

I take a deep breath. "I do." Might as well fess up and get it over with. "I missed the last step."

He nods slowly. "And?"

"It was a pretty small difference, I think, but that meant I fell out of sync with the other girls." It's okay, Mia. It happened, and there's nothing you can do about it now. I just have to keep telling myself that.

"Do you think anyone in the audience noticed?"

I look down at my lap, emotions bubbling up in my throat. He's not going to make this simple. I stay silent.

"They all cheered, they all appreciated your beautiful performance, but was it as good as it could have been?" Monsieur Dabrowski's tone gets harsher, disdainful, even.

I shake my head.

He sighs loudly, and I look up to meet his stone-cold gaze. "It was not. You may think my standards are too high, Mademoiselle Jenrow. You may tell yourself that almost no one can achieve the level of perfection I expect from my students. And in many ways, that is true."

He pauses, but I don't think he's waiting for me to say something. I did miss a step. Deep down I knew I was going to fudge it before I even did.

"I'm sorry," I finally say, trying to fill the silence.

"I'm not here for apologies. I want to make sure that you understand exactly what is going on here."

"I won't do it again," I say, "I promise." It's a silly thing to say. No one can promise that they'll never lose control. Not even a ballerina. We can train incredibly hard and practice steps hundreds of times, but we'll never know for sure what will happen once the spotlights turn on and we enter the stage.

Monsieur Dabrowski grimaces. I glance up at the clock over the door of the studio. Our class is about to start at the other end of the corridor, but he doesn't seem in a rush to get us both there.

"See, the moment I saw your failed step, I knew I had a problem, which means you do, too. You're one of my leads.

My Black Swan. I've given you the opportunity to spread your wings in front of every apprentice program director in the world."

I gasp, understanding now what he's trying to tell me. "Please, Monsieur Dabrowski, don't take my role away from me."

"It isn't 'your' role, Mademoiselle Jenrow. Hundreds of ballerinas have held it before you, and hundreds will hold it after. You are not owed anything."

He's right, of course, and I want to kick myself for saying that. I'm not sure what I can do to make up for it, but I have to try. "Tell me what I need to do, and I'll do it."

He pauses, considering me. "I need you to focus. Do not let yourself get swept away."

My fingers go to my mouth. I can still feel Louis's lips on mine. It's too late for that: I already got swept away.

I nod. "I won't let you down."

Monsieur Dabrowski clicks his tongue and gets up from his chair. For a moment, I think he's just going to walk out, but instead he starts pacing the room, slowly and gracefully, in the black leather slippers he wears every day.

"You have already let me down. I saw great things in you, and I was very disappointed to learn that I was wrong."

My insides twist in fear. "It was just one step. Haven't you ever missed one?"

He sighs. "I have. More than once. One time, I was performing *Sleeping Beauty* in Moscow, and I almost dropped my partner in the middle of our *pas de deux*." He walks slowly toward the window before he speaks again. "But this isn't just about that one mistake. It's about you throwing your future away for a summer fling. And that is all on you, Mademoiselle Jenrow."

I freeze. My mind goes blank as I try to process what he just said.

"Your life is not my business outside these halls. But if you are my Black Swan, and I find out that you're wasting your energy every night, flirting around the city when you have just a few weeks to learn one of the most difficult roles in ballet, well . . . *that* is my business."

I gulp, unable to speak. There's no way Louis told him about us. Why would he? He knows that impressing his dad is incredibly important, not just to my success here, but to my future as a dancer. If Monsieur Dabrowski doesn't believe that I'm fully dedicated to ballet, then he's not going to recommend me to the apprentice program directors. Or worse, he's going to tell them to steer clear of me, and my career will be over before it even begins.

"It's not what you think," I say. "What's happening between Louis and me—"

"Happened with other girls before," the *maître de ballet* cuts in sharply.

"Excuse me?" My voice is so weak, it's almost a whisper. The tears I've been holding back run down my face, and I don't bother wiping them off. This cannot be happening.

He lets out a deep, irritated sigh. "I told Louis to stop hanging around school. He just . . . well, he doesn't have his own dreams. He doesn't get it. But these girls, they have a purpose, a future. And then they ruin it all for a bit of fun."

"What girls?" I demand, realizing too late that I've crossed a line. Am I seriously discussing my love life with the artistic director of the Institute of the Paris Opera? I must have lost my mind, and, judging by the bitter look on Monsieur Dabrowski's face, it's too late to get it back.

More tears follow. I have to wipe my face now, because I can't see through them anymore.

He grimaces, then looks away, giving me the tiniest bit of privacy. "I didn't mean to make you cry . . . but, Mademoiselle J—Mia," he continues, his voice softer, "you need to decide what is more important to you. And you need to do that now. I am not taking you off the role for that one mistake, but I will not tell you this twice: you have an opportunity to shape your career as a dancer. Are you going to waste it?" I don't move as he makes his way to the door. "Take some time to compose yourself," he says. "We'll see you in class in a little while."

And then I'm alone. I slide onto the floor, letting out loud, messy sobs, not caring that anyone might walk by. Louis was so understanding when I told him that I didn't want people at school to know about us. I was charmed by how kind and respectful he was. But maybe he wanted to keep us a secret, too.

How many other girls has he done this with? And then it dawns on me.

Maybe he's even seeing other ballerinas right now.

How can I have been so stupid?

I look around the empty studio, at the black glossy piano, and the light streaming from the windows. The sound of a honking car reaches me. Outside, it's just another day. My well-worn pointe shoes peek out of my bag on the bench along with my spare white leotard—my badge of honor. But I'm not worthy of it. I've wanted to attend a program like this for years; I've dreamed of a role as important as Odile's for as long as I can remember. I promised myself I would never let anything get in the way of my dream. But that's exactly what I did.

CHAPTER TWENTY-ONE

A LONG TIME passes before I move again. My muscles ache as I rise from the floor, my knees creaking as I unfold them beneath me. I stop by the bathroom, splash some water on my face, and smooth my hair. I don't know how I find the strength to show up to class, but when I walk in halfway through, Monsieur Dabrowski gives me a subtle nod, letting me know that it's okay for me to take my place at the barre. This is the only time he's allowed a student to come in late, and several of my classmates sneak confused glances at me.

I've danced with the flu before. I've danced with sore legs and swollen toes. But I've never danced with a broken heart. I wish I could run back to the dorm, crawl inside my bed, and stay there all day. But that would mean losing valuable practice time, and letting Odile down. I think I've done enough of that already. I'm so mad at Louis for making me believe that I was special, but mostly I'm angry with myself: I let a boy distract me from my biggest dream.

For years I've been telling my parents that I would do anything to become a professional ballerina. I've asked for dance gear for every single birthday since I can remember. I've given up all my weekends. I've been diligent, motivated, focused. I've read the biographies of famous principal dancers, and they all write the same thing: the only way to make it in this world is to want it more than anyone else.

It's not just about talent or time spent in the studio. It's about that hunger, the limitless ambition that will obliterate everything else in its way. That's exactly what I thought I was doing, right until the moment I arrived in Paris. And when my dream needed my attention the most, I just let it drop to the ground, where it shattered to pieces.

That stops now. For the rest of the day, my steps get sharper, my legs move with more precision, and my gaze does not drop, even for one second. And I'm not the only one who notices.

"Wow, Mia," Fernando says to me after our *pas de deux* rehearsal. "You were amazing. Whatever happened to you . . . you should keep doing that."

I nod. "I will," I say. "I'm going to make Odile proud."

"I believe you," he replies as he sits on the floor, his legs spread apart, stretching out his inner thighs and rolling his ankles. Then he gets up, slips on thick knitted socks, and zips up his bag.

He walks away, leaving Audrey and me alone in the studio. I'm massaging my feet as she removes the pins from her tight bun. She stares at me for a moment too long.

"What?" I ask, getting back up and making my way to the center of the room.

Our rehearsal is finished for the day, but I'm not.

"Nothing," she replies after a moment.

I stay long after she's gone. I stare at myself in the mirror, lifting my chin with my index and middle finger, checking my *port de tête*. I lift one leg onto the barre and fold myself over it, releasing my hamstrings and my lower back, and repeat with the other leg. And then I get back to dancing. At some point, the school janitor wheels his vacuum into the studio, and I plead with him to give me a little more time. I play the music for my solo on my phone, and, with no one else to watch me, I'm free to fail, to curse, and to let tears fall down my face midway through the sequence. I perform *fouettés* until I feel like I might fall over.

Just last night I was skipping through my Parisian summer with hearts in my eyes. I thought my life was falling into place, but it was just the opposite. I knew I'd missed that step, and I tried to pretend that it didn't happen. That's the worst part of it. Did I really think that Monsieur Dabrowski wouldn't notice? Did I honestly believe it wouldn't matter? If I did, then the joke's on me. I challenge myself to another ten takes of my solo, promising myself that if I can dance it twice flawlessly from the first *arabesque* and *tendu derrière* to the last, I could go home. But I don't dance it twice flawlessly. Instead, I manage it five times in a row.

By the time I walk out of school, I almost think I'm okay. I even trick myself into believing that I've put Louis out of my mind. Except that when I find him waiting outside on the steps, in the exact spot where we first met, I realize once more how foolish I am.

My heart knocks against my chest. I want to ignore him, to pretend that I don't see him. I could walk away and never speak to him again. But then I'd never get to express how much he hurt me. And right now, all I want is to hurt him back.

"I know I'm not supposed to be here . . . ," he says, "but you haven't responded to any of my texts, and I was starting to worry about you." He gets up and brushes off his pants, then leans over to kiss me. I pull away sharply.

"Is everything okay?" he asks.

I take a deep breath, flared nostrils and all. "Everything is very *not* okay."

He reaches for my waist. I push him away. "Don't," I say. "This is over." And even though I mean them, the words rip another hole through my heart.

Louis's frown grows deeper. "What's going on? I thought we had an amazing time last night."

"Let me ask you something, Louis. How many amazing nights have you had with other students? How many times have you sat on these steps, checking out ballerinas, and just picked one you liked?"

"What are you talking about?" One more time, Louis tries to grab my hand, but I cross my arms. "Let's go get something to eat. We'll talk, okay?"

"Did you want to keep us a secret because you have another girlfriend here?"

"What? No, that's ridiculous."

I shake my head with rage. "So you've never dated another girl from this school?"

A small part of me still hopes that this has all been a terrible misunderstanding, and that Monsieur Dabrowski was just annoyed with me about the performance. He could have made up that story to bring me back to reason.

But Louis doesn't deny it. Instead, he just sighs. "Who told you that?"

I want to crumble to the ground and scream. Someone please wake me up from this nightmare. "That's all you care about?"

"I care about *you*, Mia. You have to know that. It's different than the others. . . ."

The other*s*. Plural. "I never want to see you again." I bark this so loudly that a couple of passersby turn to look at us, but I don't care. Two older students—probably from the yearlong program—come out the front door, and I catch Louis glance at the petite blond one.

"Her?" I ask way too loudly.

"Stop it," Louis says without raising his voice.

But I'm shaking with disgust. I take a few steps toward the girls who are walking down the stairs. "Excuse me," I say. "Do you know this guy?"

They both look a little scared as they glance over to Louis. "Hmm," the blond one says, one eyebrow raised.

Louis comes closer and positions himself in between us.

"Louis Dabrowski? He dates every girl in this school, apparently."

"Mia!" Louis says. "My dad is going to kill me."

Then he turns to the girls. *"Désolé,"* he mumbles, his chest heaving.

"Not as much as he destroyed me!" I say.

The girls open their eyes wide and freeze.

Louis says something else to them in French, but I'm too upset to even try to understand. Before they turn the corner of the street, they look back at me, giggling to themselves.

I turn to Louis. "You don't know what it's like to have a dream. Something to live or die by. Do you think it's funny to distract girls? To get in their way?"

Louis's mouth drops open. "I never stopped you from doing anything you wanted to do."

"But you lied to me."

He shakes his head. "Maybe I didn't tell you everything about my past, but—"

"Stop!"

"No! I'm not stopping. I want you to succeed, Mia. I want you to get picked by the ABT director, even if it means I'll never see you again." He seems on edge himself, vulnerable even, but I don't trust anything coming from him anymore. His words just glide over me, my anger stripping them of any meaning.

"You're right about something, Louis. You don't understand how hard I've worked to get here, because you don't care about anything. I'm done throwing my future away for someone who thinks this is just a game."

Louis swallows. For a moment, I'm certain that he's about

to yell at me just like I did at him. Instead, he just looks on bitterly, shakes his head, and walks away. A moment later he straddles his Vespa, snaps his helmet shut, and drives off without looking back.

That night, to keep my mind busy, I decide to break in yet another new pair of pointe shoes. It feels good to bend the wooden shank relentlessly. I bang the toe box against the floor repeatedly, probably harder than I need to. After I burn the ends of the ribbon and sew on the elastic just the way I like, I put them in my dance bag, satisfied. Now I'm ready for my next rehearsals.

There, at the bottom of my bag, are the pictures of Élise Mercier, my ancestor. I sit on my bed, and, as I stare at them, it dawns on me that Louis isn't the only mistake I've made since I arrived in Paris. Something else knocked me off my path: I let this family legend get to me. I somehow believed that my future was out of my hands, that it had been decided for me centuries ago.

But Mom was right: it doesn't matter if it's true or not. Whether Élise Mercier was painted by Degas, or whether she was even an important ballet dancer in her time, my past does not define me. Only I can shape who I'm going to become, by doing exactly what I had been doing until now: working hard, keeping my focus solely on what I really want, and then working harder. I place the pictures at the bottom of the drawer in my nightstand and turn off the light. From now on, and until the moment I'm on a plane heading back home, I will think of nothing else but ballet.

CHAPTER TWENTY-TWO

OF COURSE, IT'S not that easy. I wake up several times throughout the night all weekend, wondering where I am. Then I lie there, replaying our conversation in my head. I don't regret what I said. I just regret . . . everything. On Monday, I'm already awake when my alarm rings, exhausted but restless. I turn it off and drag myself out of bed. Today cannot be over soon enough.

At breakfast, Audrey is even quieter than usual. In fact, she's barely said anything to me since my date with Louis. It's not like we used to stay up and chat for hours before, but sometimes we'd talk about what part of the ballet we were working on and which sequences were giving us trouble. She's avoiding me. And I want to know why.

"Do you want to rehearse together today?" I ask, surprising myself.

"I'm leaving now," she says. Then she looks from me to my half-eaten breakfast. The message is clear: it's now or never. I gulp down the rest of my raspberry-topped yogurt, clear my plate, and run after her, kind of surprised that she tolerated the few seconds it took me to do this.

Once we're in the studio, she looks on absentmindedly as I practice my solo. When I fudge a *relevé,* she says nothing. Halfway through, I feel a sharp cramp in my calf and grimace, but she doesn't tell me off for losing my composure. The Audrey I know would click her tongue or shake her head in disapproval. But that Audrey is not here today.

After I finish, it's her turn to take position in the middle of the room. She nods at me, and I press "Play" on my phone. Her music filters in through the speakers, but I turn it off before she takes her first step. I need to get something off my chest.

"Do you have something to say to me?" To my surprise, she doesn't protest the interruption, but she doesn't respond, either. "Because I'm going to find out at some point, and I'd rather hear it from you."

It's been nagging me since my conversation with Monsieur Dabrowski. How did he find out? "You told Monsieur Dabrowski on me," I say, feeling my face grow hot.

Audrey rolls her eyes. "Play the music, Mia."

But I don't move, so she makes her way to me. She tries to grab my phone, but I pull it away.

"You told him!" I say.

"I have no idea what you're talking about," she spits. "Are we going to practice or what?"

"We're not," I say, making the decision as the words come

out of my mouth. I've played this in my head over and over, and the only person who could have told our instructor about me and Louis is right in front of me. I don't know how she found out—maybe on the boat, maybe she overheard me talk about him with Vivienne and Madeleine. But one thing is certain: she never believed my story about hanging out with my aunts all those other times. The night of the party, I thought the girls were just joking about me and the mysterious cute French boy. But what if they knew all along? In any case, it's obvious why Audrey ratted me out: she wanted both roles all to herself, the White *and* the Black Swan. She must have been so miffed when I took Odile away from her. "You betrayed me," I continue, my voice shaking. "And I'm not like you. I can't pretend that everything is fine."

Audrey sighs again. She walks over to the bench and sits down. She shakes her head a few times, then looks up at me. "I know you can't pretend. You're terrible at it."

I grunt. "I'm sorry if I have feelings."

"You have so many of them," Audrey says, rolling her eyes, "there's not enough space for me in our room. You're just *feelings, feelings, feelings*! Look, I told you before: I'm here to dance, not to share gossip or wander around the city. I don't want to know what happened with your boyfriend, or whatever. I'm not here to deal with your drama."

"I can't believe you told his dad, Audrey. That's low, even for you."

Audrey lets out a sharp laugh. "How would I know his dad?" Then it hits her. "Wait, you're going out with

Monsieur Dabrowski's son?" The disbelief in her eyes is apparent, even from across the room.

"Not anymore."

"You have to be kidding me. Of all the boys in Paris, you decide to go out with our instructor's son, and when it goes badly, you blame me for it? Do you really think I would have gone to Monsieur Dabrowski? I'm scared to even talk to him."

"Who else could it have been?" I ask.

For someone who has difficulty showing her feelings, she looks genuinely shocked.

"That's not really my problem," Audrey says loudly. "But I'd never sabotage a rival. Especially not a worthy one."

I search my brain for a snarky comeback, but then I stop. Did she just say . . . something kind of nice?

Audrey takes off her pointe shoes and starts stretching her feet one after the other. "I guess we're not doing any more dancing before class," she grumbles.

I look down at my phone, still paused on her solo music. I set it down and walk over to the bench.

I sit down next to her. "You think I'm worthy?"

"Yes," she says sharply, not looking at me.

I wait for the *but*. There isn't one.

Instead, she adds, "Sometimes I worry that you're going to catch the attention of the ABT director and not me."

"He or she could notice both of us," I say without much conviction. Because let's be honest: the chances that they like one of us enough to offer an apprenticeship are slim enough, but two? That's not going to happen.

"I didn't tell anyone about your business. I don't even know anything."

"Okay," I say. I believe her.

"But you know what annoys me the most?" she asks, turning to me. "You have fun!" she snaps, like it's the worst crime in the world. "You go out at night with your mysterious guy, come back all rosy-cheeked and happy, and I think, She's not going to get up tomorrow to practice. She's too tired, too in love, too whatever. But you do. Every day. I *hate* that."

This is the first time I've heard what Audrey really thinks of me.

"You hate that I have fun? Well, I hate that you don't." She looks as surprised as I am about what I just said. It doesn't make a lot of sense when I put it like that, but it's true. "Audrey the Robot, that's how I think of you. It seems like all you need to do is press a button and there: perfect posture, excellent technique, never a false step. You don't even blink when you dance."

"I can't afford to blink," Audrey says. "There's too much at stake."

I let out a bitter laugh. "We're human beings, Audrey! Blinking is not optional."

Audrey sighs. "You haven't met my mom."

"I'm sure she's proud of you," I say, but I can tell from the look on Audrey's face that it's not that simple.

"I don't know about that. I'm doing everything she expects of me, but it's never enough."

"You're the best dancer I know," I say, not quite believing that anyone could think that Audrey Chapman is not doing enough.

Her lips tremble for a brief moment, but she regains her composure before she speaks again. "She's had this plan for me ever since she took me to my first ballet class. I must do everything she's done, exactly how she's done it. I wanted to go to the ABT summer program, but no, it *had* to be Paris, because that's how the Bolshoi Ballet noticed her. She thinks I should move to Moscow, like she did at my age, and have the same amazing career she had. She doesn't think ABT is good enough."

My eyes grow wide. "Every dancer in the U.S. dreams of ABT."

She just nods sadly, then looks down at the floor. We sit in silence for a few minutes. And then I realize what I've done. I brought my private life to school. I took the one person who always made it very clear that she didn't want things to get personal, and I forced her into it. I'm suddenly overcome by a wave of guilt. I really have lost my mind these last few weeks. And I don't know how to get it back. But I can at least try.

"I'm sorry I called you a robot," I say after a while.

Audrey shrugs. "And I'm sorry I'm jealous of you."

"You're not jealous of me," I say, shaking the thought away.

"Don't make me say it again."

We're quiet now, for a long moment.

"You were really dating Monsieur Dabrowski's son?" she asks, incredulous, after a few minutes have passed.

I nod slowly. Tears have wanted to roll down my cheeks since the beginning of this conversation, and I finally let them. "I made a terrible mess."

Audrey sighs. "Do you think you can clean it up?"

I laugh. And I cry some more. I didn't just create a mess. I *am* a mess. "I don't know."

"I have an idea," Audrey says, getting up.

I check the clock above the door. It's almost time for class.

"We could help each other," she continues, sounding a bit unsure. "You help me learn to have fun or *feel* things. . . ." She says this last part with a sort of disgusted shrug.

I can't help but smile. "That's not a good start."

"Fine, let's put it this way: you teach me how to be more like you. The good, dancing part of you, not the messy part, I mean," she adds. "And I'll help you be more like me."

I frown. Is Audrey really suggesting what I think she's suggesting? "Like a team?" I ask.

She seems to consider it for a moment. "Like a team." And then of course, she adds matter-of-factly, "It doesn't mean that we have to like each other."

I laugh, but she's right. "No. We just have to respect each other."

"Exactly," she says as she extends her hand. I hesitate, and not just because mine are still covered with tears and streaks of mascara. But Audrey's hand is still stretched out to me, so I shake it. We have a deal.

"But for what it's worth, Audrey?" I look her in the eye. "I think I do like you."

CHAPTER TWENTY-THREE

"**YOU KNOW THE** rule," Audrey tells me as we begin what feels like our hundredth practice session together. We've been at it every morning and evening. Often it's just the two of us, but Fernando sometimes joins in as well so we can practice our duets. Audrey glances at the phone in my hand, which I'm gripping hard.

"I'm turning it off!" I say, showing her the dark screen.

For days, my heart has skipped a beat every time my phone has chimed, but it was never Louis. No texts, no sign of life. It's like I made up our time together in my head.

Audrey nods. "Good. Let's get to it."

A picture flashes in my mind: Audrey Chapman, twenty years from now, wearing all black in this exact studio, badgering students who haven't yet mastered the flick of a foot or the rounding of an arm. They'll be terrified of her, and she'll love every minute of it.

We warm up for a few minutes, from our necks down to

our toes, and finish off with a round of *pliés*. I peel back my layers—my cozy cardigan, my leg warmers, and my puffy slippers—until I'm only wearing my white leotard, skirt, and tights.

"Let's start with the *fouettés*," I say, quickly putting on my pointe shoes.

Audrey's face lights up. Even though she'd never swap roles with me, I bet she'd welcome the challenge of the Black Swan solo, those thirty-two *fouettés*. But it's mine to tackle alone.

I get into position, and without music or further ado, I begin spinning over and over again.

"That leg!" Audrey snaps, a little too loud. "It should be whipping through butter, not concrete!"

"I'm whipping!" I yelp. "Whip, whip, whip!" I say with every turn.

I stop and attempt to laugh while catching my breath. That, too, is quite technically challenging.

Audrey rolls her eyes. "Come on, Mia, focus!"

"I'm here to bring the fun, remember?"

Audrey pretends she didn't hear me. "What did I tell you?" she asks, seriously.

I sigh. "That I can't think, even for one second, that I might not be able to do them."

"Exactly. The moment you doubt yourself, you've lost the battle. Your body knows when your mind fails you. That's when it gives up."

I nod gravely. At the start of this week, my *fouettés* were still a work in progress. They were getting there, but slowly. And now, thanks to the Audrey Chapman school of thought, they have *almost* arrived. I've developed much better control over my standing leg. I can keep my hips and leg more level throughout. I can and I will.

Every day my technique improves, and with it my time in Paris comes closer to an end. But I won't let myself get sad about it. I'm doing exactly what I came here to do: refine my skills, learn to be a better dancer, and get a shot at impressing an apprentice program director. Even if I jump a little every time my phone beeps, it's a win all around.

"You've made so much progress," Audrey says as we towel off after getting out of the showers.

Just a few days ago, my jaw would have been on the floor. But something has changed between Audrey and me. A barrier has been lifted.

Which means I can be as honest with her as she is with me. "And you haven't made any." She looks at me funny, but I think she knows exactly where I'm going with this. "We've been working on my technique all week long," I add.

"And it worked!" she says with a genuine grin.

"That was only half our deal: you help me be more like you, and I help you be more like me. Every time I tried to get you to loosen up, you sent me off on another round of *fouettés*."

"You can never do too many *fouettés*."

"That's not the point," I say, putting on my skirt.

Audrey slips her belt through the loops of her jeans. "Fine." She pauses, her T-shirt in her hand. "We can stay if you want."

"Oh, no," I say, running a comb through my wet hair. "What I have in mind cannot happen between these walls."

Ever the dutiful student, Audrey agrees to follow me. When we step outside, the evening breeze has already taken over the streets. It has rained a lot over the last few days—at least that's what I saw from inside the studio—but tonight the sky is clear, and everyone is out again. We walk through the Marais, sneaking glances at the pretty shop windows, and turn onto Rue de Rivoli, the main street on the right side of Paris that goes all the way beyond the Louvre. But we stop way before then, at the main square in front of Hôtel de Ville, the city hall.

"A concert? That's what you had in mind?" Audrey asks, pointing at the stage. It hasn't started yet, but hundreds of people are already gathered around.

"Not quite." I checked the schedule earlier: tonight's act is a French reggae band that covers Bob Marley songs, among others. While most of the crowd is huddled up in front of the stage, a smaller group hangs a bit to the side, in plain view of Notre-Dame.

The band comes onstage, the music starts, and the crowd erupts in cheers.

"I want you to join them," I say, pointing to the small group. I noticed this the last time Louis and I drove by here: there are outdoor concerts here all summer long, and people dancing their hearts out in the middle of the square. It's the exact opposite of the kind of dancing *we* do: these girls and guys just move their bodies however they feel like it, swaying along and making silly faces. They don't care about how they look or who's watching. It's perfect.

"That's not going to happen," Audrey says, stepping back as if she's scared that she might catch whatever disease they have.

"You," I say in my most authoritative tone, "are going to dance right here, in front of all of these people, and you're not allowed to even think about your steps."

Her eyes open wider as she shakes her head. "No way."

The ground vibrates with the bass of the speakers, and Audrey's expression grows more worried as she looks around. "I'm not really a reggae kind of girl," she says.

No kidding.

"You have to get out of your comfort zone."

But she just folds her arms across her chest. "You need to find something else."

"Fine," I say with a shrug. "There are other bands playing tonight. So if not here, then you have to dance at the next one."

Audrey takes in the extra large crowd around us and sighs. "Okay."

"The next one," I say, "no matter what kind of music it is."

"I said okay!"

We keep walking along the banks of the Seine for a few minutes, until we come across another gathering. As soon as we can hear the tunes coming from a small patch by the water, Audrey grunts. I try not to smile as we make our way closer. This crowd is smaller, but they are all standing in a tight circle around a singer crooning into a microphone. A woman in a red flowing dress dances around him while a few couples show off their moves.

"Salsa it is," I say, barely containing my laughter.

Audrey gasps. "It's couples' dancing. I'm not a couple."

I shrug. "Should have thought of that a few minutes ago."

I give her a little shove, which she resists. Right in front of us, a man and a woman our parents' age rub their bodies together while casting each other hungry looks. It's kinda gross, but they're very good. When the song stops, he swings his partner back and plants a big wet kiss on her lips.

The look on Audrey's face is worth the price of admission alone. I shove her once more, and she reluctantly takes two steps forward. She casts me yet another pleading glance, but I have no mercy. In fact, I cannot wait for this show.

That's how a tall, graceful yet suddenly very awkward American teenager finds herself attempting hip shimmies, barely able to move in the tiny space she carved for herself among middle-aged couples. I'm not saying it's funny, but several people around me try, and fail, to suppress giggles while whispering to each other. This isn't an audience plunged in darkness underneath the stage; we're standing right there. But Audrey soldiers on, focusing on the dancers' feet as her face turns different shades of red. And, as much as she tries to shake that booty, I think it's fair to say that salsa is not her calling.

I start to wonder if I should rescue her, but someone else beats me to it. The woman from the couple we were just observing points at Audrey and whispers something in her partner's ear. Nodding, he steps out to the side as the woman takes Audrey's hand.

Regarde-moi, she mouths to Audrey, pointing to her feet. *Watch me.*

Audrey does, and together they practice a few steps back and forth. Then, the woman points at her hips, shifting them from left to right, showing her how it's done. Audrey's French has room for improvement, but she understands the language of dance.

So she learns. The woman nods encouragingly, placing her hands on Audrey's hips to guide her as they go. There's still tension in her eyes as she focuses, but her shoulders relax, and she's no longer clenching her jaw. The crowd, who has been studying them closely, starts clapping with a beat. The claps get louder as the woman lifts Audrey's hand into the air, taking her for a spin. After another go-around, Audrey breaks out into a huge grin. Then she turns to me, beaming. "I'm having fun!" she screams over the music.

I laugh, and so do a few others around. I glance at the crowd, which is only getting thicker. Everyone cozies up together on the narrow sidewalk, young and old, couples or larger groups of friends. That's when I see him, on the other side of the small circle. Black hair, loose shirt, holding another girl's hand. I can't breathe. I never wanted to see him again, but now my heart crunches as I pray he turns around and sees me. It's been like that since the moment we met: everything I've felt about Louis has been completely contradictory. Simple and complicated. Impossible, yet natural. Another song ends, and people shuffle about, including Louis. I clench my fists, trying to figure out what to do.

He turns toward me.

But it's not Louis. Just someone who looks like him. The realization hits me hard, and I exhale deeply.

Audrey comes over to me, pulling me out of my thoughts. Her partner has gone back to her man for the new song, so she's alone again.

"Don't worry, I'm not leaving the dance floor," she says before I have time to protest. "But now you're coming with me."

She grabs my hand and guides me into a dance.

"I want to go home," I say, my eyes full of unshed tears as I glance back to the Louis lookalike.

"Not happening," Audrey says with a laugh.

I try to smile, but it probably comes off as a small grimace.

"Come on, Mia," she says, shimmying around. "Show me what you got."

I take in the result of my handiwork: Audrey Chapman goofing around on the street, for all of Paris to see.

"Thank you, Mia," Audrey says as she spins on the spot. She bangs into the couple next to her, but doesn't seem to care. "This is actually fun. We should do it again."

I smile, for real this time. I didn't find love with the perfect French guy, but it looks like I gained an improbable friend along the way.

CHAPTER TWENTY-FOUR

AFTER OUR FRIDAY-NIGHT session of street dancing, we agree to take a break from rehearsing for the whole weekend. Strangely enough, it was Audrey who suggested it.

"My body needs to reset once in a while," she informs our group over breakfast.

Eye rolls are exchanged, then plans are discussed for the day. The girls decide to take a trip to Jardin du Luxembourg, a manicured park with a large pond not far away. We've been there before, and I couldn't believe my eyes the first time. Green metal lounge chairs circle it, making it a perfect spot for sunbathing or picnicking. It's also a popular spot for children to play with miniature boats—with sails in bright shades of blue, red, green, or yellow—that they push around the water with wooden sticks. Even though the weather is perfect for it, I don't feel like joining the girls. I don't feel like anything, in fact. I decide I need a day all to myself.

I start by doing laundry, and then check the state of my pointe shoes. They look pretty tired, but half a bottle of glue and many stitches later, they're ready for Monday, and our last full week of the program. Then I paint my nails, call my parents, and answer texts from a few friends at home. They all think I'm having the time of my life in Paris, so I don't mention that I'm spending a beautiful summer day inside in my yoga pants. Our dorm provides sandwiches and salads for weekend lunches, which are left in the fridge for us to have on our own schedule. No one else is around, so I eat a sandwich while standing in the empty kitchen in complete silence.

More excitement awaits in the afternoon: after a long nap, I fold the clothes that I've scattered around. When I open the drawer of my nightstand to put away my jewelry, I find a small envelope inside. At first I wonder what it is. And then I remember.

It feels like months have passed since Vivienne handed me those pictures. I remember the look on her face that day, full of hope that I would resolve the mystery that's been on her mind for decades. I sigh as I sit on my bed, studying the photographs. I quickly debate with myself. I only have a short time left in Paris, but I can't get distracted. I still have the details of the Musée d'Orsay curator that Louis gave me, but I don't have a "Louis" to do this with anymore. My heart grows heavy as I think about our aborted adventure. But this is my family legend, my history. I don't need a boy to help me figure out where I came from.

• • •

A phone call and a métro ride to the other side of Paris later, I'm perched at the counter of a colorful kitchen, sipping iced black tea opposite Charlotte Ravier, aka Dr. Pastels, a young-looking woman with buoyant red curly hair.

"There is a record of an Élise Mercier dancing at Opéra Garnier from its inauguration in 1875 to 1886," she informs me. I didn't tell her much on the phone. As soon as I mentioned Louis's mom and Degas, she immediately invited me over, saying it'd be easier to discuss it in person. She's composed and speaks quietly in perfect English, like this is just another day at the office for her. Still, I'm impressed that she managed to find this information since I called her. I guess that's why she's the curator of one of the most famous museums in the world.

"You know, Degas didn't paint as much there," she adds, pushing a plate of biscuits in front of me.

I frown as I take one.

"There was another building before, Opéra Le Peletier," she explains with a smile. "That's where he was all the time, painting ballet scenes. Degas didn't like Opéra Garnier as much. It was too grand and too glitzy for his taste."

"Oh," I say, feeling deflated. "And what happened to Opéra Le Pel . . ." I struggle to pronounce the name. Dr. Pastels helps me out.

"Pe-le-ti-er," she enunciates clearly. "It burned down."

"That's terrible." I shudder as I picture Paris engulfed in flames.

"That means all the records are gone. Which is why there are many gaps in our knowledge."

She seems way more bummed about that part than the fire itself.

"I have something that might help," I say, opening my bag. Dr. Pastels perks up as I retrieve the envelope.

"Are these the photographs?" she asks, not so patiently waiting for me to hand them over.

I frown. I didn't get a chance to mention them on the phone.

"Louis told me about these, but then he said he wouldn't be able to bring them over," she explains as she opens the envelope carefully, pulling out the photographs with the tips of her fingers.

"Louis came to see you?" I ask, my forehead scrunching up in surprise.

She nods. "He was here just yesterday. I said I couldn't help much if I didn't see the pictures, and here you are. *Parfait!*"

"Yesterday?" This doesn't make sense.

Dr. Pastels smiles but doesn't take her eyes off the pictures. "Well, first he came about a week ago, to ask me some questions. He said he'd bring his friend and the photographs the next time. But then he just came back alone. He sounded very sad about it. I thought maybe he'd lost them."

Louis was here. He came to see this woman about *my* mystery, *my* family legend, even after we broke up. After I said all those horrible things to him.

"Hold on a moment," she says. She walks out of the kitchen and comes back a minute later carrying her laptop. "After Louis explained the story, I made a list of all the paintings your ancestor might be in."

"Really?" I ask, my eyes growing wide.

"Actually, I removed all the paintings that she definitely wasn't in, based on the time period and what we already know about Degas's models. You see, he kept some records himself, but they are far from complete. Sometimes he'd write down the actual name of the dancer, but others he'd scribble something in a code that only he could understand. Artists aren't the most organized people."

I nod. "But with these photos . . . ," I start.

"I may be able to narrow it down," she continues, turning her laptop toward me. On the screen is a detailed spreadsheet including painting titles, locations, dates, and names of the models featured. That column is filled with many question marks.

"These photographs are perfect," she adds, turning the screen back to her. "They're dated, and there are several identifying elements. That chandelier looks very much like the ones in Opéra Le Peletier, for one. And I'm pretty sure I recognize at least one of the girls."

I lean in to look at the screen.

"That's amazing," I say, as her software program continues filtering results.

"That's art," she responds with a small smile. "And lucky for you, my only plans for tonight involved watching an Alfred Hitchcock movie with a glass of red wine while my husband is out of town. This is way more interesting."

"So should I come back?" I ask, but she's turned her attention to the photos again, looking from them to her computer screen.

"If you'd like," she says. "But if you have time, I could do this now. I know these are precious, and I don't want to ask you to leave them with me."

• • •

That's how I find myself flicking through a pile of style magazines in the sparse, all-white living room of a total stranger. Dr. Pastels has retreated to her office, but not before pouring me another glass of iced tea and instructing me to make myself at home.

I scroll through my phone and scan the list of my recent calls until I find Louis's name. My index finger hovers over it as I try to deal with my feelings. I can't talk to him. No matter how Monsieur Dabrowski found out, he was right. I'm not throwing my chances away for a bit of fun. Nothing is more important than giving Odile everything I have. And even if I weren't Odile, this story would never have a happy ending. I leave Paris in two weeks. Yet, everything inside me is telling me to press that button and deal with the consequences later. The only thing that stops me is remembering the disgusted look on Louis's face just before he stormed off on his Vespa. That look will haunt me forever.

I click away from the screen and open my YouTube app. Before I rushed over, my afternoon plans included rewatching clips of the best performances of *Swan Lake,* from London to Singapore, and Rio to New York City. For an hour or so, I travel around the world through Odile.

When Dr. Pastels walks back into the room, she's holding a sheet of printed paper.

"Now," she says, sitting next to me on her couch, "I need to tell you that my research is not an exact science. The only way to be a hundred percent certain that Degas painted your ancestor would be to ask either one of them."

"And that would be a little challenging," I joke nervously.

"*En effet.* Louis mentioned this was very important to you, so I don't want to get your hopes up."

"I understand," I say, sneaking a glance at that piece of paper. My heart rate quickens as she flips it over.

"That's it?" I ask when I glance at the mere three lines on the page.

She nods. "Based on all the information you gave me, and the photos, I can say that, if Edgar Degas painted Élise Mercier, it would almost certainly be one of these three works of art."

"Thank you," I say as she hands me the list.

"It's my pleasure. It's not so often that I help solve family mysteries. Oh, and, again, you're so lucky. . . ."

She pauses, and I hold my breath. Is this about Louis?

Dr. Pastels smiles. "The paintings on this list, they all happen to be in Paris."

My jaw drops. "You mean I could actually see them? Like, soon?" I run my eyes over the column indicating the location of each painting.

"It's not that simple. One may not be on display. I'll need to check. And another is part of a private collection. I'll have to call in some favors, so it may take a few days, but yes, I think it can be arranged."

I thank her about another dozen times as I get up to leave.

She walks me to her door, and, there, she has one more question for me. "Do you want to tell Louis about my new findings or should I?"

My heart stops. She can't know the turmoil this creates inside me. What if I did talk to Louis, but only about this? Would I even be able to? Every time I've seen him, all my good intentions have evaporated with just one of his smiles. Monsieur Dabrowski was very clear with me. I can't let him down again. And I won't. I've put hours, days even, into my *Swan Lake* rehearsals. I'm not going to miss a step again. So what does it matter if I use the little bit of spare time I have to track down a painting that means so much to the women in my family?

"Mia?" Dr. Pastels says when I still haven't responded.

I take a deep breath. I need to give her an answer, and deep down I know what I want it to be. The fact is, this Degas mystery is Louis's adventure, too. I'd never be this close to an answer if it weren't for him.

I take a deep breath. Stop overthinking everything, Mia. "I will."

I press the "Call" button while I go down the stairs, but the line is still ringing when I exit the building. Why would he pick up? He must hate me. But then, just when I'm about to end the call, I hear a sigh on the other end.

"Hi," he says, his voice small.

"Hi," I respond, placing a hand over my rapidly beating heart. "I have something important to tell you."

Silence on the other end. It's not going to stop me.

"I'm really, really sorry for the things I said to you. I don't actually believe that you have no passion in life. In fact, you're probably the most passionate person I know. I was hurt and I lashed out. It's none of my business who you date or dated."

"Mia, I tried to tell you . . ."

"Whatever," I say. "It doesn't matter anymore. I don't want to leave Paris feeling like I made an enemy."

"You didn't."

"Are you sure? Because there's something I want to ask you. And I completely understand if you don't want anything to do with me."

"I'm listening," he says. It's not the warm, charming Louis, but that's okay.

"First, I have to tell you about my afternoon."

I explain everything, from my call to Dr. Pastels to the list of three paintings.

"Ha," Louis says. "If I were you, I'd be racing around the city already."

"I don't want to do it without you."

Another silence. I just have to power through it. "You believed in this mystery as much as I did, even when you didn't know me at all."

"It's easy for me. I have no other passion." His voice has a hint of bitterness.

This stings, but I deserve it. "I discovered my own dream when I was so young; it's hard for me to remember that not everyone has their whole future figured out. You'll find your own way. I know it."

"Hmm, maybe," Louis says.

"But before you do, I need to ask you something. I only have two weekends left in Paris, and I know how I want to spend them. Would you like to go find this painting with me?"

CHAPTER TWENTY-FIVE

WE MEET AN hour later in front of the Musée de l'Orangerie. As Louis's Vespa pulls up, my heart knocks so loudly, it resonates in my ears. He gives me *la bise* without hesitation. The memory of our make-out session flashes in my mind as I breathe in his familiar smell. It was only about a week ago, but everything has changed since then. I've missed him. I know it's wrong. It can't work. Won't happen again. But while I'm not sure I can deal with this distance between us, I won't lie to myself: it's better than not seeing him at all.

We join the line outside the museum, which snakes across several lanes.

"Why is there a question mark in front of Musée de l'Orangerie here?" Louis asks after I hand him the list.

"Dr. Pastels said this painting is owned by the museum, but it might not be on display. I figured I should check it out anyway."

He breaks into a smile. "Dr. Pastels," he says. A memory from happier times.

"It's a great nickname." I look away, feeling my cheeks grow hot. An hour ago I would have sworn that being with Louis again was the worst idea possible. And now . . . now I need to focus on why we're here.

The line ahead moves slowly, bringing me closer to facing my great-great-great-grandmother. *Maybe*. She could be here inside these historic walls, immortalized for eternity. And maybe one day, I'll tell my daughter the story of chasing this painting around Paris, so *she* never has to wonder where she comes from.

Louis checks his watch as a museum employee walks along the other side of the line.

"Le musée va fermer bientôt. Nous sommes complets pour aujourd'hui," he announces to the crowd.

"They're about to close, and they won't let anyone else in?" I ask Louis, to be sure.

He answers with a sorry smile. "Yep. But, on the bright side: your French is really improving."

I laugh, even though I'm crushed. "Could we explain that we have an art emergency?"

Louis raises a quizzical eyebrow. "And cut in front of all these people? You really *are* turning French."

The crowd starts to dissipate, and security guards close the front door. We're not going to get inside today. "I'm sorry I made you come all the way here."

Louis shrugs. "You can buy me a drink to make up for it."

I open my mouth to respond, but I can't. I can't have a drink with him, and I can't say that to his face. But . . . he tried to solve my family mystery, even after what happened. I can at least thank him for that.

"Deal," I say.

We make our way along Place de la Concorde—which is topped by a centuries-old Egyptian obelisk—on the edge of Jardin des Tuileries. I stop to take photos along the way, trying to capture everything. I don't suggest any selfies— things are still obviously tense between us—but at least I can be grateful that, once again, I get to discover this city's many treasures through Louis.

We walk through Place Vendôme, where we also find an imposing column—this one green—standing tall in the middle of the square. It's surrounded by some of the most expensive jewelry stores and hotels in the city, including the famous Ritz. Yet there's nothing flashy about it: the creamy buildings are just a little brighter here, and guarded by men in white gloves and three-piece uniforms.

We find a lovely café on the sweetly named Rue des Capucines off the square, with a large terrace and free seats in the corner that offer plenty of opportunities for people watching. Louis orders a beer, and I try not to flinch as I remind myself that he's almost eighteen—it's a normal thing to do here. I opt for *"un Perrier rondelle,"* in memory of my first night in Paris. So many things have changed since then, including my accent. I don't want to brag, but give me a few more weeks in Paris, and I'll fit in like a local. Except I

don't have a few more weeks. Soon I'm kissing all of this—
the terraces, the paved sidewalks, the ancient buildings—
goodbye. Which means I have to get everything off my
chest now.

"Why did you contact Dr. Pastels? After what I said to
you, I figured you would never give me another thought."

Just then, the waiter comes back with our drinks. Louis
waits until he's gone to respond.

"You got it in your mind that I'm some kind of player
who stalks ballerinas and goes around the city breaking
their hearts." I open my mouth to protest, but he raises his
hand to stop me. "It really hurt that you would think that,
after everything that happened between us."

"I'm sorry," I say, not daring to meet his eyes.

He doesn't look at me, either. Instead, he grabs a paper
coaster and spins it between his fingers. The two guys at
the next table give us a strange look, probably sensing the
tension between us.

"You were right," Louis says, not meeting my eyes.

Ouch. I feel like someone pinched me really hard. The
sting remains for a few seconds afterward.

"About what?" I ask, though I don't really want to know.

Louis clears his throat and shuffles on his seat. I've
never seen him so uncomfortable. "That day we met on the
steps . . . ," he starts. He sighs loudly. "I was there to see my
ex. Well, almost ex."

My heart twists, and I feel the tears well up at the corners of my eyes. I didn't think the truth could be worse

than what I've been picturing in my head, but maybe I was wrong.

"I can explain," Louis says, glancing up at me.

"You don't have to," I reply, my voice small. Part of me is curious, of course, and wants all the details. But I don't know if I can take it.

"Please, let me," Louis replies, and before I can say anything else, he launches into it. "Two years ago, when Max was in the program, he invited me to a party with students from the school. I joked that he was lucky to spend his days with so many pretty girls, and he didn't want me to feel left out. I met a girl at the party, and we started going out. From the beginning, it was messy, complicated. We were both jealous. Possessive sometimes. There was something real between us, but . . . I don't know. It didn't really work. Still, we had fun. We all became close as a group, Max, Émilie—they weren't together yet—and a few others from the school. We hung out at each other's houses, went to movies, concerts, parties. I wasn't just in a relationship with her, but with all of them. I think that's why it worked for as long as it did. And then . . . she broke up with me. It shouldn't have been a great surprise, but I was devastated. . . ."

"You loved her," I say, my voice trembling.

He looks away and nods, before continuing the story. "So I started hooking up with other dancers, girls she knew. It wasn't anything serious, I think I was just trying to get back at her in some way. There was one party that got a bit out of control. We all drank too much, and the pictures circulated around school. My dad saw them. He didn't say anything to me that time, but he warned Max. He said something like, "This program isn't summer camp. If you have enough energy to go out partying, then you're not working hard enough."

That does sound like his dad, but Louis looks so solemn that I decide to keep this observation to myself.

"And then . . . she came back. Said she wanted to try it again."

I notice that Louis still hasn't mentioned her name. I wonder if it's because it's too painful for him.

"I asked Max for advice. He's been my best friend for ten years, since I was hanging out in the back of my dad's classes. My parents had just separated, my mom was traveling all the time, and there wasn't anywhere else for me to go."

"It must have been hard, going through your parents' divorce." I want to place my hand on his across the table, but I resist the urge.

He shrugs. "They're much happier as friends than they were before. Anyway, Max told me that maybe I was acting out because I still had feelings for her. He was right. We got back together—that was about a year ago—and it was good for a few months. We did tons of things with Max and Émilie, but when we were just the two of us, something was missing."

Louis sneaks a guilty glance at me.

"So you were still dating her when you met me?" I ask,

as neutrally as I can. On the inside, I'm shaken and bitter. That moment was one of the most exciting and spontaneous of my life. I feel cheated, though I have no right to.

"No," Louis says. "Well, yes. I mean, not really. We spent the last six months breaking up and getting back together and breaking up again. Every day I never knew if we were still a thing or not. When I was waiting on the steps outside school, I had just broken up with her, *again*. But she said she wanted to talk, and I couldn't help it. I came over to see her."

"Who is it?" I ask, trying to bring back the details of that day.

Louis doesn't hesitate. "Émilie's best friend. Sasha. She's a student teacher, too. She got stuck talking to someone that day, and I was already regretting rushing over. It was this endless cycle between us. It never went anywhere good . . . and then I saw you."

I sigh. "So you used me to get out of an awkward conversation with your quasi ex?" I sound snarkier than I intend to, but Louis doesn't mind.

"I know it sounds bad, but yes," Louis says. "You looked so panicked, and cute, and I realized I didn't want to be there. It was pointless."

I gulp, remembering the day at Musée d'Orsay when Émilie shot Louis a strange look. She must have seen Louis talk to me, and was thinking about her friend. I also think back to the day we saw Fernando talking to Sasha on the street, and the party on the boat, when the four of them hung out.

"So you and Sasha . . . ," I start. I know the question I want to ask, but I'm so scared of the answer.

"It's over. She's been texting me, and I told her I was done. For good. But I can't cut her out of my life. We have all these friends in common. I don't want to lose them."

I nod sadly. I know everyone has a past, but this seems like it's not past enough.

"I swear, Mia. Nothing has happened between us since I met you. I think she could tell that something changed in me. I didn't respond to her messages right away. I've never been distant like that before."

"So you think she told your dad? Maybe she saw us somewhere and went to him?"

I guess in some ways it doesn't matter how Monsieur Dabrowski found out, but if one of the student teachers despises me because I stole her boyfriend and is trying to ruin my last few days of the program, I'd kind of like to know.

Louis shakes his head. "I thought that at first. I know she can be jealous, but . . ."

"I just want to know how much trouble I'm in," I say with a small laugh.

Louis takes a deep breath. "It was my mom. You know how I told her about you and your family legend? I think she'd never heard me talk about someone like that. She didn't mean to get us in trouble, but my parents talk sometimes, and I guess it came up. That night, after he told you about . . . the other girls, my dad really laid into me. He told me I should spend more time figuring out what I want to do with life, and to stay far away from *his* ballerinas."

I look around us, conflicted. We shouldn't even be together now.

But Louis sits straighter as he looks me deep in the eyes. "And yes, when I first met you, I thought maybe I just have a thing for ballerinas. But I couldn't get you out of my head, and I knew it was different this time. You're not like anyone I've met. You're so passionate about ballet, but you still make room in your life for, well . . . life. So, to answer your question, the reason why I called Dr. Pastels . . . I care about solving your family mystery, because *you* care about it. I just wanted to make you happy. From the moment I met you, I thought, I love to see her smile. And if she's smiling because of me, then even better."

"This is a lot," I say, my heart swelling. Too many different feelings fight inside it; I can't process them right now. Am I really the girl Louis is describing? Until now, my life has felt like a long stretch of ballet classes. But then I came to Paris, and it's like the city opened my eyes. Or was it Louis?

The waiter comes to check in on us, and Louis waves him away.

"I told my dad I couldn't stay away from you. Not if you came back to me." Then, he purses his lips. "I was really upset about what you said. But I deserved it. When you asked me who I was waiting for that day, I wasn't honest with you."

I nod, looking down. It's true. I think on some level, I knew it. I wanted to believe that he was waiting for Max, because it all felt like a fairy tale. I played Louis up in my head as this dreamy French guy. But real life is more complicated than that.

"I'm so sorry, Mia. These last few weeks with you have been some of the happiest of my life, and I feel like I betrayed you."

I want to cry and laugh. Throw myself in his arms and walk away from him. I want to hurt him and I want to love him, and I don't want to have to choose.

"And I'm sorry about the passion stuff," I say at last. "What I said to you . . . it was awful."

"Yes, but there was some truth to it," Louis says. "Growing up, I always thought that having a passion meant that you couldn't have any fun. My parents were doing what they loved, but they were working so hard that it felt like they never had time to actually enjoy it. But what you said really got me thinking about what I want to do. It inspired and scared me at the same time. I never told you . . . but I used to paint."

"Really?"

He nods, a smile forming on his lips. "I loved it when I was a kid, and my dad would bring me art books so I could get ideas. But then I just dropped it at the start of high school. I got lazy, I guess. Or maybe I felt like I should do the opposite of whatever my parents were doing. You made me want to start again. In fact, I've been working on something. . . ."

I find myself holding my breath. "Can I see it?"

"No," Louis says firmly. "It's not ready."

I lean back, a little surprised. "I'm sure it's amazing. Can you at least tell me about it?"

Louis ignores my question and gestures to the waiter for the check. He pulls his wallet out of his pocket, but I stop him.

"It's my treat, remember?" I try to sound upbeat, like I haven't noticed the sudden change in the atmosphere.

"You don't have to worry about my dad, Mia. He can be really tough sometimes, but this is about me. Not you."

"He had every reason to be mad at me," I say. Maybe he didn't have to say it like that, but I missed that step, and he knew why I was so distracted. I don't blame him.

"You'll do amazing, I know you will," he says as I drop a bill and a few coins on the little tray.

Then he gets up. "I have to get back to it."

We part ways a few minutes later. Our goodbye is quick and slightly awkward. Louis seems deep in his thoughts, and I feel like everything has been said. For now. The sun is starting to go down as I walk home, the sky turning a hazy shade of blue. Only one question burns up inside me for the rest of the night. When am I going to see him again?

CHAPTER TWENTY-SIX

AS OUR PERFORMANCE approaches, Audrey and I double down on our rehearsals. We're at school long before anyone arrives, and long after they're gone. But, today, as the excitement for the show mounts, a few younger students ask if they can stay back and watch us.

"As long as you're silent," Audrey responds coolly. But I notice her smiling. What ballerina doesn't enjoy devoted fans?

She offers to set up the music for my variation while I go first. I try to quiet my mind as I take position, forgetting the people in front of me, the noise of honking cars coming from the street, and even Louis. I want this practice to be all about me, or at least, all about Odile. The first few notes fill the room, and I make my *entrée*. As soon as I lift my right leg up in the air, my mind blocks all the stress and confusion, allowing my feelings to inspire every move. The dance lasts about three minutes, but in my heart it goes on forever, blending the strain of my muscles with the pleasure of doing what I love the most.

I only join the real world again when it's over. The small crowd claps; even Audrey joins them. I take a bow and head over to the bench to catch my breath. Audrey doesn't waste a minute, and hands me her phone as she takes my place center stage. She gets in position, aligns her spine and shoulders, and raises her chin at the perfect angle. I play the music, and she's off. I watch, mesmerized by the elegance oozing out of her. She's the dream White Swan, destined for the role. That's when it occurs to me: Monsieur Dabrowski chose perfectly. He saw right through us from the very beginning.

I haven't taken my eyes off Audrey, but the minute she finishes, something feels different. People clap quietly, and there's a strange air in the room. Audrey's face drops. I follow her gaze, her mouth half-open, and I let out an inaudible gasp.

Myriam Ayed, the *danseuse étoile* of the Paris Ballet, is here, watching from just behind the open door. She's wearing leggings and a loose sweatshirt—under which the straps of her leotard are showing—and she's carrying her dance bag. It hits me that she must be here to do exactly what we're doing: practicing for her next performance. The school is so big, and the professional dancers' studios are in a different wing from ours. We haven't seen her since orientation.

"*Bravo,*" she says, clapping a few times and stepping inside. "Very good."

"Thank you," Audrey mutters, clearly starstruck.

"You too," Ms. Ayed says, turning to me. I blush in response. "You both dance very well."

I smile, mumbling my thanks, but that's it. I'm scared of saying anything stupid to a ballet legend.

"Now, can I make a suggestion? Switch," she says, making the gesture with her fingers between Audrey and me.

Audrey frowns at me. I frown back.

"I don't understand," I say.

The rest of the students have gone completely silent, watching how Audrey and I will handle the pressure of being watched by our idol.

"You are the White Swan," she says to me, "and you"—now pointing at Audrey—"are the Black Swan. Switch roles. Just for today, try dancing in each other's shoes."

"But . . . ," I start. I'm about to go into all the reasons why we can't. The idea of failing in front of Myriam Ayed is so unbearable that I might just stop breathing. But I don't say any of this, because Audrey shoots me a stare that seems to say, "Just. Do. It." She has a point. Am I really going to argue with the most famous ballerina in Paris?

Myriam Ayed takes a seat as Audrey clears the space for me to get into position. But I've never learned the steps. I couldn't list them if I tried. And yet, my body seems to know them. In fact, I think my muscles welcome the change as I lift and turn, twist and *pirouette*. My arms follow, wrapping around an invisible tree, led by the music and my beating heart. I'm pretty sure I'm not in charge. It's like my body told my brain, *Relax, I got this.*

As soon as I complete the last step, my eyes search Audrey's. By now, I've learned to read her face, however impassive it might be. In all its subtlety, it's saying, *Nailed it.*

Then, Audrey becomes the Black Swan. There is fear in her eyes, but the music carries her just like it moved me, and when she's done, she has the biggest smile on her face.

"Magnifique," Ms. Ayed says, smiling brightly from Audrey to me. "The thing is, ballet is a collaborative experience. Each dancer sets the scene for the next one. Even when you're doing a solo, it's not just about you: you are simply borrowing everyone's attention for a few minutes, before passing it on. Ballet is about harmony. And harmony can only be achieved in the spirit of teamwork."

I hang on to her every word, joy coursing through me. Then, I glance at Audrey, whose face is as solemn as she can force it to be. We may have only just practiced each other's solos, but I'd say we've been dancing in each other's shoes since the moment we arrived in Paris. I know she must feel that, too. I make my way to the side of the room where she is, and I can't help it: I close the distance between us and wrap her in a big hug. She's tense at first, but I feel her heartbeat slowly calming down. "This is the best day of my life," I whisper into her ear.

"No, it's the best day of *my* life," she replies. I burst

out laughing, but she only allows herself a quiet chuckle. Myriam Ayed is still watching, after all.

• • •

Sometimes I wish I could just live inside a dance studio. Reality doesn't come find me there. I'm not Mia. I'm not a seventeen-year-old girl. I'm not a high school student. I'm only who I want to be, someone who feels everything through the prism of one of the most beautiful art forms.

But as soon as we leave the building, I'm Mia again. Something is nagging at my heart. My time here is coming to an end. Paris and Louis are slipping away, and there's nothing I can do to stop it. Audrey and I walk in silence to the métro station, so much so that I almost forgot she was there.

Until she asks, "Do you want to walk instead?"

"Okay," I say.

Our dorm is pretty much right across the river, but we're usually too tired to walk home after school, even though the path takes you through some of the dreamiest spots in the city: via Place des Vosges, an elegant square surrounded by art galleries; across the Pont de Sully; and through Île Saint-Louis, right behind Notre-Dame.

I wish the beautiful view would help me clear my thoughts, but it's not that easy. Louis and I have exchanged a few texts since the other night, but things are different, and probably always will be. Now I feel weighed down by all the contradictions I'm keeping inside. I didn't want to fall in love, but I couldn't stay away from Louis. I wanted to focus on ballet, but I couldn't resist exploring my family legend. Every time I told myself we couldn't be together, and every time I ran to him as fast as my legs would carry me. I'm tired of racking my brain and messing with my heart. I'm tired of trying to keep it all together.

I take a deep breath and turn to Audrey. I want to ask her something, but the words are stuck in my mouth. I just don't know where to begin.

"What?" she asks, looking at me funny.

"I—I love this time of day in Paris. The sun goes down so slowly that it makes the light even more beautiful, don't you think?"

Audrey raises an eyebrow. "You do not look like you wanted to talk about the color of the sky. Wait, is this about . . . ?"

Am I seriously considering talking to Audrey about my love problems? The girl who I might compete with for the rest of my ballet career?

"So it's about him," Audrey says.

"Yes," I finally admit. "His name is Louis. You know, I really didn't come to Paris to fall in love."

Audrey lets out a laugh. "I hope not! But then what?"

I shrug. "We were kind of together, and I know it was wrong, but I swear that's not how I got Odile."

I stop to study her, but Audrey doesn't react.

"Yeah," she says. "You got Odile because you deserved Odile. Everyone can see that."

"Oh," I say. Would it really have been that simple all along? "Well, anyway, now we're not together anymore because of me, and I . . ."

"And you want to be again?"

"No," I say firmly. But of course I don't mean it. "It wouldn't make sense."

Audrey stops in her tracks. She gestures for me to come closer so we're out of the way of the pedestrian traffic on the bridge. Next to us, a young woman in a green dress and a colorful scarf wrapped around her long dark hair sings Édith Piaf's "La vie en rose."

"Mia, you're going to do whatever your heart tells you to. That's who you are."

"But what about the show? What about the ABT director? I shouldn't be thinking about anything else."

Audrey sighs. "What about the regrets you will have?"

I know what my heart tells me; it's been blaring the same name on repeat since the very first day. "You would never take the risk to get distracted by a boy," I say.

Audrey chuckles. "Obviously. But I still would like to fall in love. When I'm a dancer at the Bolshoi Ballet or wherever I end up, I don't plan on coming home to an empty apartment every day, and only having my pointe shoes for company."

I look around me, all the way down the river, as I listen

to the lyrics the singer is crooning. *"Il est entré dans mon cœur une part de bonheur, dont je connais la cause."*

Its meaning rings loud and clear in my heart. *A piece of happiness has entered my heart, and I know the cause of it.*

L.O.U.I.S.

I came to the most beautiful city in the world to focus on my career, and instead I found exactly what Paris promises: romance. I worked hard, and I got cast as Odile. I've rehearsed as much as I could, and I'll continue to do so until the moment I enter the stage. So what's the worst that can happen to me now? Regrets, I guess. I want to be with Louis. Even if it's just for a few days, and even if we never see each other again after that.

I'm not sure I'll forgive myself if I don't give us a chance.

CHAPTER TWENTY-SEVEN

THE FIRST STOP on our Saturday itinerary is back at the Musée de l'Orangerie, inside the Tuileries. A Ferris wheel stands still at the top of the park, along with the Louvre at the other end, with rows and rows of trees in between. Birds perched on their branches chirp away under the shining sun. Our day of Degas hunting is off to a great start.

Last night on the phone, Dr. Pastels informed me that she had arranged for us to see the two paintings that aren't accessible to the public. The third one is at Musée d'Orsay. I had taken a picture of it last time, and the dancer is looking away, so you can't really see her face. Even if that painting were the one, there might be no way to tell.

"It's funny that we're here to see a Degas," Louis remarks as we enter the museum.

"Why?" I ask, so focused on our mission that I sound a little too serious.

"This place is famous for the panoramic paintings of water lilies by Claude Monet."

He leads us into one of the oval rooms. Shades of blue, purple, and green circle around the space, with dozens of tourists gathered in the middle to admire them. Only in Paris are the museums works of art themselves—from pyramids to old train stations and round rooms to match the paintings. I'm about to study them closer when Louis holds me back.

"Wait," he says. "You forgot something."

But before I have time to ask what, he kisses me.

I grin when he stops, and then I lean in again for another kiss. I know today is all about Degas, but . . . it's too good to pass up. I'm not going to overthink it.

We roam the circular room, admiring the endless smudges of pastels that swirl and transform into a *tableau*. It's absolutely mesmerizing and makes me forget all about Degas. But not for long.

Then, we take the stairs down to the lower floor. We find a staff member—a young man in a gray uniform—and tell him that we have an appointment with Mr. Martin, the museum's archivist. He leads us to a door at the end of the hall marked *Privé* (Private), and I feel a spark of excitement as we walk through it. Look at me, using my connections in high places. Or as high as a museum's basement can be, anyway.

"You cannot touch anything," Mr. Martin tells us as we walk through rows of large black boxes standing a few feet apart. He has a thick black beard, round-rimmed glasses, and the air of someone who would do anything to protect his babies. "And you can't tell anyone you've been here," he adds, sounding like a schoolteacher.

"We won't," I say. Though, if we do find a painting featuring my ancestor, I might be tempted to slide it under my arm and make a run for it. It's very cold in this neon-lit, windowless room, and I shiver in my floral sundress. Mr. Martin explains that the temperature is kept low to preserve the works of art, many of which are several centuries old. Meanwhile, this seventeen-year-old work-in-progress wishes she'd put a cardigan in her bag. Louis rubs my arm to warm me up, and I put my hand on his. I'm still cold, but I no longer mind.

Mr. Martin stops in front of a big black box marked 57.B. and retrieves a pair of white cotton gloves from his pocket. Louis and I hold our breaths as he opens the container, and I notice how silent it is around. You can only hear the hum of the air conditioners. It strikes me that, while no one in Paris has AC in their home, the art gets to enjoy an ideal temperature all year long. Priorities.

"Here it is," Mr. Martin says, pulling out a small frame. Carefully, he brings it over to a nearby stand and unwraps the tissue paper.

"It's beautiful," I say, scanning the young woman in a sea of green tulle. Her features are sharp, her nose pointy, and her black hair is neatly tied with a matching green ribbon. She's lifting her left arm in the air, but whether she's halfway through an *arabesque* or simply stretching, it's hard to tell.

"Why do you hide this away?" I ask. I'd assumed that Degas's best works were on display all around the world, and that only his lesser pieces might be constrained to the archives. But this one is magnificent and deserves to be seen.

Mr. Martin shrugs sadly. "We have so many, and so few walls. Sometimes we'll loan pieces for an exhibition. But this one—no one has seen it in over ten years."

"That makes us extra special," Louis says with a twinkle in his eyes.

I study the painting again, hoping it will speak to me in some way.

"What do you think?" Louis asks.

I tilt my head. Am I supposed to recognize her? Will I just *know* when we find her? I ask if I can take a picture, but Mr. Martin responds with a look of sheer horror. Hey, it was worth a shot. At least he lets me stay awhile to gaze at it. I can feel Louis's eyes on me, wondering, but I'm not sure what to feel. Mr. Martin is patient enough to listen to all my questions about the painting—where exactly was it painted, what year, its history—but while he has many answers, they don't really give me the clarity I'm hoping for.

• • •

The Tuileries are bustling with people—and even more dogs—when we exit the museum.

"Our next appointment is not until this afternoon, right?" Louis asks as we begin strolling down one of the alleyways.

I notice the spark in his eyes, and smile. "What do you have in mind?"

"You, mademoiselle, are in for a treat," he says, grinning. "It's a not-so-secret secret."

After a short walk, we arrive at the front of what looks like a tiny alley. The entrance to Galerie Vivienne is barely noticeable from the street; you could easily miss the faded sign atop the curved wrought-iron door.

Once inside, it's like going back in time. It's a long, narrow passageway covered with a domed glass ceiling. It lets in all the sunlight, which reflects on the intricate moldings and colorful tiles. It feels like we've stepped inside Degas's world. The space is lined with beautiful little shops selling books, wooden toys, wine, and antiques.

Louis watches me take it all in. "Thank you for showing me this," I say, feeling strangely proud to have my very own tour guide.

"I wish I could show you more," he replies. "There are many of these hidden passages around the city. I love that you have to know where to look. They're not so easy to find."

I wish we could visit all of them, too, but I'm starving.

"Please tell me that the next stop involves lunch," I say with a laugh.

Louis perks up. "*Bien sûr!* It's not a French date without food."

He takes us back toward the Tuileries and to Angélina, a renowned traditional tearoom.

"I should warn you," Louis says as we stand outside, waiting to get in. "This is a pretty touristy spot. Not my usual go-to."

"Oh, so you're just making an exception for your American girlfriend?" I ask, checking my hair in the shop window. And then I realize what I just said. *Non*, Mia! What is wrong with you? You can't call yourself someone's girlfriend. Especially when things are so complicated already.

But if it surprises Louis, he doesn't let it show. Instead, he moves right along. "Exactly," he says. "It's my duty as a French person to make sure you taste their infamous hot chocolate and decadent desserts. But we'll have salads first, so we can pretend like we're not just in it for the sweet stuff."

"I only have a week left to try every raspberry tart in the city," I say. "I can't waste time on pretending." I mean it as a joke, of course, but a shadow passes across Louis's eyes.

"Just a week, huh?" He's not really asking, though. We both know the deadline we're facing. Louis sighs and puts his arms around my waist, pulling me close. It feels so good, so right, so perfect, to be against him. Then he kisses me.

• • •

He was right about the desserts, and lunch practically puts us in a sugar coma. I love American pastries, and I'm not picky: donuts, carrot cakes, brownies, I'll have them all. But there's something special about the French ones, from the shiny glaze on top to the delicate placement of fruits, or the funny names like *"religieuse"* for a double cream puff pastry, or *"Paris-Brest"* for what I think might be the ancestor of the Cronut. But, forever brave, we soldier on for part *deux* of our Tour de Degas.

• • •

Painting number two is even harder to access. It's housed at the headquarters of Givenchy, a famous French fashion house, and displayed in the head designer's office. Under normal circumstances, we wouldn't be allowed to just pop by, but, luckily, Dr. Pastels helped the company acquire this piece many years ago.

Since it's Saturday, the building is empty. The only person here is the designer's assistant, a young guy named Vincent who is wearing a black suit and has a shaved head, and who, thanks to Dr. Pastels's insistence, has been assigned the task of shepherding us through the building. As we walk past a room-sized closet in which hundreds of couture dresses are hanging, I realize that I could never have found this painting by myself. If Louis hadn't given me the hope that we could, I'd never be here, so close to coming face to face with yet another masterpiece.

This one is actually a sketch, framed simply in black and taking up half the wall behind the desk. It features three dancers and is so simple—just charcoal on a white canvas—

yet incredibly precise. The girls are captured doing a *plié,* and every detail—from the position of the tutu to the curve of their arms—makes it obvious that Degas wasn't just an observer. He really understood ballet.

"This is it," I tell Louis. I can't explain how I know it. I just do.

The girl in the middle looks so familiar, and soon I realize why. Still, I need to be sure. I pull the picture of Élise Mercier and her two friends from my bag. Louis takes it from me and places it on the wall near the drawing, while Vincent frowns at us. I'm guessing he's not a Degas fan.

"Look," I say, comparing each girl in the photo with one in the drawing. "Their height matches."

We stare at each other, smiles gradually spreading over our faces.

Louis studies the sketch again, and then nods slowly. "This is your ancestor."

I take a deep breath as my eyes well up. I haven't forgotten what Dr. Pastels said. There's no way to be certain. But my heart knows. Louis knows. We're standing in front of a Degas sketch of my great-great-great-grandmother, a *danseuse étoile* at the Paris Opera. My family legend is true. There isn't the shadow of a doubt in my mind.

"See," he whispers in my ear, like he can read my thoughts, "ballet is your destiny."

Louis exchanges a few words with Vincent, and mentions me taking a picture. Vincent's eyes grow wide with disgust, as if Louis had asked if I could just scrunch up the sketch and put it in my pocket.

"*Ah non!*" Vincent says sharply. "*Ce n'est pas possible!*" *No way! That's not possible.*

"*Je comprends,*" Louis replies. *I understand.* But then he winks at me. As he continues talking to him, I notice that Louis is slowly turning his back to me, obstructing Vincent's view of my hands. Seizing the opportunity, I slowly slip my phone out of my bag and take a few discreet snaps. I can't quite see what I'm doing, but when I glance at my screen before putting my phone away, I see that it worked. Élise Mercier's Degas will be with me forever.

• • •

"How do you feel?" Louis asks, taking my hand in his when we're back outside, walking along a busy boulevard.

Nervous about the upcoming show. Over the moon that we found the Degas we were looking for. Sad about leaving Paris soon. Excited about this wonderful day with him. And then confused about all of the above.

"Happy," I finally say, smiling. It's definitely the word that sums it up best.

"Me too," he replies, running a hand through my hair. Then he presses his lips on mine. The usual Mia would feel self-conscious about all the strangers witnessing this moment. But Mia *la Parisienne* just fills with glee and butterflies.

I want this day to go on forever, but since that's not possible, I opt for the next best thing: making it unforgettable.

"You're going to call me a tourist again," I start, immediately bringing a smile to Louis's lips, "but I can't see a Ferris wheel and *not* go for a ride. I've been thinking about it ever since we walked past it the other night."

"Going up in the sky is not touristy," Louis replies seriously. "It's romantic."

• • •

Louis and I sit next to each other in the pod, admiring the view. Every time I spot a monument I know—the Arc de Triomphe, the Sacré-Cœur, or the Tour Eiffel—I can't help but squeal, making Louis laugh. His body feels warm against mine, and I shiver as his lips press against my neck.

"Today has been amazing," I say with a sigh.

"It really has."

"Every day with you has been amazing," I continue, my voice catching in my throat. "I don't want to leave."

My heartbeat goes on a ride of its own as Louis just stares deeply into my eyes.

"Then don't," he says, so quietly that I almost wonder if I'm imagining it.

I take a deep breath, but I know this isn't the moment for promises or life decisions. I just want to enjoy what Louis and I have, for as long as we have it. And right now, what I have is the chance to kiss Louis in the sky.

CHAPTER TWENTY-EIGHT

ON MONDAY MORNING, we're all a little giddy as we get to school. For once, we won't be putting on our leotards and heading straight into a dance session. Instead, the entire cast of *Swan Lake* is scheduled for our final costume fittings. I, for one, have never been so excited *not* to dance.

I beam as I pull mine out of the garment bag. The piece I tried on before is now pristine—from the intricate beading to the layers upon layers of tulle gathering around the waist. After weeks of wearing only white—and in a room filled with white swans—it's a special treat to get into the skin of the maleficent Black Swan. Valérie and her team did a wonderful job; the costume fits perfectly. But the *pièce de résistance* is yet to come. I open the box that came attached to the bag, and retrieve the headpiece. I put it on, and two beaded feathers wrap around the back of my head, covering my ears.

"Mamma Mia, Mia!" Lucy says in an exaggerated Italian

accent as she skitters toward me. She's in her own costume, a pared-down version of Audrey's.

"You look amazing," I say.

Lucy smirks. "If you like my costume so much, I'm happy to swap. I'll be the Black Swan, no problem."

I roll my eyes and she laughs. We're all assembled in the biggest studio, the only one that can fit us all. Drapes hang loosely from the corners as makeshift change rooms, so we can get in and out of our costumes. Seeing everyone all dressed up for the performance fills me with so much pride. You can rehearse choreography dozens of times. You can listen to the music on your phone every break you get. You can reread the story, digging deep inside of it to explore your character's motivations. But it takes a room full of white birds—and this little black one—to drive it home. The program is rapidly coming to an end; what may or may not come next, no one dares to talk about. We'll be performing onstage in front of the apprentice program directors from around the world in just a few days.

Instead, as we wait for Valérie and her team to inspect each of our costumes and perform last-minute tweaks, we chat about what comes now.

"What are you doing tomorrow?" I ask Anouk and Lucy. Except for Audrey, Fernando, and me, everyone has the day off before the dress rehearsal. All of the principal dancers, myself included, will meet with Monsieur Dabrowski tomorrow afternoon for a final run-through, but he's giving us the morning off so we can rest before the final push.

"I'm going shopping," Lucy says, an excited spark in her eyes. "I've been saving money for months so I could treat myself in Paris. But I still haven't gone. What have I been doing?"

"Hanging out with Charles?" Anouk answers in a gently mocking tone.

"Yeah, okay," Lucy admits. Then she laughs. Every night at dinner she's been giving us updates on her adventures with him. She's even talking about coming back for a weekend later in the summer, before school starts, so they can see each other again.

"What about you, Anouk?" I ask. "What's on your must-do list before you leave?"

"I'm going on a street art tour with my friends in the afternoon. It's a bummer you can't come."

I nod, and then, of course, I think about Louis. When we're out in the city, he always points out the pieces of art painted on the walls. Often it's simple graffiti in black and white tucked in a corner, but sometimes it's an impressive mural with incredible detailing. Louis talks excitedly about how the museums are in the streets now, and I find myself wondering if we'd have time to take one of these tours together. Probably not.

Lucy turns to our White Swan in residence. "And you, Audrey?" She's been loosening up a little bit more every day. By her standards, it means staying back at the dinner table to chat with us, rather than going straight to bed with a book and a face mask on.

"Well, hmm," Audrey starts.

There are still half a dozen students in line before us, so we have plenty more time to wait. And to tease.

"Audrey's Paris plans are all about Russia," Anouk says to Lucy and me with a wink. "Bol-shoi, Bol-shoi, Bol-shoi," she repeats in a chanting tone.

Lucy laughs, but I don't join in. I know Audrey's story now. Her mother has called her every day throughout the summer, reminding her that she *must* impress the Bolshoi Ballet apprentice program director. There's no alternative. Still, I'm not sure that's what Audrey wants. Every time she talks about the Russian company, her face falls a little.

I wouldn't go as far as calling her my bestie, but things are so much better between us now. We practice together. We help each other. And since we're hoping for different ballet companies, we're not even really competing against each other.

"Who knows what will happen anyway? We might get surprised," I say, more to deflect the subject.

But Lucy catches on immediately. "What are you saying?"

I glance at my reflection in the mirror. Whenever I look that way, I wonder who the girl covered in black feathers is. It takes me a second to recognize myself. I've changed since I arrived in Paris. My dream is the same, and yet it feels different.

"There are other companies," I say vaguely, feeling myself blush.

"Yeah," Anouk says, readjusting a strap on her shoulder and stretching out her arm. "I'd take an apprenticeship anywhere. Copenhagen, Beijing, Sydney. It'd be a great excuse to travel. Ballet is ballet everywhere. It's always going to be an amazing opportunity to learn."

I agree with her in theory, but it's so much more complicated than that for me. "Wouldn't you miss your family?" I ask. "If you get an apprenticeship somewhere, then, if all goes well, you'd probably just stay with the company. Maybe not for your whole career, but at least for a few years."

Lucy and Anouk look at each other and shrug. "So?"

"It'd be hard, being so far away from my parents and everyone else," I say.

Lucy gives me a devilish grin. "What if you found a good reason to stay here?"

I shake my head meekly. "ABT has always been my first choice."

"But then sooomebody came along," Lucy says in a silly voice.

"Shhh!" I glance around to check that no one has heard her. Last night I finally admitted to Anouk and Lucy that there was indeed a cute French guy named Louis. I told them he was a friend of Max but left out his *other* connection to the school.

"I don't know," I say with a shrug. "If there was an opportunity here . . . I guess living in Paris for a while could be nice."

I can feel Audrey's gaze on me, but I don't look at her.

I still want to get an offer from ABT. But I want more time with Louis.

"Speaking of your boyfriend," Lucy says quietly. I still shoot her annoyed look, but she ignores it. "You should call him. We all have the morning off tomorrow, right?"

"Yeah," I say, looking at Audrey to check, in case she wanted to do our own rehearsal. But, to be honest, we're reaching the point where we're all practiced out.

"So call him," Lucy says. "Tell him we want to party."

"On a Monday night?" Audrey asks, slightly shocked.

"Why not?" Lucy answers. "Please, Mia," she says to me. "Ask him to find us something fun to do tonight. We all deserve it."

I sigh and glance at Audrey. I expect her to double down and complain about this absolutely terrible idea, but instead, I read a little excitement tinted with envy in her eyes. We've all worked so hard. We're ready. And if we want to have one last night of fun in Paris, Louis is definitely the right person to call.

CHAPTER TWENTY-NINE

AS IT HAPPENS, one of Louis's friends from high school is having a party at his house tonight. Raphaël has just come back from his summer vacation, but his parents are still out of town.

"I wasn't going to go, because I wanted to hang out with you," Louis says on the phone after he explains all this.

I beam as the three girls stare at me, waiting.

Our fittings over and done with, we're now having lunch in the cafeteria. Yes, even Audrey. Like I said, she's really living on the wild side these days.

"But if you girls want to go out tonight," Louis adds, "I'm sure my friend would be more than happy to have you."

"Count us in," I say.

After we hang up, I give the girls the what's what: a house party just north of the Marais, lots of handsome French guys. And Louis's friend is apparently an aspiring DJ with great taste in music. I can practically see Lucy's and

Anouk's mouths water. Audrey plays it cool, but she doesn't miss a word of what I say.

After rehearsal, Audrey and I rush back to get changed. Louis told Raphaël he'd help set up, so I'm heading over with the girls. Lucy and Anouk are already dressed and ready to go, their own rehearsal having finished an hour before ours.

"Hi," I say when the door to the apartment on the fifth floor opens and a young guy greets us with a bright, *"Bienvenue!"* Welcome!

"I'm Louis's . . . ," I start, then catch myself. I have no idea what he's told his friends about me, or if he's even said anything. "Louis invited . . ."

"You're Mia," Raphaël says with a warm smile.

Lucy and Anouk giggle behind me as we step inside the apartment. The ceilings are extra high, with a large sculptural pendant hanging in the mostly sparse living room. The focal point of the room is the fireplace, painted black and filled with unlit candles. It's modern, oh so cool, and nothing like suburban Westchester.

On the way over here, Lucy piled on the questions about Louis—how did I meet him, again? Have we talked about the future?—but I managed to get away with vague answers. A simple glance at Audrey told me she'd kept my secret, but, as our time in Paris comes to an end, I'm less concerned about people finding out about us.

Swan Lake is in just three days. I've been on my best behavior at school, I've done well at every rehearsal, and

Monsieur Dabrowski hasn't said anything else to me—about Louis, anyway. Maybe Louis was right, and his dad's outburst had less to do with me and more to do with him. Maybe he wanted to scare me a little after I missed that step at the showcase. It worked.

"Louis has cool friends," Anouk whispers in my ear after I introduce them all, and we take in the room of well-dressed people our age. The girls wear an assortment of short skirts and flat sandals either in fun colors or metallics, while the guys are mostly in slim-fit jeans and shirts. There's no one from school here. Louis doesn't spend all of his life with ballerinas after all.

It turns out that French teen parties are very similar to the American ones. There are no red plastic party cups or kegs, and the baguettes and cheese platter are a dead giveaway, but everything else is pretty much the same: loud music, people dancing everywhere, and groups gathering in the tightest corner of the kitchen or in the hallway. Anouk and Lucy mingle with others on the dance floor, and even Audrey seems at ease. In fact, she's talking to a guy on the other side of the room.

"Are you having fun?" Louis asks me as he wraps his hand around my waist.

We've been hanging out by ourselves in a corner.

"Hmm," I say with a small shrug. I *should* be having fun. I'm with my friends. I'm with Louis. This is a great party.

"Me neither," Louis says into my ear. "Do you want to get out of here?"

"What about your friends? And what about mine?"

"No one will even notice we're gone. And the girls won't mind."

I hesitate for a moment, but I know I want to get away, too. Louis and I have so little time left together. We've been talking about all the things we'd like to do in Paris, all the places I still want to visit, and the ones Louis wants to show me, but I realize we were just happily daydreaming.

Now reality is catching up with us.

• • •

It's dark outside now, and a little chilly. I'm only wearing a light top, but I warm up as soon as we start walking.

"Where are we going?" I ask.

Louis shrugs. "Paris seems so big, but it's actually really easy to walk around. In fact, that's the best way to see it; just wandering down streets and letting your feelings guide you."

"Okay," I say, taking his hand. "Let's turn right here, then."

We walk without a purpose or a destination for an hour, maybe longer. We pass by a large square called Place de la République, then find ourselves heading down winding little shopping streets. But we're both quiet. I have a suspicion that we're thinking about the same thing. I'm leaving. And there's nothing we can do to stop it.

"This piece is by a really cool artist from the south of France," Louis says as we pass a mural of a girl in dungarees and an Afro made out of colorful umbrellas. She looks like she's going up the stairs on her way to the banks of Canal Saint-Martin.

We walk past a train station I haven't seen before, one of four in Paris, and come across several centuries-old churches. They seem to pop out of even the smallest corners like hidden jewels of ancient times. I'd like to visit them all, but that's not going to happen.

A bus stop advertisement announces back-to-school deals, and I think about how the yearlong students will be taking over for us soon. In the last couple of years, I've toyed with the idea of switching high schools to attend a dance-specific program in New York City, but I always abandoned it before I even brought it up with my parents. I wasn't sure I was ready to live just forty minutes away from home, and I felt pretty certain that Mom wouldn't let me go anyway.

"Would you come back?" Louis asks, like he's reading my mind.

"To the school?"

He shrugs. "To Paris in general, I mean."

"I would love to . . . one day." I look away. I shouldn't have said that last part, especially now that I see the shadow of disappointment crossing his eyes. But it's the truth. I would love to come back to Paris, but it probably won't happen any time soon. This trip already cost my family a ton of money. During the school year, I spend many of my evenings and weekends dancing, which makes it impossible for me to get a job. Aside from the odd babysitting session here and there, I've been relying on Mom and Dad, with some help from Grandma Joan, for all my ballet expenses, including this amazing treat of nonstop dancing in Paris.

"Hmm," Louis replies. He stares down at his shoes. "One day sounds a little far away."

I don't want to tell him what I've barely admitted to the girls. Yes, it would be amazing to come study in Paris after high school, but by then, Louis will have forgotten all about me. I feel a tear coming on and discreetly wipe it off. I've been asking myself the question a lot over the last few days. Is there a future for Louis and me? The reasoning varies, but the answer remains unchanged: no, probably not. I'm going home for my senior year. Louis is starting college in September, as an English major at the Sorbonne, a prestigious college near where he lives. Our paths are simply not destined to cross again.

Suddenly I realize we're at the bottom of the stairs of the Sacré-Cœur once again, and we both look up in awe at the Basilica. Even though it's really late now, there are dozens of people sitting on the stairs, and even more all the way up, admiring the city by night.

"Let's go up again," I tell Louis. "I want to see that view one more time."

He smiles. "Anything you want."

The climb is even steeper than I remember. I'm supposed to take it easy and let my muscles recover in between rehearsals, but my glutes just have to take one for the team.

We're both a little out of breath when we get to the top

and turn around to face the vastness of the city beneath us. I've been in Paris for weeks, but I've barely scratched the surface. "I wish I could just spend my last few days exploring the city."

Louis lets out a laugh, but it sounds kind of sad. "No, you don't. You're going to spend your last few days performing the role of a lifetime in front of all the right people. That's what you're supposed to do."

I shrug. "I know, but this," I say, taking in the gorgeous panorama of the city once more, "has to be the most beautiful and romantic place in Paris."

A smile forms on Louis's lips. "The most beautiful, maybe," he says, "but for the most romantic, there's a lot of competition. Come on, let's go."

He pulls on my arm, and I follow him down the backstreets of Montmartre. It's quiet at this hour—both the portraitists and the tourists have gone home. Yet it feels so familiar to me now. We shared our first kiss right here. I'll always think of Montmartre as ours.

A few minutes later, we arrive on Rue des Abbesses, which is lined with restaurants, cafés, and more charming shops. Louis leads us to another smaller square that looks like it's straight out of a movie, with its green wrought-iron métro entrance, a colorful carousel, and a small gated park.

"Here it is," Louis says as we cross over to the other side. It's pretty dark, and I don't see what he's talking about at first. But then, as we stop under two streetlamps, I see it: a large wall spanning at least thirty feet long and over ten feet high, covered in blue tiles with white handwriting and red little squares all over it. I step forward to get a closer look.

"What does it say?" I ask, trying to read some of the words on the wall. "This isn't in French."

Louis turns to me. "I love you."

My heart stops.

"That's what it says," Louis continues. "'I love you' in dozens of languages. This is the 'Mur des je t'aime,' and I think it's a pretty good contender for the most romantic spot in Paris."

My heart starts beating again. In fact, it knocks against my chest at a rapid-fire pace, while my mind is trying to deal with what I *thought* Louis just said to me, and how much I wanted to hear it.

"So?" Louis asks, gently shoving me. "Do you like it? I think it's cool."

I take a deep breath. I can feel Louis tense next to me. "I love it," I say.

He doesn't say anything for a moment or two, and just looks into my eyes, breathing slowly.

Je t'aime. That's what I really wanted to say. But I'm too chicken to do it, too scared to deal with the consequences of my leaving Paris—and Louis—in just a few days. But I *am* definitely a bit braver than I was when I arrived here. So I pull him toward me, and, before I can think any more about what I should have said or what I want to say, I stand on the tops of my toes and brush my face against his. Then I kiss him for all the world's "I love you's" to see.

CHAPTER THIRTY

TODAY IS THE day. The end of the program and the start of a new life. In between: showtime! Costumes, music, and the entire cast performing *Swan Lake* from curtain to curtain for a very special audience.

The magnitude of what I've accomplished in the last weeks hits me even harder when Audrey and I arrive at school. As the leads, we're given our own dressing room to get ready, away from the commotion of the *corps de ballet*. For the first time in my life, I feel truly special, and I'm not ashamed to admit it. I've worked hard. I rehearsed for hours and hours and hours. I want to believe that, whatever happens today, I will have no regrets.

Audrey and I sit in total silence next to each other, facing our own mirrors. I apply a thick layer of foundation, glittery eyeshadow across my lids, but when I try to move on to lipstick, my hand shakes too much.

The apprentice program director for ABT is going to be

in that room. My lifelong dream is up for the making . . . or breaking.

Audrey shoots me a glance in the mirror. "You got this," she says firmly. "You're ready."

My bottom jaw trembles, and I have to put my lipstick down. I can't steady my hands. "What if I'm not? Or what if I am and it's still not enough?"

Audrey takes a deep sigh. "I can't let you freak me out."

She gets up and starts pacing the room, her chest rising and falling with every breath. "You think I'm not scared about what's going to happen in there?"

I sigh, words catching in my throat. We stare at each other for a moment, tension thickening the air between us.

"Wait!" I say, suddenly. "I have an idea."

I grab my phone and pull up my music app.

As the first few notes fill the room, Audrey shakes her head. "You're kidding me," she says, but a smile forms on her lips.

It's salsa music, a memory from when I taught Audrey Chapman a thing or two about chilling out.

I get up and take Audrey's hands in mine. She rolls her eyes, but doesn't resist me as I attempt the few steps she performed that night by the Seine. One foot forward, one foot back . . . we quickly fall in sync. Audrey lifts my hand and makes me spin. Then I do it to her, too. When the song ends, we fall back on our chairs laughing.

"Thanks, Mia."

"For what?" I say with a smirk.

"For being you."

• • •

Of my friends, Lucy and Anouk are the first to take the stage. I give them each a warm hug before they go, just behind the curtains. "You will be great," I say with a huge smile.

"You better be right," Lucy jokes. Anouk crosses her fingers with a nervous grimace, and then they're off. After that it's Fernando's turn, and, finally, Audrey's. She sighs and gives me a nod as she watches for her cue. I take her hands in mine, and we just look into each other's eyes, silently sharing our strengths and our determination to make today our best performance yet. The spotlight can only be on one of us at a time, but we're in this together.

For the first two acts of the ballet, I watch from the wings, trying to simply enjoy the show. I force myself not to peek at the audience. I don't want to see the look on the apprentice program directors' faces. I don't even know which one is from ABT. What happens now has already been decided, I'm sure of it. I beam as the "Dance of the Four Little Swans" begins. Like many people, it's one of my favorite parts of the ballet. The four beautiful swans dance seamlessly together, sweeping across the stage from right to left, while our small orchestra plays one of the most recognizable songs of all time. It's a beautiful, delicate moment, the calm before the storm brought about by . . . well, me.

Just before it's my turn to make my entrance, I take a deep breath and send a kiss up to the sky, in the direction of Élise Mercier.

Thank you, I think. I hope you're watching, because you, as much as anyone else, got me here. I stretch into a few *pliés,* feeling incredibly happy. This is what I want. No matter how many times I might find myself in this exact position in the future—ready to take the stage as one of the greatest roles in ballet—I will never take it for granted. I will treat each performance as my last, enjoy every minute, and give it absolutely everything I have.

And I do.

I sweep onto the stage, my heart ready to burst out of its cage, but my mind sharp. My muscles have memorized every part of every step, and I feel them deeply. I blend into Odile's skin, her motives and actions becoming mine. A mischievous young girl trying to steal a prince's heart. I feel her dedication as Fernando and I spin across the stage under Rothbart's watchful eye. As I edge closer to my *coup de force,* the thirty-two *fouettés,* I'm not scared. In fact, I'm excited for them, knowing that I can do this. They're not absolutely perfect—they were never going to be—but I feel the strength in my standing leg at every turn. I'm in control of my hips; I hold my composure. In other words, I nail it.

Taking my bow at the end of the show, I catch the lingering look of Monsieur Dabrowski on me. I don't see surprise or disappointment in it. In fact, I'm pretty sure I read at least a touch of pride. But I don't have to guess for too long, because he asks to see each of his leads in private afterward.

"What finesse, Mia," he starts calmly when it's my turn. "That was wonderful."

Yesterday, I might have asked if he really meant it. I may have even registered a little shock. But not today. I know deep inside that this was the best performance of my life. Until the next one.

"I'm very happy with my decision," he says, his voice softer than usual. "It's not always easy to know how things will turn out, but you are the perfect Black Swan. In fact, I think you would have been a gracious White Swan as well."

I smile. I appreciate the compliment, but I think he's wrong about that. "Audrey was a dream Odette," I say. "I liked being Odile. She has an attitude and a dark secret. It was more fun this way."

The *maître de ballet* smiles, but then his face grows serious again. "I'm not supposed to tell you this. . . ." He stops and looks like he's thinking about what to say next, or how to say it, anyway.

I hold my breath. Rumor has it that the apprentice program directors will make calls tonight, inviting their top picks for auditions tomorrow. I know I shouldn't get my hopes up, but I don't care. What I felt dancing on this stage, it was powerful. I've always known the path ahead of me, but now I can see it so clearly.

"It's not really in my hands," Monsieur Dabrowski adds,

careful with his choice of words, "but any company would be lucky to have you."

I exhale, feeling a little light-headed. Does that mean he talked to the ABT apprentice program director about me? Is he trying to tell me that he helped open that door, and that the rest is up to me?

"Thank you, Monsieur Dabrowski. You have been the best mentor I've ever had." My voice shakes as I say it. And I mean it. He's been downright harsh. Almost cruel on occasion. But I'm not sure I'd be standing here right now if he hadn't pushed me in the right direction.

"And you have been a very good student. We all make mistakes at times, and that includes me. But you did the right thing. You stayed true to yourself." He pauses, letting me wonder exactly what he means. His face softens as he continues. "I saw you and Louis the other night. He thinks I have no idea what he's up to, but I pay more attention than he gives me credit for."

I stand still, unsure of how to react. But then he breaks into a smile. "It's all right, Mademoiselle J . . . Mia. I know what you're capable of now. And I look forward to seeing you do it all over again tomorrow, at your auditions."

I gasp. Am I getting more than one? I know he won't tell me. He'll let the apprentice program director share the news directly. But, with Monsieur Dabrowski's stamp of approval, I have everything I need to be the best I've ever been.

But I still feel the need to clear the air between us. "About Louis . . . ," I start.

He waves it off. "I can't blame you for following your heart. Both of you. It all worked out in the end."

My throat tightens with emotion, and for a moment I worry that I'm going to start crying happy tears. Because here's the truth. I did follow my heart. I chased my dream. I put all my trust in my feelings, and now I'm exactly where I'm supposed to be. Just a few graciously executed steps away from an apprenticeship at the American Ballet Theatre. Come with me, Odile. I'm taking you to New York City.

CHAPTER THIRTY-ONE

IF I THOUGHT the day couldn't get any more exciting, I soon find out that I was wrong. As I walk back to the dorms with my friends, Louis is waiting in front of the door with a bouquet of dark red roses.

"Oohlala," Anouk whispers into my ear, and I'm pretty sure my face turns the exact shade of these flowers.

"Sorry," Louis says quietly as he hands them to me. "I didn't mean to embarrass you in front of your friends."

I roll my eyes. "They're embarrassing themselves," I say, glancing at Lucy and Anouk, who are not-so-subtly staring at us. "You are just . . . perfect."

"Come on, girls," Audrey says, gently pushing them along. "Let's go inside."

Then, just before she walks off, she turns back to me. "I can put these in water for you, if you'd like."

I smile and bring the roses to my face. Their scent is strong, intoxicating. I don't want to let them go, but

I also yearn to take Louis in my arms, so I hand them to Audrey.

As soon as we're alone, Louis beams. "You were incredible. I wanted to stand up and scream about how amazing you were onstage."

"I'm glad you didn't," I say with a laugh.

I almost want to share what his dad said to me, but I can't jinx it. Until the apprentice program director calls, I don't know anything for sure.

So instead, I lean forward and kiss him. I will need all the strength I can get for tomorrow, and that's exactly what kissing Louis gives me.

"Okay," Louis says afterward, grabbing my hand. He pulls me in the direction of his Vespa, parked next to the bus stop. "There's something I have to show you."

"What? Now?" I ask, resisting him. "Louis, I can't. Not tonight. The auditions are tomorrow. . . ."

"I know!" Louis says, his eyes sparkling. "But that's exactly why you need to see this. Remember how I told you I was working on something?"

I nod. In fact, I tried to bring it up a couple of times since, but Louis brushed me off, saying he wasn't ready to show it to anyone.

"I'm ready now." He smiles brightly, then bites his bottom lip.

I'm not sure I've seen him this excited before.

I need to stretch, have dinner, and get an early night. The only hot date I should be having is with my foam roller.

But then I think about the roses. About him watching me from the audience. About his hopeful eyes and devastating smile. I need to be with Louis more.

"You have one hour," I say, trying to sound like I mean business. Of course, I'm smiling deliriously, so it probably doesn't work so much.

"Really?" he asks. I'm sure he thought it would be much harder to convince me. But I don't want to spend my last moments in Paris arguing with Louis about whether or not we should spend time together. I know what I want. I want Louis.

Our ride on his Vespa takes us halfway across Paris, to the outskirts of the city. As the streets and buildings become less familiar and more sparse, I realize that I didn't even ask where we were going. I'm starting to wonder about this big secret project of his. And when, finally, he stops in an industrial zone in front of what seems to be an abandoned warehouse, more questions swirl in my mind.

This is not the dreamy Paris I fell in love with. In fact, it's pretty much the opposite. The building is gray, drab, and looks like it might fall apart. There's trash littered on the ground around it: old tires, boxes of junk, even the skeleton of a car. But, as we remove our helmets, Louis is buzzing with excitement.

"Are we going in there?" I ask. What I really want to say is *There's no way I'm going in there.*

Louis takes my hand, a huge smile across his face. "Trust me, Mia."

I do, even though he didn't answer my question. Louis stops as we're about to go around the corner of the building. "I need you to close your eyes," he says solemnly. I look down and see crushed cans and bits of broken glass. "I'll watch out for you," he adds.

"I trust you." I close my eyes, and we walk slowly, carefully. I focus on the warmth of Louis's hand in mine, and on the soothing sound of his voice as he tells me that we're almost there. A minute or so later, he spins me around to face him.

"Open your eyes," he says.

But it's only him in front of me.

"Remember when I told you I liked to paint when I was little?"

I nod.

"You inspired me, Mia. I hadn't touched a brush in years, but seeing your passion, your love for what you do, it really made me question what *I* was passionate about, what *I* loved. I saw what you had, and I realized I wanted that, too."

I hold my breath, waiting for the rest of the story, but this is it.

"Turn around."

I do what he says and let out a gasp. There's a ballerina in front of us, over ten feet tall. She's painted on the wall of the building, straight onto the concrete, wearing a black beaded costume, black feathered headband, and white pointe shoes. Her arms fly up to the sky as she stands on her right leg, the left one raised behind her in *arabesque*.

She looks down with a smile at what would be the end of the Black Swan *pas de deux*. Her red lips are the only touch of color on the wall.

"You did this," I say.

Louis searches my eyes. "Do you like it?"

I look back at her in awe. "It's the most amazing thing I've ever seen."

"Not as amazing as the real one," Louis responds. I can almost see his heart rising in his chest.

"This must have taken you hours," I say, still processing that Louis painted the entire side of a building with . . . me.

A cloud covers his eyes as he nods. "I started it the day after the showcase."

Just before I broke up with him. I take a deep breath, trying to clear my mind. But all I can do is look back at her. The lines are sharp yet delicate. He's captured Odile's essence—*my* essence—so perfectly that I can't take my eyes away. Forget Degas. Louis Dabrowski has just become my favorite artist.

Once I can bring myself to look away from this larger-than-life Black Swan, I notice more pieces of art on the adjacent wall, some small and colorful, others more graffiti-like.

"If I was going to paint again," Louis explains, following my gaze, "I wanted to do something different. And then I discovered this spot, where street artists come to practice, and just have fun experimenting. It's not the most charming place, but . . ."

"I think it is," I say, wrapping my arms around his neck. "This is the most beautiful gift I've ever received."

Louis beams back at me, pulling me close against him. "I've been coming here almost every day, and I just finished it last night. I had to show it to you now."

"I'm glad you did," I say, and then I kiss him.

Louis sighs when we pull away. He has more things to get off his chest. "Before I met you, I had no idea of what I wanted to do with my life, but now I think, well . . . there's an art school I might be interested in . . . in New York."

I hold my breath. I don't want to appear too excited but . . . what the hell. I grab his face with my hands and kiss him. "Really?"

He nods. "I talked to my mom about it. The application process is pretty intense, but I could use this piece in my portfolio, and then . . ."

He doesn't finish his sentence out loud, but I fill in the blanks in my head. We could be together, for real.

"I don't know how you feel," Louis says, gazing into my eyes, "but this isn't really a summer fling. For me, anyway."

He holds his breath as he waits for my reaction. There's a mixture of nervousness and anticipation on his face, a vulnerability I haven't seen before. This isn't the Louis who makes little jokes and is quick with snappy comments. This is the unvarnished version.

I need a moment to respond. Because I didn't come to Paris to have a summer fling. But I didn't expect to find . . .

him. Still, there are a thousand reasons this shouldn't work. I take a deep breath. My mouth goes dry. I want to say it right, and I don't mean just the words, or my accent.

Finally, I'm ready to let it out, what I've been feeling all along. *"Je t'aime, Louis."*

He smiles, and his eyes sparkle as he says, "I love you, Mia."

Our kiss is the most delicious thing I've tasted in the whole of Paris.

• • •

"I have something for you," I say as we walk back to Louis's Vespa. "Well, for us." I fish inside my bag, retrieve a tiny brown paper bag, and hand it to him.

He pulls out a padlock with two keys, and frowns at me.

"When I was little, I heard about the Lock Bridge on the Seine. I thought it was the most romantic thing, all these couples attaching a keepsake with their initials on it and throwing the key in the river."

Louis smiles. "It *was* very romantic. Until the bridge almost collapsed from all the extra weight."

"I know. But to me it's just a sign that there is so much love in Paris. I want ours to stay here . . . even after I'm gone."

Louis looks down at the padlock. Then he fishes inside his satchel to retrieve a black marker.

MIA + LOUIS he writes on one side.

I take the padlock and the marker, and add MILO on the other side. Then I draw a heart around it.

"Where should we put it?" I ask, looking around.

"I want to lock it right here," he says, pointing at the front of his Vespa. "This way it will always be with me, every time I drive around the city."

"I love that," I say as he hands me one of the keys. He puts the other one in his pocket.

Then he pulls me toward him. "And I love you. I just wanted to say it again all by myself."

I open my mouth to speak, but he presses his index finger against my lips. "We need to get you back to the dorm. You have a big day tomorrow."

I nod and put on my helmet, then take my spot at the back of the scooter. In fact, I grin so widely that my cheeks brush against the inside of the helmet. Pressed tightly against him, I giggle to myself. I feel like my heart might burst with joy. I know I've said this several times since I've landed in Paris, but *this* day is the best day of my life.

Louis drives off the abandoned park and onto the main street that will take us back to the city. The traffic is heavy, each lane packed with cars almost bumper to bumper. I hang on tight as he swirls around, getting us to the front of the line at the next red light. On the other side of the cross-road, a rectangular sign announces "PARIS" in black letters framed in red against a white background.

We're home, I think. Louis glances at me in the rearview mirror and gives me a wink. I squeeze his waist tighter, my heart knocking against his back.

The light turns green, and Louis zooms ahead. In just a

few minutes, I'll be back at the dorm, having dinner with my friends before the auditions tomorrow. Except . . . I see something out of the corner of my eye. A car is coming from the right, speeding toward us. There's a bang, strong and sharp. And then everything goes black.

CHAPTER THIRTY-TWO

WHEN I WAKE up, the first thing I notice is that my body doesn't feel like it belongs to me anymore. My eyes are dry, like they've been scrubbed with sandpaper. My mouth is pasty, my lips stuck together. My limbs are heavy, unwilling to move. I don't even care where I am. I already know that my life is over.

I doze off, but whether it's for ten minutes or ten hours, I couldn't say. I wake up again to a quiet, continuous beeping sound, and open my eyes to find a man in a white coat towering over me.

"Mia, can you hear me?" he asks in a thick French accent. "You had an accident. You arrived at the hospital last night."

I glance down at my wrist, but I can barely move, and I don't see anything. Someone took my jewelry off, including my watch. "What time is it?" I ask. My voice is so croaky that I'm not sure he can hear me.

"It's six in the morning. You've been asleep since the ambulance brought you here. Do you have any memory of what happened?"

I try to shrug but it hurts. It's not that I don't remember. It's just that I don't want to.

"I'm Dr. Richard. And you're in one of the best hospitals in Paris. You're going to be okay, Mia."

I look away, tears prickling at the corners of my eyes. The only way I'm going to be okay is if I can walk out of here on my own two legs and meet with the ABT apprentice program director today.

I try to sit up, and pain shoots down my entire left side. Tears spring to my eyes.

"You broke your collarbone, but it was a clean break. We'll keep you overnight just to be safe, but you were very lucky, Mia. You won't need surgery. It should take you a couple of months to heal with some physical therapy, but I'm confident you'll get back to normal."

A clean break. You were very lucky.

He smiles again, convinced he's giving me good news. He also says that the hospital called my parents and reassured them that I was okay.

I am not okay.

Tears roll down the sides of my face, making their way down my neck and through the pillowcase. I can barely listen as the doctor tells me that we were almost at the other end of the crossroad when a car to our right went through the red light. I went flying a few meters away and landed on my left side. Louis toppled over the top, hitting the tar flat on his face. His helmet is battered, but he's fine. He only suffered a minor concussion—a small miracle—but he's still under observation.

The neon light above me is blinding, like the truth of my diagnosis.

Since I can't bring myself to say anything, the doctor tells me to get some rest and that he'll check in on me in a couple of hours.

"You're going to be fine, Mia," he says, turning back to me when he reaches the door. Except he doesn't know me at all. I'm not going to be fine. I want to scream, but even that feels out of my reach.

I close my eyes, and again, I'm not sure how much time passes before a soft and familiar voice comes to me from the other side of the room.

My vision is blurred, and my eyes slowly adjust to the bright sunlight coming in through the window. There's a woman sitting in the chair in the corner, talking quietly on her cell phone.

"Mom?" I say, thinking I must be hallucinating.

Mom leaps from her chair. "Mia!" she says, rushing to me.

I try to shuffle up in my bed, but I can't really move. "Am I still in Paris?" I ask, looking around the room.

My head feels like concrete has been poured inside of it.

My mind is fuzzy, unable to focus. I want to go back to sleep and wake up ten years from now, when all of this will have stopped hurting so much. Maybe.

Mom nods sadly. There are bags under her shiny eyes. "I jumped on the first flight over. They said you'd be fine, but I couldn't stand the idea of you waking up alone here."

My throat tightens. I don't know what to say.

"Do you need something?" Mom asks, her voice laced with concern as she carefully sits on the bed and grabs my hand. "Some water? Juice? They gave you something for the pain, and they said you might be thirsty."

I look down my arm, which is connected to an IV drip. More tears roll down my cheeks.

"Talk to me, Mia," Mom says again.

"What time is it?" I ask, scanning the top of the nightstand for my phone, and not seeing it.

Mom tries to look casual as she checks her watch, but there is worry all over her face. "It's just after two p.m."

I shake my head and try to sit up straighter. "Maybe if I . . ."

Mom presses her hand harder on mine. "I know what you're thinking, Mia. But it's not going to happen. I'm sorry, I really am," Mom continues. "The police talked to witnesses. This would never have happened if that car hadn't gone through a red light."

No, I think. This would never have happened if I hadn't been on the back of Louis's Vespa the night before my big break. It would never have happened if I hadn't met him.

Someone knocks, and the door opens. In walks Louis. His shirt is ripped at the elbow, and he has red marks on his chin and cheekbones, but he's standing on his own two feet. Uninjured.

"Mia!" he says, rushing to the side of the bed.

Mom leaves my side and goes to look out the window, giving us privacy. She seems to know Louis already, or at least of him. But I don't want to be left alone with Louis. I can't look him in the eye right now.

Still, he stands by the edge of my bed. "I'm so sorry, Mia. I should never have asked you to come with me last night."

"And I should never have said yes."

"My dad . . . ," he starts. "He stayed here most of the night. He was so upset about the whole thing, and he was hoping to see you, but he had to go . . ."

"To the auditions," I finish, my voice breaking halfway.

Louis looks down, but I can see tears along the sides of his cheeks. "You got one with ABT." He wipes his eyes before adding, "And with the Royal Ballet and the Opéra de Paris. I'm so sorry, Mia."

I thought I was already dead inside, but this ends me. I catch Mom glancing back at me, her face stricken with worry. I start sobbing, quietly at first, but then my whole body shakes. It hurts my chest, everywhere. But I don't care about the physical pain. That I can manage.

"I am so so so sorry," Louis says.

I think he's crying, too, but I can't see clearly through my own tears. They keep falling and falling, with my hopes and dreams, until the edges of my nightgown are soaked through.

Mom turns to Louis. "Maybe it's best if you leave now." Her tone is kind but firm.

Louis casts another glance at me, but I can't look at him. He tries to grab my hand, but I move it out of the way.

There's nothing left inside me.

I rest my head on the soggy pillow, facing away from him. I'm not sure how long it takes, but finally he walks the few steps to the door, and he's gone.

And then I realize, I'm never going to see Louis Dabrowski again.

CHAPTER THIRTY-THREE

I'M STILL IN the hospital when I wake up again. My collarbone is still broken; my life is still over. I lie there for a while, not moving, trying not to feel anything, until a nurse walks in with a breakfast tray.

"Bonjour, vous allez bien?" she asks as she places my meal on the table by my bed. *Hello, how are you?* She uses the formal *you*, which is normal in French when speaking to someone you don't know, but it hits me again that I'm stuck in a hospital room, so far away from home.

She checks my chart at the back of my bed. "The doctor," she starts, searching for her words. "He says you can go."

I nod, and she makes a move to leave, but I stop her. "My . . . *maman?*" I ask.

She smiles and walks back over to me. "She comes soon."

I nibble on my breakfast after the nurse leaves, but the salt of my tears is the most flavorful thing on the tray. I check the time on my phone: the dorm's dining room must be abuzz for the very last breakfast. I try to picture myself there, sharing jokes with my friends, but my mind is blank. My heart is empty.

Until a knock resonates on my door, and three beautiful faces pop in. Shocked, I try to sit up, but it hurts to move. Lucy, Anouk, and Audrey come tumbling in, swarming around my bed, their familiar scents and warm smiles filling the room.

"We didn't bring you flowers," Lucy says, searching inside her tote bag.

A memory from that night flashes before my eyes: Louis offering me a bouquet of fragrant red roses. I thought they were the most beautiful I had ever seen.

"I don't need flowers," I say, my voice flat.

"We thought of something much better," Anouk adds.

Lucy produces a greasy paper bag and hands it to me. I don't need to open it to know what's inside. I'd recognize that buttery scent from a mile away. Even though it smells heavenly, I'm anything but hungry.

"How are you feeling?" Anouk asks as I tear off a piece of the croissant and pop it in my mouth. At least it gives me something to do.

Audrey winces behind her. She knows how I'm feeling better than anyone else. Tears roll down my cheeks, doing the talking for me.

"No, no, no!" Lucy says, sitting on my bed and grabbing

my hand. "You know, my cousin broke her collarbone a few years ago, and she's running marathons again."

"Yes," Anouk adds. "With a good physical therapist . . ."

"I'll go back in time and attend my audition with ABT?" I ask.

"I'm sorry, Mia," Anouk replies, looking contrite. "I didn't mean to . . . I know this sucks."

"Yep," I say, letting out a bitter laugh through my tears.

"But you *will* dance again," Lucy says, rubbing my hand.

I know it comes from a good place, but I'm not strong enough to take it. Still, I try to sound lighthearted. "When do you all go home?"

"Now," Anouk says, checking her watch. "But we wanted to see you one last time."

"Thank you for coming," I say. "It means a lot."

"I'm sorry we can't stay any longer," Lucy says with a guilty smile. "I'll miss you almost as much as I'll miss Paris."

Lucy giggles at her own joke, but all I can manage is a weak smile.

Paris. I just want to forget that I was ever in this city, just a few steps away from my lifelong dream. Until a car crashed through it.

"Hey, girls, do you mind if I talk to Mia for a moment?" Audrey asks suddenly. She's been sitting at the foot of the bed, quietly waiting.

Lucy and Anouk exchange a look and get up. They both hug me and promise to stay in touch. Tears fill my eyes again as it dawns on me that this is how my summer of ballet is ending. Not just in a hospital, but also ripped away from my friends a little too soon.

After they leave the room, Audrey comes to sit closer. "Does it hurt?" she asks, shuffling uncomfortably.

"My collarbone? Yeah, a little. But the rest . . ." I trail off. I don't need to say it. She knows I would take the physical pain over the devastation of missing my chance with ABT any day.

"I'm really sorry, Mia. I was in shock when I found out. I'd never wish . . ."

"I know," I say.

Audrey bites her bottom lip, then looks up at me with a heavy sigh. "Listen, I wanted you to hear it from me. . . ."

She pauses. My breath turns ragged.

"ABT offered you an apprenticeship, and I bet the Bolshoi Ballet did as well," I say. Audrey got all of the auditions. And of course she knocked them out of the park.

Audrey's face wrinkles. "I'm going to ABT."

I nod, trying to inhale deeply. I need to be brave.

"I wish you would come, too. It would be so great if we did this together." It's hard to believe, but she sounds genuine. This summer has definitely changed us both.

"You deserve this, Audrey. I'm happy for you." And strangely, I mean it.

Her bottom jaw quivers, and, for a moment, I think she's going to cry. Instead, she does something even more surprising. "I'm scared," she says. "My mom was pretty mad that I didn't pick the Bolshoi Ballet, but that's not just it. I'm terrified to mess it up. What if I get to ABT and I'm just nowhere near as good as all the other dancers?"

I let out a laugh.

"What?" she asks, a frown forming between her eyebrows.

"Audrey Chapman is feeling feelings and admitting it out loud. My work here is done."

• • •

Mom comes about an hour after Audrey leaves. There's a smile on her face and a skip in her step. Maybe it's because I'm on drugs, but I don't get it.

She sits on the edge of my bed, offering me a cup of water. "Do you feel ready to go?"

I nod slowly as I take small sips. I've been dreading this moment—going home, back to normal life—for weeks, but it's taken on a whole new meaning. While I'm still here, I can hold on to the pretense. I know it's silly, but deep down I still hope that I will finally wake up from this nightmare and make it to my audition.

"What time is our flight?" I ask Mom as she gets up.

She pulls out an outfit from my duffel bag. She must have gone to my dorm to pack my things.

"Five-thirty p.m." She starts packing the few things I have here—my bag, my phone, the clothes I was wearing the night of the accident. "Two days from now."

"What?"

A smile brightens her whole face. "I'm so sorry you didn't get to go to your auditions, Mia. I know how much it meant to you."

I thought I had cried all the tears I had in me, but more find their way down my cheeks. I wonder if I'll ever stop feeling broken.

Mom hands me a tissue. "I wish there was something I could do to change this, but I spoke to Dad, and we both agreed. This can't be the end of your summer in Paris. I know this won't change everything, but I have a surprise for you. Your Paris adventure is not over yet."

There is joy and excitement in her eyes, and, as hurt and confused and devastated as I am, I can't help it; a small current of hope courses through me. Where are we going now?

CHAPTER THIRTY-FOUR

OH. MON. DIEU.

As our taxi slows down in the middle of Rue de Rivoli, passing the Louvre and the Tuileries, my heart skips a beat.

I look over to Mom. "What did you do?"

She just laughs in response, looking quite pleased with herself. We come to a stop in front of a stone corridor leading to the entrance of Le Meurice. I've walked past it before on my Degas hunt with Louis, but mostly I know it because the girls were talking about it the other night at dinner: it's one of the fanciest hotels in all of Paris, where celebrities stay.

Even though I'm acutely aware of my dirty hair and the sling across my chest, I feel a little lighter as a porter opens the door for me. He also retrieves our bags and follows us into the grand foyer. Opulent glass chandeliers dangle from the ceiling, and antique mirrors hang alongside museum-worthy paintings on the walls. It takes my breath away.

"Did you rob a bank?" I ask Mom when we're finally alone in our room.

The plush armchairs are covered in pink velvet, and every piece of furniture is punctuated with gold. Thick curtains in a silky fabric frame the floor-to-ceiling windows, which let in a soft, glowing light. I feel like a princess.

Mom chuckles. "Nope. I just used every single credit card point I had and then some. But I didn't book a suite. The concierge must have taken pity on you and upgraded us," she says, nodding toward my sling.

Going over to the window, I notice a balcony. I open it wide, step outside, and gasp loudly.

"Mom! You're not going to believe this."

Mom rushes over and gasps. Before us is all of Paris, its creamy buildings, flowerpots hanging from railings, and slate rooftops. We can see the full splendor of the Tuileries leading up to the Louvre and the Musée d'Orsay's famous clock directly ahead. That itself would put a smile on my face, but it's the Tour Eiffel, standing proud in all its glory just to our right, that makes me forget all my troubles.

"Thank you, Mom," I say. She smiles as she runs a hand through my hair. Her eyes get shiny, and she presses her lips to my forehead.

"I'm so glad you're okay," she whispers. We stand there holding hands for a long moment, a soft wind brushing our faces as the Tour Eiffel glints in the sun.

I'm still feeling a little tired, so Mom suggests we splurge and enjoy lunch in one of the hotel's renowned restaurants.

"Are you sure you didn't rob a bank?" I ask.

Mom laughs again. "I haven't visited Paris since before you were born, and I'm only here for two days. I figure we might as well enjoy ourselves."

· · ·

The white tablecloths, intricate cutlery, and fine china would normally intimidate me, but today I'm not sweating the small stuff. Instead, I try to focus on the flavors—the freshest baguette I've had so far, and the salt flecks in the butter that melt on my tongue.

"Why were you always talking to me about a plan B, Mom?" I ask after the very formal waitress takes our order.

Mom frowns, but she doesn't try to change the topic. "I only wanted to protect you."

"But why? You knew I wanted to become a ballet dancer. It was my one and only plan. And now I do need a plan B." I blink back tears. "How did you know?"

Mom takes a deep breath and looks around the room. Most tables are occupied, but it's still pretty quiet. People speak at a low level and eat with measured, sophisticated gestures. Next to us, a man lunching alone picks up his white cloth napkin and carefully dabs the corners of his mouth. Then he lifts his wineglass by the stem with only two fingers.

"I was a dancer, too," Mom says when the silence between has gone on too long. "I saw firsthand how competitive and ruthless it is."

I knew that already, but I stay silent. I want to hear the rest of it.

"I don't think I ever told you this, but I wanted to become a professional, as well. You and I are a lot more alike than you think."

Our first course arrives. My gazpacho looks so beautiful, with an artful drizzle of olive oil on the surface, that I think twice before dipping my spoon in it.

Mom smiles sadly as she tucks into her *salade niçoise*. "I was so passionate, so eager." She looks away before adding, "When I went to my audition at ABT, I was certain I would get in."

"You auditioned for ABT?" I asked, my eyes growing wide.

She nods. "Many, many times."

"What?" I say, trying to keep my voice low.

She takes another bite. "This is amazing! If I stay in Paris too long, I won't fit into my clothes."

I'm not letting her change the subject. "What happened with ABT?"

She grimaces. "The same thing that happens to most dancers who audition: I didn't get in. I never made it past the second round. I went to California and auditioned for the San Francisco Ballet and the LA Ballet. Nothing. I was good. I had talent and ambition. Just not enough."

I freeze, unable to keep eating like this isn't the biggest news I've ever heard about her. Mom has never shared this with me before. No one in my family has.

happened to me, and what life will look like for me in the next few months.

"I want to become a professional ballet dancer. This is what I've always dreamed of," I say, more to convince myself. "But what if it doesn't happen?"

Mom nods slowly. "Then you will be okay."

"Will I?" I take a deep breath and bite my tongue. What kind of faux pas would it be to start crying in such a fancy restaurant?

"Mia," Mom says, determined. "Look at me. Soon this will just feel like a small bump in the road. Trust me."

"I missed my chance with ABT. Twice."

"I thought I wanted this more than anything else; then my life took a different path, and it was perfect. This isn't about missing chances. It's about enjoying the journey. You should pursue your dream for as long as you want to, but you should also allow yourself to change dreams along the way."

I nod and silently get back to my meal. I want to believe she's right, but I can't shake off everything—and everyone—I've lost in the last couple of days. Still, I know t deep inside me: I'm going to dance again.

• • •

just gone back up to the room when my phone rings.
going to lie: my heart breaks all over again when

I realize it's an unknown number. Louis hasn't texted or called since I left the hospital. But then again, neither have I. My feelings are still too raw, and everything has been said between us. Maybe it was always meant to end this way. A clean break, just like my collarbone.

"Hello?"

"Madem— Mia," a male voice says, sounding a little uncertain. "It's Monsieur Dabrowski."

I take a seat in one of the armchairs, my heart racing. "I'm so sorry . . . ," I say. "I promised I wouldn't let you down, and . . ."

"You didn't," he responds firmly. "You can't control everything, Mia. Yes, I wish you and Louis hadn't gone out that night after the show. And I definitely wish that car hadn't gone through a red light. But things happen. No one lives in a bubble, unfortunately."

"So you're not mad at me?" I ask, trying to keep the surprise out of my voice.

"I know you're mad at yourself already, and that's enough. What's done is done."

"I missed my audition with ABT. I ruined my chances," I say, stating the obvious. It hurts to admit it out loud again, but I need to accept this new reality.

"Yes," Monsieur Dabrowski answers, serious. "The apprentice program director was stunned when I gave him the news. He didn't know what to say."

"I'm sorry," I say again, just because I feel the need to

fill the void. It's my future I screwed up, but it's clear I disappointed so many people around me. The people who mattered the most.

Monsieur Dabrowski takes a deep breath. "I talked to him some more. I don't normally like to meddle in these things, because it's not up to me how companies recruit their dancers. Still, I asked him if he would give you another chance."

"Oh," I say, wondering if I'm understanding him correctly. I can't picture Monsieur Dabrowski pleading my case, but it sounds like it's exactly what he did.

"He said no," Monsieur Dabrowski adds in a whisper. "While he was impressed by your performance, he'd invited other students to audition and felt that they should get priority, given your injury. So many dancers want to join ABT. . . ." He trails off, and I'm sure that, like mine, his mind goes to Audrey. She must be back home now, already preparing for her new life in New York City. I shake off the twinge of jealousy before it becomes too much to bear.

"Thank you for trying," I say, the words catching in my throat. It's no surprise, of course. Why would ABT give me another chance when I didn't even turn up at the audition?

"There's another reason I called," Monsieur Dabrowski says. "The program director at the l'Institut de l'Opéra de Paris called me yesterday. She was also told what happened to you, of course, but she thought about it again overnight. She saw great talent in you. She comes to New York a few times a year, and she said she'd like to see you there next time, if you've recovered. She hasn't made any promises, but . . . sometimes students get an offer with a delayed start. Exceptions can be made. I know it's not ABT, but the Opéra de Paris has a pretty great reputation as well." He adds the last part with a chuckle.

I let out a scream, and Mom looks at me with concern. I quickly smile at her, letting her know that I'm fine. I'm better than fine. I don't know how long it will take me to heal, or what my life will be like in a year's time. But that open door, that chance to meet with the director from l'Institut de l'Opéra de Paris again, is the only sign I need.

CHAPTER THIRTY-FIVE

THERE'S SO MUCH to do and see in this neighborhood, Mom and I don't even take the métro for the next two days. It's called *le premier arrondissement*—the first neighborhood—for a reason: it's got everything.

We stroll through the Jardin du Palais-Royal, and stop to take photos at a modern art installation in the palace's courtyard—black-and-white-striped columns of all lengths that contrast with the classic architecture surrounding it. They're fun and unexpected, another sign that Paris is so elegant, but with a definite edge. Later, at Ladurée, we try almost every macaron flavor, because why not? Rose is my favorite, while Mom is all about the strawberry-marshmallow combo.

Even though I can't bring myself to talk about ballet, Mom insists we visit the Repetto boutique on Rue de la Paix. She thinks I need to treat myself, that I should bring something back from Paris for when I'm finally ready to dance again. I don't tell her all the reasons why it hurts to go back there—for one, it was my first thrilling, scary, and magnificent adventure with Louis. But it seems important to her that I leave Paris feeling good and happy, or at least better and not as sad. Mom insists on buying me a new white leotard. I don't protest, and I wait until she's turned around to stop smiling.

Mostly we just wander around without a plan, turning down pretty streets, stopping for drinks at charming cafés, listening to street performers singing French songs we don't know, and going inside stunning little churches to admire the intricate stained glass from up close. There's a lightness in the air, sweet and hopeful. Summer is still well and truly here. We FaceTime Dad and Thomas, too—who seem kinda jealous of our little adventure. Thomas makes us promise to bring him back macarons, but Dad is quiet. I see concern in his eyes, so I do my best to sound upbeat, but I know he's worried about me.

I am, too, honestly. When I hung up with Monsieur Dabrowski, I didn't know how to feel. ABT didn't want me. They were right not to. They offered me an audition, and I didn't turn up to it. It doesn't matter how much the apprentice program director liked my performance. I'm sure he's forgotten all about me by now. As Mom said to me before: there are so many aspiring ballet dancers. All talented, determined, ready to give it everything. And most of them don't get run over by a car the night before their big break.

And while I'm grateful that the apprentice program

director for l'Institut de l'Opéra de Paris is open to seeing me again, I'm not quite sure what to make of it. Is she just doing Monsieur Dabrowski a favor? He swore up and down that it came from her and that he had nothing to do with it, but the more I think about it, the more I wonder if she'll even remember me in a few months' time when she visits New York.

Putting that aside, do I really want to come back to Paris next year? If you'd asked me throughout the summer, during my best times with Louis, I would probably have said yes. But that's when I thought my life had suddenly transformed into a fairy tale. I believed that I could have everything I wanted. That I never needed to compromise. I could stay up late and get up early. Hang around with my friends and sneak out with Louis every chance I got. Uncover a family legend and give Odile all of my attention.

But now I'm not so sure about this idea of having everything. It always sounded too good to be true, probably because it is. Yes, I will heal. One day. I'll have to work hard to fully recover, and even harder to make up for lost time. I'll have to take it one day at a time.

•••

Our last afternoon is here in a blink, and my hands shake as I pack up my things. The cardboard tube with my Degas poster sits in the corner of the room, waiting to go home and retrieve its rightful place above my childhood bed.

"That's everything," Mom tells me when our suitcases are by the door and ready to go.

I nod sadly. This has been a wonderful interlude, given the circumstances, but as soon as I leave this gorgeous room, I'll be back to real life with a broken collarbone and shattered dreams.

Mom sighs, like she can read my mind. "Why don't I go check us out?" she says. "Take your time. We don't have to leave for another forty-five minutes. I'll be downstairs, catching up on my emails. I'm sure my boss has had at least one or two emergencies in the last hour."

When she's gone, I go to the window one last time and step onto the balcony. My heart crunches as I face the Tour Eiffel for the last time. Is it possible to miss a metal structure? I bought a small key ring featuring it from a vendor on the Champs-Élysées yesterday, but nothing can replace the real thing. I snap a picture and post it to my Instagram. Looking through my feed, I realize that I've only shared a handful of photos of my summer in Paris. I've been too busy enjoying it to feel the need to share it with the world.

Au revoir, Paris. I write in the caption. Je t'aime.

I linger on the balcony for a while, feeling a sense of peace. I was lucky enough to experience an incredible summer in the most beautiful city in the world. Even if I'd do anything to change how it ended, how many seventeen-year-olds can say that? How many aspiring dancers have done what I did?

Once I get back to Westchester, and things are a little

clearer in my head, I'll write to Louis. Maybe he won't want to hear from me. Maybe the accident was just the universe's way of closing this chapter. Maybe he'll have realized our story was always supposed to end at the end of the summer. I just wish it hadn't ended with me crying in a hospital bed while he walked away, bruised and confused.

A light knock on the door startles me. Mom must have given her key back already. I go to open the door, but what I find on the other side makes my jaw fall to the floor.

"What . . . ," I say.

Louis's hair is a mess, like he just removed his helmet and forgot to put it back in place, as he usually does. He has a few scuffs on his cheeks and bags under his eyes. But he's here.

"I thought you were gone," he says, looking at me like I might not be real. "I thought you left Paris just after the accident. And then I was checking Instagram and . . . I got here as fast as I could."

And then it hits me. I didn't tell anyone I was staying here. No one knew that I was still in Paris. I wasn't *supposed* to be. Mom's surprise came about after my friends left, after I saw Louis for the last time. Or what I thought was the last time. When Monsieur Dabrowski called, he must have assumed I was back home already.

"I—I . . . ," I start. The words struggle to come. "I thought we were . . . over. When you left . . . I thought . . . it was the end of us. That it was always meant to be the end of us."

From his pained expression, I can tell that I was wrong.

"I felt so horrible after the accident," he says. "I thought you didn't want to speak to me again."

"What? That's not true. It wasn't your fault," I say. "I should have told you I hadn't left yet."

"I don't care," Louis says, grabbing my face with his hands. "You're here. Right now. With me. I love you, Mia. I couldn't let you leave Paris without telling you again."

"I love you, too," I say, kissing him through tears.

I know this will hurt all over again when I'm on the plane, but I'm okay with it. Love is like ballet in that way: to be worth it, it has to be painful at times. Exquisitely so.

EPILOGUE

I'M NOT RUNNING this time, but I have a definite feeling of déjà vu as I step into the Charles de Gaulle airport terminal. It's just as busy as the last time I arrived here, but I'm not leaping or *pirouetting* to get to my destination. No frizzy hair or sweat dripping down my back, either.

In fact, I stop halfway through to duck into the bathroom. Dropping my things against the wall, I claim the sink in the corner to freshen up. I brush my teeth, my hair, and the food crumbs off my tracksuit pants, before pulling out a clean set of clothes. I wash my face, apply a thick layer of moisturizer to soothe my skin after the long flight, and study myself in the mirror. I look totally presentable now, freshly pressed and almost rested. In fact, I remind myself of someone I know.

Back in the terminal, I take a selfie with the taxi sign behind me. I click to send it as a text message.

Guess where I am? 😊 I write. I keep walking toward the exit when my phone rings.

"Isn't it the middle of the night in New York?" I ask as soon as the video call connects.

Audrey shrugs back at me. Behind her, I can make out lit-up skyscrapers and the silhouettes of a few people.

"Are you outside?" I ask, incredulous. I do quick math: It must be about one a.m. there.

"Yes!" Audrey says with a bright smile, her cheeks flushed. "We just came back from a music festival in Brooklyn." She moves her phone around to show me the group she's with. Three girls and one guy wave at me. "Hi!" they say in unison.

"Guys, this is my friend Mia," Audrey says, turning the phone back on her. "She just moved to *Pareeeee*."

They laugh, and I do, too, until I realize it's me they're talking about. It hits me all over again: I just moved to Paris.

Turns out, l'Institut de l'Opéra de Paris really did wait for me. My last year of high school went by in a blur. And while it was a long and grueling road to recovery, I was back to dancing in a few months. I couldn't believe it at first, but my body remembered every move. I met with the apprentice program director in New York in the spring, and she was over the moon to learn that I'd been back in the studio for a while already. "This was meant to be," she said as we hugged goodbye. I think Élise Mercier would have agreed with her.

"What about your beauty sleep?" I ask Audrey.

"Oh, I'm fine," she says with a laugh. "A friend of mine taught me that enjoying life can make me an even better dancer."

"She sounds very wise."

Audrey nods. "I miss her already."

I've almost forgotten that Audrey and I weren't exactly friends from the start. But we are now. I took the train to New York to visit her, and saw her dance with ABT. At first I was worried that it would be too painful, but I made my peace with it. In fact, Audrey helped me see that, like Mom had suggested, the original plan isn't always the best one. Her mom always wanted her to attend the Bolshoi Ballet, but Audrey followed her heart. Deep down she knew what was right for her, where her life should be.

I hang up with Audrey just as I step outside the Arrivals terminal. I scan the crowd, my heart trumpeting in my chest. There's a long line of people holding signs with passengers' names on them. None of them are for me.

When we'd texted last week, he said he wasn't sure if his class schedule would allow him to pick me up from the airport. I told him that it was fine. Louis and I never made any promises to each other. That day at Le Meurice, we said goodbye through tears, and appreciated our time together for what it had been: an amazing summer that would give us memories for life, no matter what happened next. We texted and called, but it wasn't the same, of course. Time